Housebroken

Leona Gom

NeWest Press
Edmonton

First edition

Canadian Cataloguing in Publication Data

Gom, Leona, 1946-
Housebroken

ISBN 0-920316-93-X (bound). — ISBN 0-920316-95-6 (pbk.)

I. Title.
PS8563.04H6 1986   C813′.54   C86-091101-2
PR9199.3.G64H6 1986

The quotation from *The Psychoanalytic Theory of Neurosis* by Otto Fenichel is by permission of the publishers, W.W. Norton & Company, Inc.

Credits
Cover design: S. Colberg
Typesetting: T. Marx
Printing and binding: Friesen Printers Limited

Financial Assistance
Alberta Culture
The Canada Council

NeWest Publishers Limited
Suite 204, 8631 - 109 Street
Edmonton, Alberta
Canada   T6G 1E8

for Dale

One

When I open the door, Whitman is standing there, holding the cat. Of course I ask him in.

He stands inside the door, looking in his usual worried way at my right ear. Whitman cannot look people in the eyes, throws his glance instead at their ears, as though his aim is off by about four inches. When I came home from meeting him for the first time I had to look in the mirror to see what was wrong. It's something about him I've never gotten used to.

The cat has been here before and is not particularly alarmed, although he struggles to get down and then pads off to examine the rest of the house.

"I thought you might want him," Whitman says. He looks down at his empty hands as though they are something odd, as though they have just grown there.

"Want him?" I repeat stupidly.

"I never really cared about him. I suppose you know that. He was Susan's. And now he keeps yowling around the house, goes from room to room. It just drives me crazy."

"Well," I say, stalling. "I don't really know. I'm not much good with pets."

"I thought you said you had a cat once."

"That was years ago," I say, "and a dog got hold of him and we had to have him put down. It wasn't, you know, very pleasant. Getting attached to something, I mean, and then losing it."

"Say no if you want to," Whitman says. He sounds impatient. "I won't take him to the pound or anything awful if you don't want him. It's just that, well, he was Susan's cat, you know what I mean?"

"Of course," I say, "of course." And I do know. But does he think it will be any easier for me?

"Look," he says. "How about if you take him on trial for a week? You can give him back if it doesn't work out."

I consider that. "Okay," I say finally. "That sounds fair."

"Good," he says. "He's a nice enough cat, I suppose. You shouldn't have any trouble with him." He begins backing awkwardly out the door, watching the cat, who has sat down now at our feet, listening to what we are saying and looking up at us with his bland cat face, his alien intelligence. "Well, I'll bring his stuff over, then."

I watch him go, down my walk, hunching against the rain. He crosses the street without looking, goes into his own house directly across from mine. From here I can read the plaque above the door. Whitman and Susan Jervis.

The cat comes and rubs against my leg, leaving a swirl of hair on my slacks. What have I done? I don't really want a cat. Susan's cat. I think of the time I was over at her place, and suddenly it threw up, a slimy, turd-like mess, on the kitchen floor.

"Oh, Jesus," Susan said, jumping up and ripping half a dozen paper towels off the rack. I suppose I should have offered to help her clean it up, but I didn't.

"Furballs," I said.

"Bulimia," Susan said.

"What?"

"Oh, you know. It's that eating disorder, when you gorge yourself and then make yourself throw up." She went back for more paper towels.

"Oh. But would a *cat.* . . .?" Of course, I think now, she must have been joking. With Susan it was never that easy to tell.

"You live with crazies, you get crazy." She dropped the wad of paper towels in the garbage and turned on the hot water tap, dangling her hands under the limp stream as she waited for the water to get hot, although even at best I knew it would only be tepid, because Whitman did not want to waste money by keeping the hot water thermostat higher. The cat sat on the floor beside her, cleaning himself too, licking his fur, making more hairballs.

The phone rings, startling me, pushing away the memory. The cat has shaped himself into a tidy loaf on the toe of my shoe, and I carefully wriggle my foot free and step over him as though it were important not to disturb him. When I pick up the phone, Whitman's voice is in my ear.

"There's something else. Do you want to have Susan's writing, you know, her poems and stuff?"

"To . . . keep, you mean?" I am not sure what he is asking. I pick up a pencil, as though there is something I should be writing down.

"I thought there might be things there, you know, worth saving, and maybe you could look through them, see if there was anything. . . ." His voice grows fainter, as though he is moving the receiver away from his mouth.

"Well, okay," I say, not sure what exactly I am agreeing to. I realize I have coiled the phone cord around and around my fingers, like thick black rope, and I pull myself free.

Ten minutes later Whitman is at the door again, with a cardboard box under one arm and a large shopping bag in the other. He sets the shopping bag down on the floor and carries the box to the kitchen table.

Something cold lays itself along the back of my neck. The box is piled to the top with papers, file folders, scribblers. On top of everything are two framed pictures of Susan. One is a formal portrait of her taken when she was about twenty; another is a snapshot of her on the beach at English Bay. And there is a third photograph, a wedding picture of her and Whitman. I pick it up, slowly. My hand is shaking a little.

"You don't really want to give me this."

He sits down, lights a cigarette. He folds his long legs under the chair, his ankles collapsing in a way that makes it seem a pair of shoes has been dropped untidily between them.

"It's okay," he says. "There are other copies." He takes a deep drag from the cigarette. I can almost feel the smoke shouting into my own lungs. "It's just that, you know, these were sitting around the house. I couldn't stand to see them every day." He picks up the one of Susan on the beach. "This one was on the dresser in the bedroom." I remember seeing it there, but of course he wouldn't know that. "In the morning it was pretty well the first thing I saw when I woke up. You know what I mean? I just couldn't stand it."

For a moment his voice trembles. I am both afraid and hopeful that he will cry, feel myself preparing my response. But he only takes another pull on his cigarette and turns to look out the window at the thin rain. The day is the colour of concrete.

"Of course," I say, "of course I know." His ash drops onto the table. He pushes it around in tiny circles with his thumbnail. I want myself to ignore it, but I get up, bring a saucer from the kitchen, and quickly brush the grey pile into it. He doesn't seem to notice.

"But the rest," I prompt. "I didn't think there'd be so much—"
The box sits impassive between us. My voice catches on the
corners. I reach out to touch it, warily, as though it were a wild
animal, sleeping; I am curious, but it might be dangerous. I
wonder how much of what is in the box Whitman has read. I
recognize one of the scribblers at the top as a journal Susan had
been keeping—surely he must know what it is.

"Don't you think this might be, well, too private? Don't you
think you should go through everything first, sort of edit it?" Now
he will have to tell me if he has already done so.

"What does it matter?" His voice is angry. "What does it matter
now?"

"I suppose," I say after a moment. "Okay. I'll look at it. I'll see."

He stands up. "Good," he says, sounding relieved. He shoves
his long, bony fingers into his jacket pocket. Susan once told me
she was amazed that any pocket could be big enough to hold all
those fingers. "Look, I appreciate this. I didn't want to throw the
things all away, but I didn't want to deal with them, either."

I almost say it is only a few days, too soon for him to make such
decisions, but I decide not to.

"Whitman," I say. He has his back to me, preparing to leave. He
doesn't turn around.

"Life is shit," he says.

"Life goes on," I say, our voices overlapping each other. He
turns, and suddenly we laugh, metallic little sounds that clatter
into the air between us.

"Yeah. Well," he says.

At the door he stops beside the shopping bag, and I think for a
moment he is going to take it back with him, but he only begins to
empty it, like someone who has brought me presents. There is a
half-full package of kitty litter and the shallow box with the
domed cover; I remember helping Susan pick it out. "The *toilette*,"
she called it. There is the scratching post, which the cat has never
used, a brush, two food dishes and a water bowl, an unopened flea
collar, the jar of vegemite which Susan got with the cat and which
is still almost full, and a few cans of cat food.

"You sure you haven't forgotten anything?" I say.

"Don't think so," Whitman says, serious, looking at the pile of
things on my floor. He folds his bag up neatly along the original
creases and points at the cat food. "I think he'll eat other brands,
but this one was his favourite."

The cat sniffs at the pile of things on the floor as though they were the least familiar in the house.

"Well, Dong," I say, "it's you and me."

Whitman pulls his mouth up into a grimace that is sometimes a nervous smile and sometimes a gesture of annoyance. I assume this time it is the latter. "You can change his name if you like," he says. "I always thought it was so stupid. Dong. Jesus."

I try not to smile. "I suppose I could," I say.

"Yeah. Well." He keeps watching the cat, his fingers running over and over the folds of the bag he is holding. Then, unexpectedly, he bends down and strokes the cat, who ignores him, is licking at the lid of the vegemite jar.

"It's a trial," I remind them both, "for a week."

"Sure," he says. His knees creak as he stands up. "For a week."

After he has gone and I have put away the cat food and set up the litter box in a corner, the cat insists on being let out. When I open the door uncertainly he squeezes past before I can really decide if it is wise to let him go. I watch as he crosses the street and lies down on the front step of Whitman's house. I leave him there for about an hour, and then I go over and bring him back.

Two

For two days the box Whitman brought me sits on the table. I know that touching it will be the beginning, and I am nervous, want to put it off, feel I have not committed myself until I start reading, and then I will not be able to stop. I sit at the table and stare across the street, as though I am waiting for Whitman to come out of his house. I wonder what he is doing, thinking, behind the closed curtains, what else he is packing away in boxes because it reminds him of Susan.

I remember when they moved in less than a year ago, how I sat at this same table and watched them unloading their van, not knowing then how they would change my life.

Finally I take the three pictures out of the box and lay them on the table in front of me. Susan. I pick up the wedding picture. She looks so young, squinting a little into the camera, her arm around Whitman's waist. Her blonde hair was long then, in elaborate curls over her head. She is slim and beautiful in the way all wedding pictures are beautiful, the way they catch people at their most promising. Even Whitman is smiling here, looking like someone I would not recognize. But it is the smile of a man in a soldier's uniform whose photograph sits on his mother's bureau twenty years after the war is over and he hasn't come home, the smile of a man who senses his own future but will do what is expected. It is harder for me to look at Whitman than it is to look at Susan.

I turn the picture over, pick up the formal portrait of Susan, a graduation photo, I suppose. Zack's Photo Studio, Fairview, Alberta, it says in gold print at the bottom. It is not a flattering photo, the light picking up both the acne on her cheeks and the too-thick make-up she has used to hide it. She is wearing the white lipstick that was fashionable in the sixties, and, oddly, it makes her mouth look too big. Already she has the pudgy jaw line that seems a bit too large for her face, that looks as though it will eventually fold into a double chin. She is wearing glasses, one of the lenses quite thick, but even so I can look into those deep-set eyes, the eyes that turned her plain, square face into one a stranger might look at a bit longer than necessary. She did not wear glasses when I knew her, and it surprises me a little to think that she may have had contact lenses, that there were such things about her I do not know.

In the last picture, she is on the beach in Vancouver. I recognize the highrises behind her. She and Whitman lived there before moving here, so it is likely a recent photo. She is wearing a bikini and looking embarrassed, not wanting to have her picture taken. She has gained a lot of weight, and it hangs around her hips like extra clothes.

I put the pictures in an envelope and set them on the mantle. I cannot postpone looking at the rest of the things in the box. I empty everything on the floor. The cat jumps down from the chair he seems to have claimed and sniffs cautiously at the pile, then crawls into the empty box and occasionally reaches out a predatory paw at me as I try to sort through things.

There are many single looseleaf sheets, most of them written in pencil, a tiny script. I realize I have not seen Susan's handwriting before. These seem to be rough drafts of poetry. Some sheets are stapled or clipped together, and they might be short stories, or some kind of prose pieces. I try to read some of the poems—"Night rattles at my door," begins one, but the tiny writing shuts me out. It is a garble of crossed-out phrases, arrows directing me to other arrows, passages inserted everywhere in even smaller writing, abbreviations I cannot turn into words. Finally I pile the loose pages all together and turn to the file folders.

Here it is as though another person had done the work, the folders all carefully labelled: "Love Poems #1," "Love Poems #2," "Short Story: The Way Home," "Short Story: Choices," "Story: Foxtail and Freddy," "Letters from Editors." I open one of the poetry folders. Inside, the pages are all neatly typed, numbered, everything centered on the page. I am relieved to recognize the titles of some of the poems from the rough drafts. I close the folder. Not yet, I think. I must get everything in order before I begin. And I know that these are not what I want to read first.

What are left are the two scribblers. I sit for a while looking at them before I can bring myself to pull them towards me. They are Susan's journals. One has a blue cover; the other is orange. There is a place for name, address, subject, but only the orange one has anything written on it. Beside "Subject" it says, "Orange Juice." I can feel my heart start to beat faster, the itch of sweat in my armpits.

The handwriting is not, I am almost frightened to see, hard to read. It is a careful, half-printed script, reminding me more of the typed pages in the folders than of the anarchic writing in the rough drafts. It is almost as though she wrote this for someone else to see. I remember the book on graphology I once read, the simplistic analyses I used to do on letters from my friends. Upper zone letters high: it means imagination, I think. Some left-handed slant: leaning towards the past. Large spaces between words: loneliness—or was that for small spaces? I am glad I have forgotten.

The first entry is dated July 1, 1983. The day they moved here. Quickly I look at the first entry in the other scribbler. December, 1983. I know Susan kept diaries before they came here; she showed them to me once, a pile of them in the back of her filing cabinet. There must have been nine or ten, going back a long way, perhaps even to when she knew Freddy. Whitman, I think. He must have found them, then. Or had he? Maybe these were the only ones he didn't want to read, which is why they are here. But why give them to me, if he knew they were diaries, if all he wanted was for me to look at her literary work? I almost begin to smile. This is so like Whitman. He never makes things simple, wants people to think he is complex and mysterious, like the heroes in Gothic romances, usually not difficult to understand, but with a reputation to defend; they have to work at being enigmatic or people might lose interest.

I go back to the orange scribbler. I must make myself begin.

> Friday, July 1, 1983: well, here we are. Chilliwack. Lordy. haven't unpacked anything yet, just keep wandering around the lumps of boxes and suitcases. the house is so fucking huge, three bedrooms, a second bathroom in the big bedroom (*master* bedroom, must get the language right, so many rooms here, I'll have to find names for them all). we're both exhausted, but don't feel sleepy, still pumped up with adrenalin. a house of our own, after all these years. please, god, let us be happy here, I'll be good, I promise.

I close the scribbler. It is like hearing her talk. "The house is so fucking huge." I can remember her saying that to me, exactly those words, the first time we met. She's testing me, I thought then;

"fuck" is one of those touchstone words people use to assess others, the world, they think, being made up of people who are either offended by the word or not. I skip ahead a few entries, want to see what she has said about that day.

> Tuesday, July 5, 1983. finished unpacking today. amazing how much kitchen stuff we have, considering my fear and loathing of cooking. wish dishes would go out of style, like clothes, so you could throw some of the damned things away. memo for next fight with W.: throw dishes. still no phone hook-up, after my waiting all a.m. for the asshole from B.C. Tel. to show. went out in p.m. to the little grocery on Yale Road, must try to find a better shopping district in town. if only I had my own car. met the woman across the street as I was coming back. quite a gorgeous woman, considering she must be over 40, something kind of pompous, prissy about her, though. and me and my mouth. I had to say "fuck" to her, just the thing to do to charm your neighbours. she didn't faint, but I can imagine the story spreading through the matronly Chill. circles, "did you hear about those new people on Macken? Well, she says the f-word."

A smile is fiddling with the corners of my mouth. "Gorgeous," I think. I have never thought of myself as gorgeous. The men who have called me beautiful always followed this with some sexual demand; I did not really believe it was anything more than obligatory foreplay. Brenda says my face is "interesting," a word that is always a euphemism. Both my parents were tall and gangly people, not attractive, really, with their bones that seemed too close under their skins, their long faces that stretched their features thinly, not enough flesh to be sensual. When we were young, Claudia and I resembled them, accepting ourselves as not ugly but not beautiful either, just somewhere in between, ordinary children who did not stand out. When puberty came, pulling at us, Claudia changed very little, but my body rounded itself everywhere, filling in angles, adding weight until I was sure I was too fat. My face changed and softened so much people no longer recognized me, and my breasts swelled until I thought they would never stop; I was sure they must only seem vulgar. Thinking of it now, the way the boys looked at me, I suppose I had become attractive, but I was, and still am, used to thinking of myself as inconspicuous, a person of whom there are no expectations.

I looked at the other words Susan has used to describe me.

"Pompous, prissy"—somehow they are not as hurtful as I might have thought. I remember a professor at the university saying that when you mark a student essay, if you begin by saying something positive, the student will be much more willing to accept criticisms. Gorgeous, I think, almost laughing out loud, but pompous and prissy. Why not? There are worse ways to see me.
I go back to the journal. Now that we have met, it will be easier.

Wednesday, July 6, 1983: almost a week since we moved, already I'm starting to feel that what-am-I-doing-here. I walk around and around the house, through all the rooms, thinking *my* house, *my* house, remember my father on the farm walking around the fence, to see if anything had fallen on the wire to ground the fencer, my mother saying, "oh, he does that to check out his property, make sure nobody's stolen any of it, maybe he pees on the fenceposts like the dogs do, who knows with him." Property. Homeowner. maybe I should pee in the corners of all the rooms, would have to save up a big load.

Thursday, July 7, 1983: finally got phone connected this morning. sat there listening to the dial tone, the sound of the outside. I dialed Connie's number, got a recording saying you-have-dialed-a-number-to-which-long-distance-rates-apply, I was stunned, it hit me for the first time how Connie and Beth and Jim weren't just a few blocks away, that the phone line went for miles and miles, how if we talked now every word would be costing us something, would have to pay its way. the recording kept repeating in my ear. "fuck you," I shouted, "fuck you." really mature.
W. was late again, supper was cold and tasted like rubber cement, but I didn't give a shit. ask me how my day was, I thought, and I'll shove my fork in your ear. I asked him how his day was, he said there was so much new to learn, he didn't like all this overtime, didn't want to get behind in his thesis. ask me how my day was, I thought, and I'll give you shredded thesis sandwiches for lunch tomorrow.

Friday, July 8, 1983. worked a bit in the backyard, some nice shrubs and flowers there, it's good to dig in the earth, the hot yellow gravy of sun, *my* garden, connection to something primal, dirt under my fingernails, ground into my pores, don't get carried away, you hated this on the farm, don't get romantic.

Saturday, July 9, 1983: weekend. W. hermitted in his study, digging at the damned thesis. at least I had the van, went for a drive to Cultus Lake, full of tourists from Van. getting away from it all. noticed a college on the way out of town, maybe there'll be courses there I can take if I can't find a job, but, shit, I'll be able to find *something*.

Sunday, July 10, 1983: bizarre episode today—

Of course I remember this day. Bizarre, she says. That's a good word for it.

—couldn't drag W. out to play so decided to take up the offer of that woman across the street, Ellen what's-her-name, to "drop in sometime." she didn't seem like the kind who would get too kaffee-klatschy, and I was still feeling like such a shit for saying "fuck" to her, thought I should clean up my image in the neighbourhood. it was okay until this friend of hers arrived, a real born-againer. W. says I should get used to these attitudes, this is a Bible-belt town, etc., but I-mean-really.

I suppose I should be grateful to Margaret, or blame her, depending on how I look at it. There is nothing to bring two people closer than to meet a third person who seems to them both to have grazed in the pastures of lunacy.

I look at the journal again. It says Susan "decided to take up the offer" to "drop in sometime." I cannot remember saying that. It nags at me. Somehow it is important for me to know exactly how it began, who made the first move, who was responsible.

In any case, I was not displeased to see Susan at the door, although I felt the same wariness she did at encouraging that daily visiting routine the other women in this neighbourhood have. I had been careful to avoid that all these years, even though it probably meant I was considered snobbish or eccentric. I was not as nervous about Susan, though, because for one thing I had concluded she did not have children and would not be asking me to babysit or to contribute conversation about toilet-training. And during our first brief meeting I had, quite simply, liked her. I think it was partly because she *had* used the "f-word," had not been polite and safe, was someone who would take chances.

By the time Margaret arrived, I had learned that Susan was born in northern Alberta, that she met Whitman at university in Edmonton, that they moved to Vancouver so Whitman could do his Ph.D. in Psychology and now had only his thesis to finish, but she didn't see much point to it because there were no academic jobs any more, anyway.

"I have a B.A.," she said. "Big deal." She ran her forefinger along her chin, a funny gesture that made me notice her fingers, the nails that were not untidy but all different lengths. "I finally got a part-time job at a bank in Vancouver, but then I got laid off, so Whitman had to look for work and, would you believe it, he gets a job as loans officer at the very same branch that laid me off. He says it's because he worked in a bank for a year before he went to university, but if you ask me it's got more to do with the fact he's got hair on his chest and I don't—well, not enough hair, anyway."

I laughed. It was interesting listening to her talk, her voice deep in a way that made me think at first she had a cold, her language one that swung from tough to plaintive, with unexpected inflections, almost a dialect.

"So why did you leave the city?" I asked.

"Oh, the bank is into transferring its middle-management types around as much as possible to get them more experience. I think it's just a test to see how loyal they are, and whether they've got the proper kind of wives, who'll put up with all this moving shit."

"I guess I was that kind of wife," I said.

"Oh? Why?"

"Well, I mean I didn't really want to move out here, but Gordon—he was my husband—insisted. It was too expensive in Vancouver, he said; the pace of life would be easier in Chilliwack; I'd like it really-I-would—"

Susan gave a little snort of laughter. "All the usual bullshit, in other words."

"I guess so," I said, laughing too. I thought of the little book-keeping and report-writing business I had started, of how well it was doing, and of how when Gordon's accountant said I should incorporate myself, Gordon looked at him as though he had betrayed some secret and said, "Oh, now, that shouldn't be necessary," and a few weeks later he was saying "Chilliwack" and saying it over and over. But I had agreed to come; it was my fault, too, for giving in. I wonder if I would do the same now, if I have changed at all. Then, it seemed clear that if I could not convince him, he would have to prevail, and that was that. So I left my work, my house, my friends, and we moved to Chilliwack, into a new house on a dead-end street east of town. "With a little imagina-tion," the real estate agent had said, waving at the square and practical and off-white rooms, "you could do wonders with this place." I have not, I think, looking around me now, done wonders with this place. It is still the same plain two-bedroom house it was then.

After the movers had finished, after Gordon's sister Paulette had left the bottle of champagne, Gordon took my hands into his and said, "It's all right, then, isn't it? Sure it is." He looked at me with such eagerness I couldn't bear it, to let him not be guilty.

I pulled my hands slowly out of his, looked away from him. "I'm glad it's what you want," I said.

"So how long have you lived here?" Susan asked.

I had to think for a moment. "Ten years. Good heavens. I would have been thirty-four then, and Gordon would just have turned fifty-six."

It amazed me. Ten years. And I was still here, after all this time. I remembered how miserable I had been at first. The only people we saw regularly were Paulette and her husband, and Gordon's two sons from his first marriage, John and Gerald, and their wives. They all had numerous children, loud and destructive and normal, but fortunately they did not bring them over often. Gordon's relatives were all pleasant enough; like him they seldom had opinions that could either offend or interest anyone. We often played cards, and that at least was something I enjoyed, probably because I played to win and usually did. Gordon's first wife had died three years before he married me, but her memory leaned over us all because they took such pains never to mention her. It was as though Gordon were a bigamist, and I wasn't supposed to know. Sentences would begin, "That was the time you. . . ." or "You remember the house on Young Street. . . ." and then drop into embarrassed silence. Gordon said it was because they did not want me to think they were comparing us.

His son Gerald was older than I was, and it added to our discomfort. Neither he nor John would ever stay alone in the room with me, as though mere opportunity would turn us into sexual animals eager to attack each other. When they visited, the house always seemed to be full of guilty secrets.

For a while, I would drive in to Vancouver at least twice a week, sometimes just to park outside our old house and feel miserable. My friends slowly packed up the space I'd had in their lives with something new. It wasn't the same as it had been when I could simply drop by for coffee; now the visits had to be planned and formal.

"If you hate it out there so much," said Brenda finally, "why don't you just move back here?" Brenda Wikally was my best friend.

"Move back?" I had never considered it. "Gordon wouldn't do it."

"Then leave him."

"Oh, God, I couldn't do that."

"Well, think about it."

So I had to think about it. All the way back that day, I thought about it. *Welcome to Chilliwack*, said the sign at last, *Country Living at its Best*. I thought about it. Down Yale Road, past the big anti-abortion sign telling me not to murder babies, through the perpetually-remodelled downtown struggling against the big shopping centre outside of town, I thought about it. I turned onto Macken Avenue, into the driveway of this house, and Gordon came down the steps and opened the car door and held out his hand to me and said, "Hi. How was everybody?" I didn't have a chance.

"But it got better, didn't it?" Susan asked. "I mean, you did finally get used to this place?"

"I guess so," I said. "We made some new friends, and we did some travelling, to Europe once, and Australia. It was, you know, an undemanding life."

"But then he died," Susan said, not making it a question, as though she had been reading my mind.

"Two years ago," I said. "A heart attack in the evening, watching TV. He just stood up, holding onto the arm of the chesterfield, and said, 'Oh, God,' and an hour later he was gone. Funny, you know—when I think of it what I always see most clearly is his hand on the chair, how broad his fingernails were and the look of the chesterfield arm between his spread fingers."

"The mind will do that," Susan said. "It'll clench around some detail, the grain of sand in an oyster, and expect you to go on from there. You make what is necessary, I guess."

"What a good way to put it," I said.

"Yeah?" She looked pleased, surprising me that such a simple compliment could affect her, that she had, after all, the same vulnerabilities as we all did. "Is there more coffee, by the way? I love the evil stuff."

"Oh, sure." I got up and walked over to the stove, and through the kitchen window I glimpsed something moving, sliced off by the bottom of the window, a half-moon of wild white hair that

could only belong to Margaret. Margaret was coming up the walk.
"Oh, good grief," I said.
"What?" Susan asked. But there was no time to explain about Margaret, even if she could have been explained. It was almost funny, that she should have arrived when she did, like a continuation of my history, because it was after Gordon died that I met her, that I had more or less inherited her.

She was Gerald's mother-in-law, a round and rumpled-looking woman in her early sixties, "not getting the pension yet," she assured me, and she was persistent. "We're related," she would say in answer to my vague excuses. She was what people would call "strong," the domineering strength that is acceptable in men but not in women, and she inserted herself into my life as though there were no question of my needing or wanting her.

In spite of myself, I rather like Margaret. We do not think alike on a single issue, and she is a gossip, hungry for other people's emotion as though it were pure protein, but, after the bland agreeableness of the rest of Gordon's family, she could at least entertain me. And there is a grim resourcefulness about her that makes me glad she is on my side. The first time she came over, my house was busy with a coup of red ants. I had killed dozens of them at a time, pinching them one after another into a paper towel, but the next day Margaret brought me some ant traps, little round boxes, and set them up around the house.

"Don't kill the little devils one by one," she said. "Let them get into the bait and they'll carry it back to the nest and kill the whole works." It was the kind of efficiency that satisfied her. After two days there was not an ant anywhere, and I imagined a hill of tiny corpses somewhere, perfect long-distance genocide.

"It worked beautifully," I told Margaret. Nothing pleased her as much as gratitude.

Another time, not long after Gordon had died and I was faced with taking on the mysterious chores of men, I hired a roofer to reshingle part of my roof, and when he did not fix the leak and ignored my polite complaints, it was Margaret who went over to his office and said she could see to it that he never got another job in this town, and the next morning he was back on my roof with new shingles, and the leak was fixed.

"You have to stand up for your rights," she said, cutting into her piece of pie with such determination that flakes of crust leapt onto the tablecloth. "People take advantage of widows."

And here she was, coming up my walk, Margaret.

"What? What?" Susan was saying.

"Oh, it's a little hard to explain," I said, opening the door.

"Well, hello," Margaret said, coming in without being asked. "And who's this?"

So of course I made the introductions, and then Margaret, not even waiting for me to finish pouring her coffee, began to tell us about the new church she had been to that morning.

"It was the most exciting one yet," she insisted, "and I've been to a lot." I could attest to that.

"Oh, really," I said, wishing she would leave. I could see Susan's face go stiff and anonymous, like those faces on TV of bank robbers with stocking masks; you could almost see their features but not quite, had to imagine the expressions that must be there.

"This one was in Abbotsford," Margaret went on, "Sevenoaks Alliance, you know, the one Pastor Bob is at, the famous Pastor Bob, you've heard of him."

"I think so," I said. I hadn't.

"Well, it was a wonderful sermon. He explained so clearly—the man is so *intelligent*—what the anti-Christ is, and it's not communism like Rev. Schmidt says, it's *Humanism.*" She turned to Susan. "Do you know what Humanism is?"

"Oh yes," Susan said.

Margaret was a little disappointed; a part of her lecture would have to be cut out, but she quickly reshuffled her material. "And he explained all about 666. You know what 666 is, don't you, the number of the beast? Well, did you know that in computers 666 is the basic programming number? Everywhere people are getting forms and credit cards with 666 on them."

"Maybe it's the computer, then, that's the anti-Christ," I said, "not Humanism." I tried to catch Susan's eye, hoping she would see I was not being serious.

"Well," Margaret thought for a moment. "They're related. Humanism is the philosophy of the people who build the computers." She was no dummy.

"Of course," Susan said.

"And it gets worse," Margaret continued. "You know how in the big grocery stores the price has been replaced with those computer lines, how they run it over a scanner to read it? Well, Pastor Bob has *proof* that those scanners are also set up to read individual identification numbers, which will be tattooed with a laser beam, and they'll be invisible to the naked eye, into a person's right hand or forehead! And that, of course, is exactly what the Bible prophesies. It's the mark of the beast, whose number is . . ."

"666," I said. "Well, it certainly does all fit nicely together."

"Amazing," said Susan. "Did you know that in Vancouver all the federal government phone numbers begin with 666?"

"You see, you see!" cried Margaret. "Of course the government has to be in on it."

"And come to think of it," Susan continued, "there's a philosophy prof. at UBC, who I'm sure teaches Humanism, who lives at 3666 West 6th."

I thought she was pushing it, but Margaret did not seem anything but delighted to have found someone else who believed.

"Look," she said before she left, "I must leave these books with you," and she dug several paperbacks from her bag and shoved them into my hands. "This one Pastor Bob wrote himself. Can you believe he'd have the time? *Apocalypse*, it's called, and then there's this one, *Satan's Mark Exposed*, and *How to Recognize the Anti-Christ*. I haven't read them yet, but Pastor Bob probably explained it all well enough to me, so you can keep them if you want. Oh, and here, *The Humanist Manifesto*. You *must* read them," she said, touching Susan on the arm.

When she was gone, Susan and I stared at each other across the room. I did not know what to say.

"I only want to know one thing," Susan said. "How the hell would you get your forehead across the checkout counter onto the scanner?"

And then we were both laughing, laughing for weeks afterwards, every time we saw a license plate, an address, with even two sixes in it, the way friends laugh when they have a private joke, laughing as though the insanities of the world could never touch us.

Once I told her I thought she had been overdoing it with Margaret, with the phone number and address business, and she said, "but I wasn't. That's really true."

"Oh, sure."

"It is, really."

I did not believe her, of course, but when I got home I called Vancouver information and asked for the number of Canada Post and Canada Customs. "666-3531, 666-1545," the operator said. It was a bit startling. I have always wanted to see if there is a philosophy professor living at 3666 West 6th in Vancouver, but that would involve a bit more work than a joke is worth, and perhaps I don't really want to know.

Three

It is the next day. The journal is open on my lap. I am brooding over an entry dated Tuesday, September 6, 1983.

> another job interview, just for a bloody typist's job at an insurance company. had to take a typing test, so humiliating, only got up to 30 w.p.m. I could tell that smarmy "we'll-let-you-know" meant "forget it." Ellen drove me to the interview as usual—I worry that I'm using her, always expecting her to drive me around. but then I tell myself that she's just lonely, that maybe I'm doing her a favour spending time with her, that maybe I'm a bit like the daughter she couldn't have.

I am hurt and upset by this. Doing me a favour, she says. How could she reduce our friendship to mutual exploitation? I know it wasn't like that. But this is only September, I tell myself, glancing at the other scribbler. Maybe it did seem to her then that I was lonely, was . . . pressing. And she was depressed when she wrote this; perhaps that is why she is being hard here, on both of us.

Her last statement puzzles me: "the daughter she couldn't have." I have never wanted children—it was not a matter of my being unable to have them. I try to remember the conversation from which Susan might have taken this, but it is all a blank. What a strange thing for her to misunderstand. And whatever Susan meant to me, I don't think "daughter" comes close.

The next item is dated Thursday, September 8.

> went shopping and to a movie with Ellen, trying not to think about not getting a job, being stuck in this town forever, well, Ellen's done it, ten years for gawd's sake and she's still moderately sane.

Moderately sane. Well, that is a relief at least. *Moderately sane* is the best Susan could say about anyone.

"Vancouver is just far enough away for me to really miss it, to feel connected because it *seems* close, but then you look at that two-hour drive in and you might as well be in the interior somewhere, know what I mean?"

I knew exactly what she meant. Gordon had promised that living a hundred miles from the city was no distance at all, that we would still come in for plays and movies and to see people. But I knew even then what it would be like. I had been born in Vancouver, but a few years before my mother died we moved out to the suburbs, to Surrey, which was just country then. We lived in a big old house on Hjorth Road, which is now called 104th Ave. and is an ugly four-lane commercial street. Our friends in the city slowly shifted away from us, and eventually Vancouver became just somewhere we had once lived. When I moved with a girlfriend into an apartment in Vancouver's west end to go to university, I felt as if I had come down from Inuvik, except that coming from Inuvik probably had more prestige than coming from Surrey. Once, when someone accused the Surrey MLA of representing only the lunatic fringe, he protested that they needed to be represented too, and I laughed along with everyone else at my psychology professor's joke about Surrey with the lunatic fringe on top. It is so easy to betray your past.

"It'll get better," I said to Susan. "A job will come along. You'll find Chilliwack isn't all that bad."

"Yeah, sure," she sighed. "You know 'Chilliwack' used to be spelled with an 'h' in it: Chilli*whack*, right?"

"Yes."

"Well, they changed the spelling because all these people came here and said they couldn't wait to get the 'h' out."

"Oh, Susan!" I began to giggle, like a girl, and people around us in the Zeller's looked at me indulgently, smiling a little themselves.

"It's true, it's true," Susan insisted. "I read it in a Chamber of Commerce brochure. Hey, I'm going to buy this. Whitman will love it." It was an ashtray with the words *Stop Smoking* engraved on the bottom. I thought she was joking but she took it with her to the cashier and set it beside the batteries she was buying.

"It won't really help, will it?" I asked. "To stop Whitman smoking, I mean."

"Oh, hell no," Susan grinned, bouncing the ashtray lightly up and down in her hand.

We walked around the store a bit more, both of us reluctant to go home. Susan wanted to look at microwave ovens, but when she saw the price of them she shuddered. "If I pay that much for anything," she told the salesman, "it has to be able to give me orgasm." Back in the mall, she bought us each an ice cream cone, and we sat on one of the benches eating them, like children, swinging our legs and watching people pass. When I think of my days with Susan, it is such times I want to remember, the way she made me feel young again. I had spent so many years with Gordon learning to be older than I was, a dutiful grown-up, and Susan was the tomboy who moved in next door and said, "Come on, I dare you."

Finally we wandered out to the parking lot, where my car had gotten itself lost, and Susan said I should train it to come when I called, and she embarrassed me by standing in the middle of the lot shouting, "Here, car, car, car, car." I found it at last, and we headed home, arguing about seat belts, Susan insisting it was better to be thrown clear, but I don't think she believed it, was only arguing that way because I was arguing the opposite.

As we drove past the downtown movie theatre, she suddenly shouted, "Hey, I don't believe it! *Woodstock!* I take back all the rude things I said about this town. Stop, stop—let me see when it's playing."

"There's no room to pull over," I protested.

"Oh, just double-park," she said, impatient. "I'll only be a second."

I put the flashers on and waited while she ran back to the theatre. Even such a minor traffic violation made me nervous; I suppose I expected an immediate accusation of horns and police sirens, but the one car behind me simply changed lanes and went past me as though I had every right to stop in the middle of the street.

"Ellen, listen!" Susan, excited, was at my window. "There's a show starting in ten minutes. Let's go, okay? Or have you seen it already?"

"Well, no, but. . . ."

"Then let's go, okay? It's a great movie, really, you'll like it."

Excuses welled up in me, but I realized my main reason for hesitating was only that it was so unexpected, and that might actually be a good reason for me to go.

"Okay," I said. "I'll park and meet you back here."

Inside the theatre, which had that worn-out smell of old popcorn, I said, "I vaguely remember hearing about this movie. It has a lot of rock 'n' roll music in it, doesn't it? You realize that's not exactly my style."

"Aw, you'll love it. The part when Joan Baez goes a cappella is just wonderful."

"You mean you've *seen* it?"

"Just once. It's the kind of movie you don't mind seeing twice."

I could not imagine wanting to pay to see any movie twice. In fact, after this one started, I couldn't imagine wanting to pay to see it once. I'm not sure what it was that made me uncomfortable—maybe the drugs, maybe just the general dishevelment of everyone, their odd arrogance that they were significant simply because they were all here in the same place, Woody Guthrie's son saying over and over, "The New York freeway's *closed*, man!" as though that were an important accomplishment. But there was some interesting music, I had to admit that, even if it *wasn't* exactly my style, and by the end of the movie I was actually glad I had come.

Outside, I said, "Well, that was entertaining."

Susan didn't answer, and when I looked over at her I saw she was wiping tears from her face.

"You're crying!" I exclaimed. I am not usually that tactless, but it was so surprising—why should anyone cry after a movie like this?

"Well, yeah," Susan said, embarrassed. "Dumb, eh?"

"But why? It was such a happy movie. Nobody dies at the end."

"No, you're wrong—everybody dies at the end. All those wonderful young faces and, fuck, now those women are all born-again Tupperware salespeople and the men are all corporate lard-asses, and all that idealism and anti-capitalism is just down the toilet. I mean, that film is fifteen years *old*, and so are we that much older, so am I, maybe that's all it is."

"Oh," I said. "I didn't realize it was that long ago." And I hadn't. I had thought the film was perhaps four or five years old. Fifteen years. It shocked me, that I was so out of touch. The people on the screen could almost have been my contemporaries. By the time we were back at the car Susan was making some joke about parking meters and I was the one who was depressed.

It was late afternoon by the time we got home, and I could see Whitman was already back from work and mowing his front lawn. Susan waved at him and he waved back. But when she got out of the car, instead of heading back across the street she said, "Mind if I come in for a minute?"

"Sure," I said, even though I was still feeling depressed about the movie and not really in the mood for anyone's company. "Shall I make some coffee?"

"Oh, well. . . . I shouldn't really stay." But she walked over to the kitchen table and sat down. I put on the coffee and came over and sat down, too, both of us watching Whitman across the street pushing the lawnmower back and forth, back and forth.

"I should get home and make supper, I guess," she said, but she didn't get up. "I mean, mowing the lawn is such shit work."

"I guess I wouldn't know," I said. My own yard is rather wild. The farm boy who sometimes comes to cut the grass says he will soon have to bring a combine.

She laughed. "A speck of dust in your house would cut its wrists out of loneliness, so how come you're so, ah, casual, shall we say, about the grass? Jesus, people could lose children in it."

I considered her question for a while. "Gordon always used to keep it so neat. I'm not sure why I don't. Maybe it's one of his chores I resist absorbing. I don't want to make myself that independent." I got up to bring us our coffee.

Susan watched me, pulling her mouth sideways in the way she sometimes did when she disapproved. "My mother told me once when I was a little girl and wanted to learn how to milk the cows that I shouldn't learn, because if I did then I'd be expected to do it all the time."

"It's something like that, maybe," I said.

"When I was a little girl," Susan said. I don't know what she meant, repeating herself like that. We were silent for a moment. The noise of the lawnmower rattled through the windows, stuffed itself into our ears. "Well, shit, I'm no better," Susan said suddenly. "If Whitman dropped dead I'd probably say to hell with ours too. Lawns are a big joke, anyway—I mean, civilization gives us electricity and flush toilets and socialism, and then, just to see if we're paying attention, lawns."

We sat for a while longer, sipping our coffee, watching Whitman push the lawnmower back and forth. I could see the sweat forming a thin oval on the back of his shirt. He never looked up once, so perhaps he knew we were watching. When he was almost finished, Susan got up to go. She almost forgot her package with the ashtray and batteries on the kitchen table, and when she reached for it she picked up the salt shaker sitting there, too, and said, "Look. A salt and battery."

"Go home!" I said.

Sun., Sept. 11: got so furious at W. today, him and his goddamned
thesis, surely t'God if he was ever going to finish it he'd have done it
years ago for fuck's sake, but, no, he carries it around with him like a
stone, a big heavy excuse, Sisyphus pushing his thesis up the hill.
maybe he thinks I'm part of the hill, a big log he has to step over,
that threw up a root this morning for him to trip on, saying it was
sick of being ignored, that it's always his job or his thesis and never
me, and it sounded childish, but I didn't care, I was so pissed off,
how every weekend when we could go somewhere together we
don't. And W. with his grim sour look saying the thesis was damned
important, didn't I understand that yet, it was his way out, to something better, a Ph.D. was all he'd ever wanted. that's the trouble, I
shouted, and I slammed out, took the van and drove down Hope
River Road, parked and sat there watching the grey water pleating
past, and I thought about Freddy and felt sorry for myself.

Susan sitting on Hope River Road thinking about Freddy. The
words send a chill up my neck. The next entry, something
mundane about gardening, was written three days later. I go back
and read the lines about Freddy again, but it is useless; I cannot see
what Susan saw, cannot see the Freddy she remembered.

It was about two weeks later, in early October, that Whitman
first mentioned Freddy to me. It was a night I would remember for
other reasons. Susan had called, said she was just rushing off to
catch the bus to Vancouver, a friend was having a baby and wanted
her there, she'd be gone for three or four days, and if I felt like it,
why didn't I ask Whitman over for supper, he'd be so grateful for a
good meal, the man couldn't turn on the oven without pulling the
knobs off, etc.

I was nervous. I had never been alone with Whitman before. He
was always just a faint noise in the background when I went over
to see Susan, someone who would materialize sometimes in the
kitchen to make a cup of coffee. We would thrust awkward pieces
of conversation at each other as he waited for the water to boil.
"How's the thesis coming?" I would ask. "Slowly, slowly," he
would say, or sometimes, "Not too bad today." Then he would
slouch off back to the study with that hunched walk of tall people
unused to their bodies. "His Alan Alda walk," Susan called it,
"post-modern Quasimodo."

Once, I remember, I asked him about his job at the bank,
whether it was going well.

"I think," he said, as though he were working it through for the first time, "the manager thinks that because I've taken so many psychology courses I should know a lot of tricks about getting along with people, seeing through them, knowing if they're lying on their loan applications, that sort of thing. And I don't, of course. It makes it difficult."

Susan had been watching him in a kind of tight, intense way. *She looked at him with narrowed eyes:* it was a line from novels, but I had never actually seen anyone look that way. Until now. Susan looked at Whitman with narrowed eyes. Then she turned to me and said, with a sigh, "Whitman's life isn't working out, you see."

He gave her a look of such anger and disgust I shrank from it. He walked out of the kitchen without saying a word.

Susan gave a light laugh, waved her hand vaguely in the air, as though trying to brush something away. "Oh, dear. I seem to have said the wrong thing again."

When I think of them together, Susan and Whitman, I realize how seldom I saw them that way, how little I really knew about what went on between them.

That night in October, with Susan in Vancouver, I made supper for Whitman, a reasonably good meal, but nothing too elaborate, a chicken casserole. I did not want him to think I had prepared anything I might not have made just for myself. I began to mix a dessert that I had made once before and taken over to Susan and that he said he liked, but then I stopped myself, afraid he would remember and think I was doing it just to please him, would think I had a mind that saved up such information like a recipe box. It was almost as hard to choose what to wear: something attractive but not elaborate. I finally picked out a blue suit dress that I knew looked good on me but that was over five years old. I made a point of not washing my hair that afternoon.

During supper I dished up the usual question. "How's the thesis coming?"

"Slowly, slowly," he said.

"It's on Skinner, isn't it?" I asked. "Behaviourism?" My mind rummaged through its moldy archives to what was left of an introductory Educational Psychology course.

"Well, basically, yes." I had asked the right questions. This was what mattered to him. He leaned forward across the table, almost, for a moment, looked in my eyes. "It's about Skinner but also about Humanism," he said eagerly. "Essentially the two are incompatible in their approach to human behaviour, but I see some ways of reconciling them. Existentialism and Humanism are—what's wrong?''

I had been smiling, thinking of Margaret and the anti-Christ. "Oh, nothing, nothing," I said. "It's just that I had a talk with someone else not long ago about Humanism."

"Really?" he said. "Here, in town?"

"Well, she's not exactly a kindred spirit. She thinks Humanism is the manifestation of the devil."

"Oh Lord, them!" he said angrily, pushing back from the table, flailing his long fingers in the air. "They have to have absolutes, some crack-pot ministers giving them the one right answer. Well, wouldn't we all like it to be so easy, not have to take responsibility for screwing up because the old guy in the sky has it all figured out and is organizing everything." He paused, embarrassed. "I mean, it just upsets me when people can't face up to reality, you know?"

"I guess it's appealing to think that no matter what you do you can't ever really make mistakes." I was simply repeating what he had said, eager to be agreeable. It was, I suppose, what I thought, too, which was fortunate; I have never been good at standing up to a man in an argument. My father said to me once, "There are other ways of getting what you want," not explaining, only saying again, "other ways," and looking at me hard.

"Determinism," Whitman said gloomily. "It's why Skinner is so damned hard to deal with."

"Did Susan tell you about the time she was over here and my crazy religious friend dropped by and told us about 666?"

"I don't know," he said. "I mean, I can't remember. Actually," he hesitated. "I don't listen enough to Susan. Sometimes I know she's been telling me something and my head is still in the bank writing up a loan application or with the thesis and I just don't hear a word she's saying. Pretty shitty of me, right?" He gave a little *huh* of laughter.

I don't want to hear this, I told myself, but part of me was excited; he was trusting me with his feelings. Now I wonder if he wasn't just trying to lead me into telling him what I knew about Susan.

"It's understandable," I said, my voice like a hand smoothing out wrinkles on a bedspread. "You can't always shut out all the voices that want something from you."

He smiled. I felt stupidly pleased. "Ellen," he said then, "has Susan ever said anything to you about Freddy?"

"No," I said. "Who's Freddy?"

"Oh, just some guy she used to know when she still lived with her folks up north. I just thought that, you know, she might have mentioned him to you sometime."

"No," I said, curious. "She hasn't."

And before I could ask him any more about it, he began talking about something else, and then I brought dessert and coffee, and as soon as he had finished he got up and thanked me politely for the meal and said he would have to go.

I want to end the evening there, but it is not that easy, memory an over-zealous janitor who picks up the discarded frames of film and splices them back in. I shut my eyes against the image, but Whitman and I are still standing there at the door as we were that night. Whitman is taking my hand, awkwardly, to say good-night, and suddenly he is putting his hands on my shoulders and kissing me, and I am reaching up my hands and putting them on his waist, and then he is pushing back against the door, stumbling on the steps, and walking very quickly back to his house. And I am standing at the open door with the foggy cold climbing up my legs, my arms crossed so tightly on my chest it is as though something dangerous inside of me might escape.

I have been crying; there are small wet circles puckering the page. If I had not kissed him back, I think, if only I hadn't kissed him back. But it did not seem like a question of making a wrong choice. I thought of those Kirlian photographs I saw thirty years ago, the pure energy flaring out around fingers like the sun's corolla, and Whitman and I, standing at the door, with that energy suddenly leaping out at each other. It was the way it was with Paul, my first husband, although I do not like to remember that either. Not a question of choice, I tell myself even now, wanting it to be that simple.

I go to the kitchen and make myself a cup of coffee, walk around the house with it, holding the mug in both hands even though the heat is at the point of discomfort. I go into the study, sit at the desk. Books crowd the shelves to the ceiling along three walls, a collection Gordon and I were both proud of. I have read everything here at least once, but today it does not make me feel accomplished, only old. The books all have their backs to me, I think suddenly, surprised to see it that way. We have spines, they are saying, wrapping their covers arrogantly around them.

It is pointless to do this, but I pull out Laurence's *The Stone Angel*, the book I had been reading that day in October, and it falls open to the page with the piece of paper in it like a bookmark. Only it is not a bookmark. It is the paper I found in my mailbox the next morning. I unfold it. Typed almost exactly in the middle of the page are these words:

> "Though not free to act,
> men nevertheless behave
> as if they were."
> B.F. Skinner

"Rampant with memory," says Hagar Shipley in the book open before me. Perhaps that is who I am, an old woman looking back and misunderstanding.

"So how was the big city?" I asked when Susan got back, when she scratched on my door in her usual silly way and pleaded to be let in.

"Weird. I've only been gone, what, four months, but already it seems as if I never lived there."

"The waters seal shut behind, and, lo, no ripple tells of thy passing."

"Ecclesiastes, right? No, Rod McKuen. Glad you're reading something with a little class. Anything else new I should know about?"

It was almost funny. "No," I said. "Not a thing."

My secret sat on the table between us like a bowl of red apples, saying *eat*, saying *knowledge*.

Four

I look at my watch: 2:30. My aerobics class is at 3:00. I consider missing it, continuing with the journal, but I have missed too many classes in the last week; I must make myself resume the routines. I get out my shorts, my sweat shirt and sweat pants, although I always feel dowdy around the other women in their colour-coordinated outfits, their tights and leg-warmers. But I decided right at the beginning that I would not spend money on special clothes. I did have to buy a special brassiere, though— "industrial strength," Susan called it, embarrassing me in front of the cashier.

At the class, which is at a community hall only a few minutes' drive from my house, I am still able to go through all the exercises without having to stop; I suppose I had assumed that missing even a few sessions would reduce me to breathless flab.

"Are you having *fun?*" shrieks the instructor, an anorexic-looking woman barely out of her teens. "Beat iiiiit," the music shrieks back at a volume loud enough to homogenize our brains. Whenever I hear any of these songs on the radio, I can think only of where they appear on the aerobics tape, of how much longer I have to go.

"Looking *good*, Peggy!" she shouts at Peggy, the only woman here older than I am and about seventy pounds overweight. Peggy has only been coming to our group for about the last month, although she quit after the first two classes, disillusioned, no doubt, at being the only one here who seemed to have any need of such sessions. Several members of the class visited her and talked her into coming back. She is necessary to us, I suppose, a warning of what we will become if we break faith.

"Cool down!" And we begin the slow last five minutes, the part I like best. "Stretttch, two, three, and uuup, two, three." The last wistful notes of "Bridge Over Troubled Waters" cling to the air, and then we are finished, murmuring satisfaction to each other and wiping the sweat from our faces, like construction workers at the five o'clock whistle.

Driving home, I wonder, as I usually do, if I should stop going—it seems so foolish, jerking my body around in a roomful of people I barely know. It gives me a sense of keeping control, I suppose. But mostly I go because it helps to define my day. I first started going after Gordon died, when I was desperate for definitions, when life around me turned into a blizzard I was lost in, a white, anonymous landscape.

Of the first months after his death I can barely remember anything. The days are pasted in my memory like over-exposed photographs, people with their paces pale and out of focus. Then one day I flushed the rest of the Valium down the toilet and took inventory. I was a Widow. I said it out loud, watching my mouth in the mirror, "I am a Widow." I remembered how years ago I had stood before a mirror in Vancouver and said, "I am divorced." At least, I decided, *Widow* was a word with status; it spoke unambiguously of suffering and survival, of unjust abandonment. It also, I think now, spoke of freedom, but I have never wanted freedom when I could belong to someone.

Whatever I thought being a widow would mean, I was soon to see I was wrong. Gordon's sister Paulette dropped by only without her husband and eventually stopped coming altogether; his sons and their wives came by only two or three times after the funeral and that was all. The couples Gordon and I had befriended over our years here, the people I considered my own friends as much as his, slowly stopped calling.

"It's hard, you know," one of the women explained to me, awkwardly. "There's no one for the man to visit with."

What the women did do was press upon me the names of other widows, a more appropriate category of relationships, other women with something missing. I was always polite and uninterested, and, except for Margaret, I was able to deflect them all. These are women at the end of their lives, I thought, and I am, dear God, I am only forty-two. I have half my life left.

Brenda of course suggested I move back to Vancouver, but even she said I should give myself time, that too much change too soon was stressful. And I was afraid of the move; Chilliwack felt like home now, Vancouver a big new city I would be a stranger in. Brenda was the only one I really knew there any more, and we were both nervous about the demands I would make on her. Then there was the question of money. Gordon had left me the house and just enough in savings to live from, but even if I could sell the house now, the market was so depressed I would take a loss, and I could never afford the Vancouver prices. For now, I told myself, I'll stay here. "For now" has stretched into nearly three years.

Later, of course, there were Susan and Whitman; I couldn't leave then. But between them and Gordon's death was an awkward, restless time. I was trying to find out, I suppose, how to live my life.

"You need a *hobby*," Margaret insisted. Hers was making afghans. She must have made enough to populate half the homes in Chilliwack.

"I don't have the kind of talent with those things that you do," I said, partly because I knew it would please her but also because it was true. I do have a hobby I enjoy: reading—fiction, history, biography, poetry, and my study is piled to the ceiling with books. I must have read most of what is in the town library, and I always check out the maximum allowable and have them read well before the due date. But the books then were not enough; I found myself reading three or four pages without understanding a word, putting them down carelessly without bookmarks. I would stand looking out at the street for hours, even at night would not want to draw the curtains, as though something important might happen that I didn't want to miss.

Finally, because I am well organized and believe problems should be approached practically, I made a list of things I could do and crossed them off as I tried or rejected them. I titled the list, "Looking for Meaning," putting quotation marks around it to show myself I was being at least a little ironic.

1. Get a job.

I made a vague effort to reactivate my old business, but no one was interested in the kind of consulting services I could offer. "You have to understand," said the young man patiently at the Manpower office, as though I had the I.Q. of a hamster, "times are bad all over." I had waited in line for two hours to hear that. The only job offers I had were for baby-sitting, and I was determined not to let it come to that. I have never particularly liked or wanted children, and perhaps one of the reasons I married Gordon was that he had already raised a family and wasn't interested in starting another.

2. Join a club.

For most I was either too young or too old, and definitely too unmarried. But there were:

a) the fitness class, where I went every day except Sunday. But it was not exactly the sort of activity that gave my life meaning; it was more like making a frame for a picture I hadn't yet bought.

b) the local branch of the New Democratic Party, which I joined for a while. I am not really a socialist, am what Susan would call a wishy-washy Liberal, but in this province there is no Liberal Party, only an extreme right and an extreme left, and I suppose I was not alone in letting myself be nudged further left than I wanted simply because that is the side civilization seems to be on here, and one does have an obligation to side with civilization. But the Constituency meetings were too depressing, full of grim statistics and nostalgia for the short time years before when the party was in power. Chilliwack, we all seemed to know but did not actually admit, was a vehemently Social Credit riding where the NDP had no hope of ever winning a seat. And I would rather not play if I know I can't win.

c) the church. People here take religion seriously. Margaret insisted I attend several of the local fundamentalist churches with her; she was, I must concede, at least eclectic, and did not seem to have chosen one absolutely, but they were all rather alarming. It was educational, I assured her, but not something I thought one should do very often. I did some Sundays, out of an old atavism, go to the United Church, where I had been brought up in a rather half-hearted and innocuous way. "I don't see how it could hurt her," my mother had argued. For Margaret the United Church was really no better than atheism, and I admit that increased its appeal. The people there were nice and would sometimes invite me over after the service. It was a pity, I thought, that I was so bored by nice people.

d) the reading group. Six of us, mostly with some connection to the United Church, began a novels club, meeting every month at each others' homes and discussing a novel we had chosen. I found it interesting enough, and I still go regularly, although, since we try to restrict our selections to what we can each buy in the local bookstore, there is a problem with variety, and sometimes we have had to settle for Arthur Hailey or Stephen King.

3. Take a course at the college.

I had been an English major at university, so I decided to try something more objective. I enrolled in a Math course, thought I would appreciate the precision of it, the way there was one right answer for every problem. I was prepared to feel the awkwardness of being the oldest in the class, but I was not prepared for an instructor who had just taken a Cold Mountain workshop and decided to turn the class into an encounter group. I did not enjoy working in a "diad," as he called it, with an eighteen-year-old, telling each other how we felt about a) arithmetic and b) each other. I suppose the next class would have been better, but I did not go back.

4. Travel.

I liked travelling, but it was not much fun alone, and it was expensive. Brenda and I went on short trips together when she had the time. One summer we spent two weeks in San Francisco, where Brenda had an old friend who took us to a gay club for women. I felt voyeuristic, but it was interesting, watching women in love with other women, wondering what it would be like to want that. Certainly it was difficult to come back to a town run by fundamentalists. Travel, obviously, could offer no advice about how to live here, only an escape.

5. Make friends.

There was Brenda. There were some of the United Church women. There was Margaret. There were a few old university people I still corresponded with. It was, I thought, as much as I wanted at the moment. It is not possible, in any case, to advertise for friends with the required personality; you collect them by coincidence, by accident: who sits beside you in a class at school, who keeps phoning and coming over until you give in, who moves in across the street.

And, even as I was brooding about it, thinking that I would have to make a new list, thinking about moving to Vancouver again, stirring it around and around in my head like a gravy that won't thicken, I saw the white van pull into the driveway across the street, saw the agent in the Block Brothers car hand the house keys to the tall, worried man in his mid-thirties who stepped out of the van, saw the passenger door open and a blonde woman in jeans get out, saw for the first time the two ordinary-looking people to whom my life would belong for the next year.

Back at home after my class, I take a quick bath and wash my hair. The cat yowls at the closed bathroom door until I have to get out of the tub and let him in. He looks around, disappointed, as though he had been expecting something more interesting and then jumps up on the toilet seat and leans in to drink.

"Stop it," I yell, flicking bath water at him. I hate how he will insist on drinking from the toilet even though I put fresh water out for him.

I frighten him so much that he nearly falls in, but he recovers his balance and jumps down and gallops back to the door, where he gives me a mournful look and begins to lick the drops from his fur. He's just a cat, I think, feeling guilty, and when I get out of the tub and get dressed, I pick him up and pet him until I cajole him into his rumbling purrs. He sits slit-eyed and happy on my lap. It is amazing how easily I can stroke him into forgiveness, erase my unkindness from his memory. If only it were as easy with people. I let him stay on my lap, where he stretches out into sleep, and I reach for Susan's journal.

It was October there, I remember, a listless month drawling by, transitional, sucking the green from the leaves and the warmth from the evening air, stiffening the gardens with the first frost. But the afternoons were thick with sunshine, showing us what we would be missing by November, when the days turned brown and then grey.

I did not see Whitman again for several weeks, except for glimpses of him as he came home from work and hurried into the house. Once I saw him look furtively over his shoulder, at my window, as though he were afraid I might rush out and pursue him. *Were:* no, that is not right. It suggests unlikelihood, the hypothetical. *Was* is the right word—as though he *was* afraid— suggesting probability. I smiled when I saw him do that, but I did not think it was funny.

Susan I saw almost every day. She liked to play cards and taught me games I'd never heard of. Her favourite was an old German one called 66 ("One more six and we'd be playing with fire," she said). It was a complicated game using only half the deck and involving an option I didn't quite understand called "covering up," in which the card lying face up is turned over onto the rest of the pile, removing it from play, and you have to win by using only the cards in your hand. It was something Susan tried frequently, even when it was chancy and I would make three times the usual points if she lost. When we didn't play cards we went shopping together, trying on expensive clothes and buying polyesters. Wools and cashmeres and silks, Susan explained, never came in sizes over ten, because rich people were never fat, and fat people had to be protected from themselves; it had something to do with the Trilateral Commission. Sometimes we would go for drives in the country; once we stopped for gas near Hell's Gate, with its risky views of the white-knuckled Fraser pushing like a fist through the canyon, and we got coffees inside the service station from a vending machine with a sign on it saying "Hot Drinks," except that someone had stuck a greasy band-aid over the "r." "Hot dinks!" Susan said. "Now this is my kinda place." It was dark by the time we got home.

"Where in the hell *were* you?" I could hear Whitman's voice as Susan walked up her front steps. "I was worried sick."

"Sorry," she said. "I didn't know how late it was."

"You could have phoned."

"I know," Susan said, sounding truly contrite. "I was just thoughtless. Bad, bad Susan."

I opened the door and went into my own house, where no one was waiting, no one had worried. "Gordon," I said out loud, as though I expected an answer.

There are not many October days recorded in the journal. My eyes drift past a few short and uninteresting entries, and then they snag on this one.

Saturday, October 15, 1983: finally persuaded Ellen to go into the city to the Solidarity rally, and it was really something. the way we had lunch on Robson, waiting for them to go past, and then seeing them coming, this enormous swell of people and the big union banners, one after another after another, all those ordinary people. I was so excited, didn't want to bother with lunch, but Ellen just kept eating her damned burger, saying, "don't rush, they'll keep coming," and of course they did, all those thousands, and then we left the restaurant and stepped into it, a river of people moving west to the ocean, and then curving back down Georgia and to the plaza for the speeches. God, it was wonderful. 70,000 people, they said. it just felt so fucking *good* to be out there, because it was the right thing to do, of course, but also because it felt like . . . power, like being part of something historical, it felt the way grass must feel, a great collective of cells, taking over the whole world.

I remember Susan's excitement, how she kept talking about the rally all the way home, and how it saddened me a little since it was something I went to only because she insisted.

"I don't know what good it will do," I said, knowing it would make her angry, and of course it did.

"You have to stand up for your rights," she said, sounding like Margaret.

"I voted NDP," I said defensively. I didn't tell her I would have preferred to vote Liberal. Susan, I knew, was decisively left of the Liberal Party, and whereas I came to the NDP from a vacuum on its right she came to it from a vacuum on its left. I was never exactly sure how socialist she really was, and I suspect she wanted me to think she was more extreme than was actually the case. She had told me about her involvement at university with something called the SDU, which I understand was a left-wing group, although all I can remember her telling me about it is that she learned to stick her stamps on upside down on her letters, an apparently radical act for which the RCMP could open a file on you. "I was probably more afraid of the Post Office than of the RCMP," she admitted, which still seems quite logical to me. When Susan talked about politics, her opinions were full of adjectives like "bourgeois" and "Marxist" and "working-class," terms that frightened me a little, because when I was growing up the only thing worse than being called a "communist" was being called "on welfare." Both of these seemed to me at the time to be undesirable ethnic backgrounds. Fortunately, my parents had bequeathed to me a desirable ancestry; when people said I was "English" they said it with approval.

"So you voted NDP," Susan said. "Big fucking deal. That wasn't enough. Now we have to do more. We can't let them get away with calling it 'restraint' when it's just an attack on the poor and on social services, and when they're spending billions on a new stadium and Expo and a ski resort. A ski resort, for Christ's sake!" Of course she was not telling me anything I didn't know, but she seemed to need to make the arguments again, as though I were the one who needed to be convinced.

"Men!" she added suddenly, slapping the steering wheel with the palm of her hand. "I'm sick of being a victim of goddamned *men!*"

"But . . . well, Susan, you can't blame *all* men," I said gently, alarmed at the anger in her voice.

She took a deep breath, held it for a moment before letting it go. "Oh, I know, I know. I mean it's the male *principle* here, and women can buy into that, too, I suppose—those bullying, aggressive, unemotional values, you know what I mean—the survival-of-the-meanest bullshit."

"I guess so," I said, dubiously. "I just hate to sort of blame all men—"

"Of course," she said impatiently, as though I had missed the point. I suppose I had. "I know that."

We rode in silence for a while, a sense of strain tightening the air between us. Susan turned the radio on, but the static was already blurring out the Vancouver stations, so she turned it off again. I looked out my side window, rain beginning to blow across it like hair.

"Well, hey," Susan said finally, in her familiar ironic voice. "I should run for office, right, show them how to do it. With all the knee-jerk socialists and knee-jerk feminists, I'm the perfect jerk to vote for. And it would be good for restraint—since women make only half as much as men I'd get paid less."

I looked at her and grinned, relieved that whatever it was that had irritated her about me seemed to have passed. "That's right."

"No more incompetents in public office." Suddenly she gave a little snort of laughter. "Whitman had a good idea the other day, actually—the man does surprise me occasionally. He was frothing on about how his manager at the bank sometimes just moves into a parallel universe for a while and makes no sense at all, and Whitman says what we need is for people to have to wear little adhesive strips on their foreheads, like those things you can stick onto kids and if they have a fever the strip turns red. Well, the ones on adults would turn red when you become incompetent, and then everyone would know, okay, you can't be trusted now, your brain is in Hawaii."

"What a good idea," I said. "Except that with this government the strips would be red all the time so it wouldn't really tell you much."

"I know," Susan said, gloomy again. "That's why it's important to go to the rallies, to keep on yelling."

"They won't listen," I sighed, feeling old and cynical. "They're the government and they can do whatever they want."

"They can't ignore seventy thousand people," Susan insisted.

But of course they did. Perhaps I knew they would because if I had been them I would have done the same. When you have the power, you use it the way you want; it is that simple. The trouble with power is that it must either be exercised or relinquished.

Still, I am not sorry I went to the rally. It is, after all, a cause I believe in, and I was amused by the look on Margaret's face Sunday

when, after she repeated for me Pastor Bob's grim indictments of
the unions, who were just footmen for the anti-Christ, I mentioned
that I had been at the rally, too. But aside from such childish
satisfactions, I considered it merely something that had to be done,
like the dishes; you are pleased when you have finished, but that
does not mean you enjoyed the job. What I remember most are
things like how I worried about the car, if we could find the lot we
left it in, how I wished I had not worn such thick socks because it
was too warm, how I couldn't hear the speeches because the sound
shattered on the nearby buildings and gave me a headache, how
two dogs close to me started to fight.

And I remember—and it is something that I clutch now,
quickly, like a clue directing me to the answer I want—how Susan,
to override my objections about how I was uncomfortable taking a
car into the city, said she would drive, and how her driving
alarmed me. She drove over the speed limit most of the way,
inserting us rapidly into new lanes without signalling. At stop
lights she would rely too much on the brakes, and then on green
would ram the gas pedal to the floor. I had been with men who
drove this way, I thought, but never women. I am a cautious driver
myself, one who obeys the rules; even as a pedestrian I will turn
back to the sidewalk if the *wait* light comes on before I am at least a
quarter of the way across. When I got home, I was exhausted, less
from the rally than from anticipating accidents.

The journal has another entry about the rally, I notice:

> Mon., Oct. 17: so furious and depressed, seeing the only *Sun*
> coverage of the rally was buried in the back pages and the picture
> showed only the banner of the Marxist-Leninists. 70,000 people,
> and the fucking paper dismisses us all as Dirty Commies. really
> upsets me, that they can take it all away, so easily, Jesus, I just
> started to cry, Ellen must have thought I was crazy.

No, not crazy. It is just the difference between us, I thought. I
had not felt the excitement, so now I did not feel the pain. I took the
newspaper from her, folded it up, dropped it in the garbage and
closed the lid. Then I picked up the coffee pot on the way back to
the table and poured us both another cup, and I made Susan stop
crying by telling her a story about my uncle in Victoria whose
pension cheque got delayed, and he was so mad he filled up an old
chamberpot with perogies and brought it right into the premier's
office, saying, "You don't give a shit, eh?" The story is almost true.

I did have an uncle, and he did bring a chamberpot into the legislature once, but he was an old and senile man, and I feel ashamed still for betraying him like that, to make someone laugh.

Five

Thursday, October 27, 1983: oh, he's got to be kidding. W. announces that he's asked the people from the bank over tomorrow after work, "just for a drink." great. wonderful. he knows I'm a terrific hostess. "everyone else has done it," he says, "it looks funny if I don't." sure, I say, now they'll see you've got a wife with less personality than cauliflower. "I wish you'd stop putting yourself down all the time," he says. yeah, I say, it's just premenstrual tension. poor W., he never knows if I mean it or not. *I* never know if I mean it or not.

Susan, on the phone to me that night: "Oh, shit, Ellen, I'm awful at these things. You've got to come over when they're here, please, please, please."

"What good would I do? I don't know any of them. I don't know anything about banking."

"You think *I* do? Oh, come on. It'll be easier for me if you're there. You sort of exude poise."

I laughed. "Me? I'm no good in large groups." But I suppose I knew what she meant. People had said it to me before. I think it was only that I had learned how to reflect back to people variations of what they themselves had said, and since I never offered them the threat of a dissenting opinion I never made them uncomfortable. Of course it was easy for them to understand this as interest, but for me it was rarely that. I don't think I did it because I wanted them to like me, although they usually did, or even because it was a game I enjoyed playing, but simply because it required the least effort. I read an article about a computer program that works this way; I think it is called "Psychiatrist." You might say, "I hate my father," and it will say, "Tell me more about your father," and when you say, "He drinks too much," it will say, "Why does he drink too much?" Of course, if you say, "Xmbynthl," it will also only say, "Tell me more about Xmbynthl," because there is no real understanding or intelligence in the machine, but you do not want to believe this. The writer of the article was alarmed at tests of the program that showed people tended to be more honest and intimate with the machine than they were with their real psychiatrists, but it seemed only reasonable to me. It was what Brenda called the non-directive counsellor routine.

Brenda had phoned earlier that day, I remembered with a nudge of guilt, asking if I wanted to come into the city for the weekend, but I said no, I was busy. I had relied on her so much in the last two years, and now I was withdrawing from her. Because I had Susan. It wasn't fair, I told myself; Brenda is supposed to be my best friend. We have known each other for twenty-five years. We kept in close touch even after I moved to Chilliwack, something she accepted even if she did not understand. I know she thought it was foolish of me to marry Gordon in the first place, a man so much older than I, especially so soon after my divorce from Paul, but Brenda has that tolerance of people's weaknesses that I suppose you have to develop if you are a teacher, and Brenda has been teaching now in the same elementary school in Vancouver for nearly fifteen years. She feels sorry for me. I feel sorry for her. It isn't a bad basis for friendship.

Gordon, for some reason I could not understand, never liked Brenda, called her Brenda the Brick behind her back and sometimes to her face. She would only laugh and pretend he meant it as a compliment. She does in some ways resemble a brick; she is a thick rectangular woman barely five feet tall, and her face and arms are splashed with large, soft freckles. Her hair is a nondescript brown, but in the summer sun it turns such a rich red people have accused her of using henna.

"She's got lesbian tendencies," Gordon once said, perhaps to excuse his dislike of her and to explain in the only way he knew her disinterest in men. Brenda, in fact, was totally asexual. She had never, she told me, had the faintest interest in either men or women.

"I suppose I'm missing something," she said, shrugging.

"Not much," I said, thinking of Paul, of how *not much* was both true and not true.

It is curious, when I think of it, that I never introduced Brenda to Susan, even though Brenda has been out to see me several times in the last year. And Susan did the same thing; I know she had friends from the city who came in to see her sometimes, but, except for the man who brought her the cat, she never let me meet them. Perhaps we wanted to keep our friendship separate from the people who knew us before we moved here, people who knew us too well, knew things we wanted to leave behind.

"Well, anyway," Susan was saying, her voice jarring me back, "I really wish you'd come to the damned party. You'd get to heaven on that one good deed alone."

"Well, in that case," I said. I remember resolving to call Brenda back that evening, but I never did.

"Great," Susan said. "I'm going out to buy the booze. Want to come?"

"Sure," I said. And I grabbed my coat and purse and met her outside, and we climbed into the van and drove down to the liquor store by the shopping centre. Inside, Susan filled her cart with about a dozen large wine bottles and several of rum and gin.

"That'll be over $100," I warned her.

"Yeah, well," she said, pausing to add a bottle of coffee liqueur as we headed for the checkout, "I love leftovers."

"What about food?" I asked.

"Oh, fuck the food," Susan said. The man in the line-up ahead of us turned and glared at her. Susan smiled at him warmly and said, "Hello, there," and he turned quickly away. "A couple bags of peanuts and chips," she continued as though there had been no interruption, "that should be enough. If they want food they're shit-outa-luck."

But the next morning I made three dozen cream cheese balls, with walnuts and brandy, and brought them over to her in the afternoon.

"These are *fantastic*," Susan said, picking up another one.

"They're for your *guests*," I said, slapping at her hand. "When are they coming, anyway?"

"Anytime now, I suppose. God. Do I look all right?"

"You look fine," I said. "I like your hair like that." She had had it done, a short, curly perm.

"It's one of those instant things—shake and bake or something."

"Wash and wear," I said.

"Whatever."

"But really, you look nice." She had put on some lipstick and eyeshadow, and she wore a blue pantsuit with a frilly white blouse. "I'd hardly recognize you."

"That good, eh?" She rubbed a finger along her forehead. "I even put powder on, for Christ's sake. And look at the oil seeping through." She stared at her finger, which did look glossy. "Petro-Canada should put up a rig on my face."

Then we heard voices at the door, Whitman talking to someone, and he opened the door and ushered in two thin women in pastel dresses and high heels. They looked as if they were both under twenty.

"Joyce, Lana," Whitman said, "this is my wife, Susan, her friend Ellen." He gave me an odd look. Surely Susan had told him I would be here? "Joyce and Lana are tellers at the bank." Whitman stood with his hand on the doorknob, as though he were debating whether to come in or not, while the rest of us made the expected friendly noises and shuffled off to get drinks.

Then the others arrived—Pearl, another teller, who was about twenty-five and proudly pregnant; Eva, the secretary, a large middle-aged woman whose face looked as though it were not made for the smile her life expected it to wear; Gracie, the accountant, whose rigidly backcombed hair and thick eyebrow pencil made her look like Joan Crawford; Paul Wotski, the assistant manager, and his wife, whose name no one seemed to care to remember; and finally, the last to arrive, the manager, Mr. Matachuck, an obese, awkward man around whom the others actually trembled. *Matachuck*, I thought: the name is familiar for some reason. But I couldn't pinpoint why.

I found myself drifting into the kitchen with the three tellers and the secretary. They spaced themselves around the kitchen table and spoke in furtive and excited whispers about someone called Anne, who, it seemed, was the fourth teller and the one designated to be disliked by all the others.

"I had her till at lunch," said Joyce, "and she had the tens all mixed in with the twenties. No wonder she can never balance."

"Anne is the newest girl," Eva explained to me.

"And she's not too efficient?" I said. The others laughed eagerly.

"The only thing she's efficient at," said Pearl, giggling, "is spending time in Mr. Matachuck's office."

"Oh you're *awful*," said Joyce, laughing with the others.

Susan came into the kitchen, balancing a tray of cheese balls in one hand and carrying a glass of wine in the other. She had the slightly dazed look of someone not as drunk as she wished she were.

"Cheese balls, anyone?" she announced.

"These are *good*," said someone. "Did you make them yourself?"

"The maid made them," Susan answered, looking at me.

They laughed uncertainly, and each took a cheese ball and then went back to talking about Anne. Susan set the tray down by the sink and poured herself more wine.

"How are you doing?" I asked, coming over and pouring myself another glass, too.

"Who *are* all these people?" she said. "Jesus."

"How's it going in the living room?"

"The manager is sitting there like a termite queen and the others are gazing up at him adoringly. Suck, suck, yuck."

"Whitman, too?" I asked. I could not imagine Whitman being like that, but then I could not imagine Whitman at all in a social situation.

"Whitman?" Susan laughed. "Mr. Taciturn?" She gave a little hiccup that seemed like an answer. "God. Come back into the living room with me, make sure I don't disgrace myself."

We went back into the room and sat on the two empty chairs by the doorway. I could see what Susan meant about the manager, the way he hogged the chesterfield, with a tray of cheese balls on the coffee table in front of him. The people on either side of him on the chesterfield had to hold onto its arms to avoid sliding into him, he made such a large depression. The others in the room were grouped around him in a respectful semi-circle. He was talking in a kind of sad monotone about the last time the auditors had come and taken a whole week and how this time it would have to be better.

"Oh, it will be," Paul Wotski said earnestly, leaning forward. His nameless wife nodded eagerly, as if she, too, were convinced of it.

"We don't have that problem with the mortgages this year," Gracie, the accountant, added. Even her voice sounded like Joan Crawford's.

"Head Office was very unhappy about that," Mr. Matachuck said, and they all bowed their heads a little, as though it were a personal reprimand. Perhaps it was. Even Whitman sat with his head down, but he had been sitting that way ever since I came into the room. He rolled his glass of wine between his fingers and stared into it with great concentration. What is he thinking, I wondered;

how does he feel about these people, people he sees every day, sees almost as much as he sees Susan?

"The morons *lost* half their mortgage receipts last year," Susan whispered to me.

Mr. Matachuck was droning on again, something about the Canada Savings Bonds, and Paul Wotski would insert, "Oh, yes," or "I know what you mean," or "Good idea" periodically. Gracie made a few efforts to say something but finally gave up and drank three glasses of wine so quickly that her left hand never let go of the bottle beside her chair. When she saw me looking at her she gave me a smile that showed all her teeth, and when I smiled back she raised her glass to me a little, as though we were old friends sharing a joke. The nameless wife got up in search of, as she whispered to Susan, "the little girls' room," and never came back.

"When do you think we should start, Whitman?" said Mr. Matachuck suddenly.

Susan leaned forward in her chair; I could actually hear her take a sharp breath and hold it. I think I did the same. We were children in a classroom, waiting for the child caught not paying attention to confess. The others turned too, to stare at Whitman, but it was hard to tell if they thought as we did; perhaps theirs was the dutiful silence of students waiting for the star pupil to give the right answer. The room was quite still.

Whitman looked up, slowly. He wiped the moisture away from the bottom of his wine glass with the palm of his hand and then set it carefully on the end table by his chair.

"I don't really know," he said.

"Well," said Mr. Matachuck, sounding only slightly disappointed, "I was thinking of next week."

Susan got up and took the wine bottle from the table beside her chair and went over to Paul Wotski and said, loudly, "More wine?" pouring some into his glass before he could answer. It was a good diversion, I thought, taking the attention from Whitman, but still, she had waited, like the rest of us, until he had had to give his answer.

"Well, all right," Paul Wotski said, as she finished pouring.

Gracie started to laugh and said, "Well, *I*'ll have some more, too, please."

"You, Mr. Matachuck?" Susan asked, as she finished pouring Gracie's.

"No, no, I should get going," he said, sighing and looking at his watch. "Got some more things I should do at the bank before I get to go home." He lunged forward several times until the momentum lifted him from the chesterfield to his feet. "So, well, thank you, Mrs. Jervis. Whitman." His chins nodded at them both.

Whitman stood up, too. "Thanks for coming," he said. "I'm glad you took the time."

Susan led the man to the door, and as he went out, I suddenly remembered what I had heard about him, years ago: Matachuck, the bank manager who married a seventeen-year-old girl who told people she used to be a prostitute in Vancouver. No one was really sure if she was making it up or not, but it was what she would answer when anyone asked her how she and her husband had met. The marriage did not, I believe, last long, less than a year, and now I expect he is married to the kind of woman bank managers are supposed to be married to.

It would be a marvellous story for Susan, I thought, smiling to myself as I went to where she was closing the door, but then for some reason I hesitated. I'll tell her some other time, I thought. But I never did. I am still not sure why. Perhaps I was afraid of what use she might make of it, what it might mean for Whitman. When I think now of what happened during the rest of the party, I was probably wise not to tell her.

"Well," I said to her instead, "you're handling things well."

"Oh, *aren't* I being efficient?" she said. "One down, seven to go."

"I don't suppose they'll stay much longer."

"Christ, I hope not." She began to giggle. "Wasn't it funny how when Matachuck asked Whitman something about the Savings Bonds, he obviously didn't have a clue what the man was talking about?"

"Are you sure? I mean, did he really not know?"

"Of *course* not. He *would* have known if he'd been listening, but he doesn't bother. His mind was way off somewhere—Christ, I should know, I see that look on his face often enough. The bank is just not important enough for him to have opinions about."

"He must hate working there."

"I don't know," Susan said, thoughtful for a moment. "He does a good job, I think. They respect him there. It's just that . . . he won't let himself care. He's afraid to let it matter to him."

I wanted to ask her to go on, but the tellers and Eva and the nameless wife, whom the group had apparently absorbed on her

way back from the little girls' room, hovered into the living room
at that point, and one of them asked Susan timidly, "Is he gone?"
"The big boss?" Susan said. "Yeah, he's gone."

"Oh, good," someone sighed, and they all came back into the
room and sat down, their voices suddenly loud and confident after
the way they whispered nervously in the kitchen. They had
finished with Anne, the absent co-worker, and were now
discussing the new Instant Teller the bank had just installed.

"I had a customer today who said he didn't hold with this new-
fangled foolishness," said Pearl. The others laughed.

"I had a woman who said it gave her ten dollars too little, so she
cut up her card and handed it to me. I mean, one mistake and she
won't have anything more to do with it," said someone else.

"Well, you can see her point," said Gracie. The others looked at
her impatiently.

"These are people who are just opposed to *progress,*" Pearl
insisted.

"But don't you realize—" It was Susan's voice, loud and
irritated. *But you don't realize:* those are not the words with which
to preface a congenial conversation. I started to get up from my
seat, an instinctive movement, like when you see a child chase a
ball across the street careless of an oncoming car, but then I
gripped the arms of the chair firmly and made myself sit still. What
could I do, leap up and clap my hand over her mouth, drag her into
the kitchen, interrupt with some shrill banality about the weather?
And of course she would resent my intervention; in spite of what
she might tell me, she did not want my advice, my protection. I
remembered once when she had gone to a job interview, and I said,
"Watch your step," and she pulled a derisive face at me and
answered, "That better just be an orthopedic suggestion." No, I
thought, Susan does not want me to interfere. I let her continue.

"—that those damned machines are wiping out your jobs?"

The tellers looked at her, embarrassed, as though she had said
something so foolish it hardly needed to be answered. I could see
the way their eyes flicked to each other, designating someone to
reply. It was interesting to watch, to see how well they worked
together, a kind of instinctive closing-of-ranks against the
intruder. I had seen the same thing at a party of Brenda's teachers,
when someone who worked for the School Board had said split
classes were good for the kids; there was that moment of silence
while a kind of collective denial gathered in the room, and one of

the teachers seemed to be chosen to make the refutation, speaking for the others so well I could see their faces animated and unanimous as though they were all saying the words. The power of the group, a tribal consciousness that must have to form among people who work together: I could only imagine what it must be like.

Finally it was Pearl who answered, folding her hands over her pregnancy as though it gave her special authority. "None of us are losing our jobs," she said, enunciating carefully, the way you do when you speak to a foreigner.

"Not yet, maybe," Susan said. "But give it time. The whole point of these automated tellers is to make you unnecessary."

"No," Pearl said, patiently. "We got a lot of information about them from Head Office, and we just have to learn to work *with* them. They're to make our jobs easier, that's all. They're to supplement, not replace us." Heads were nodding in agreement around the room.

"So Head Office tells you. Head Offices tell you what's expedient, to keep you off guard. But what protection do you really have against lay-offs? You're not in a union, are you?"

It was hard to imagine the room being filled with greater discomfort. *Union* was obviously a dangerous word.

This time it was Paul Wotski who answered, in a firm and managerial voice. "No. There's no union. It doesn't seem to me like we need one."

The tellers avoided looking at each other, fiddled with their drinks or their earrings or the hems of their dresses. It was clearly an issue on which there was not quite unanimous agreement.

"Not to you, maybe," Susan persisted, impervious to the wreckage she might be leaving. "But a union is the only protection people have against technological changes that take their jobs."

"We're just a small branch," someone else protested.

"So? You can start anywhere," Susan said. "Although a really *great* place to start would be to unionize the Data Centre." And she chuckled, taking another drink of wine.

An appalled look twitched across Paul Wotski's face. He stared at Susan as though he thought she might be mad.

"How about some coffee?" I said quickly. It really was time to rescue Susan from herself. After all, I would only be doing what she had done for Whitman, although, like her, I suppose I had waited too long. It is a curious thing about people, how they can recognize the behavioural mistakes of others so much better than their own.

"Not for me," Paul Wotski said, standing up, looking at his watch. "Gotta go." His wife jerked up from her chair and stood beside him, smiling with relief. "Well," he said, "thanks for the wine and—" He glanced around the room. "—say good-bye to Whitman for me. Where is he, anyway?"

It was the first time anyone seemed to have noticed he wasn't in the room. They turned to the chair in which he had been sitting and which was now occupied by Lana, who looked alarmed and said defensively, "I don't know where he is."

"The little boys' room, I imagine," Susan said, moving to the front door, opening it, ushering the Wotskis out.

"Shit, I was just starting to have fun," she whispered to me on her way back into the living room.

"That's the trouble," I said.

"Party-pisser," she said, crossing her eyes at me. "All right, all right, I'll be good."

And as I went into the kitchen to make the coffee I could hear her ask Pearl when the baby was due, and the conversations behind me filled themselves again with the even and innocuous murmur of people saying nothing important. But it is not fair to make such judgments; perhaps the things they were saying then were the most important of all. Because things are easy does not make them insignificant.

I began to measure the coffee into the filter cone, but then I lost count of the number of teaspoonfuls and had to pour them all back into the jar and start again. The kettle was already boiling, and I unplugged it and poured the water slowly into the filter, watching it drizzle brownly out the bottom into the pot. I felt a little drunk, too, and watching the coffee felt almost as sobering as drinking it. But, no, drinking coffee is not supposed to make one less drunk, only less sleepy.

The laughter of the women in the living room, the faint splashing noise of the coffee: but there was another sound too, faint, not unfamiliar to this house, but incongruous now, somehow. I listened for it, began to follow it out of the kitchen, into the hallway leading to the bedroom. It was louder here, a clicking sound, irregular but persistent. The door to the study was closed. And then I realized what it was. A typewriter. Whitman. Whitman was in his study, typing, at the party to which he had invited the guests.

I don't know how long I stood outside the study door, like an eavesdropper, listening to the clatter of keys, the silences, then another burst of letters, like Morse code, a scene from a war movie, someone in enemy territory retreating to a locked room and taking out his equipment and sending a desperate message.

I put my hand up to the door, gently, and felt the faint vibrations of the machine. A word, space, another word, space—I imagined the sentences, eloquent and intelligent, lined up on the page above the striking keys, and Whitman speaking them over to himself, alone in his room.

Finally I went back to the kitchen and poured the coffee into cups, set them on a tray with spoons and cream and sugar and carried them into the living room, where I saw two of the tellers had already left, but the others, grateful and smiling, took the coffee and kept on talking.

I took a cup to Susan, who was sitting on the chesterfield looking almost asleep. "How's it going?" I asked.

"Whitman," she said. "The bastard."

Fri., Oct. 28: survived the party somehow, I suppose people were only here for an hour or so but it seemed like a week. drink, drank, drunk.

Saturday, October 29, 1983: HangOver. and over and over. The Power of Positive Drinking. W. had to go in to the bank for a few hours in the afternoon, and when he comes home he tells me the manager was there and said, "I hear your wife was recommending we get a union in here," and W. had to assure him I wasn't speaking for him, oh, I can just hear it: "Can't you keep your wife under control?" "I'm sorry, sir, it won't happen again." well, dammit, it serves him right. I said, why didn't you give me a list of verboten topics beforehand then, and besides where the hell were *you,* fucking off like that, leaving me to handle it alone? and he said, "I'm sorry, that was really unfair of me, I know it, there's no excuse." and what could I answer to that, what could I say? oh, I said.

"Oh, I said." It is the response you make when there is no argument possible, when what the other person says defeats you without even trying, closes a door on you, however softly and sadly, and all you can do is put your hand up to it and say, "Oh," as though you understood, as though there really had been an explanation.

Six

I have almost finished the yellow scribbler. There are only about a dozen entries in November, nothing very significant. Susan was doing a bit of writing again, but she had not found a job and was getting bitter about it. There is the entry that talks about the job at Friesen's. Oh, yes. I remember driving her to her second interview with the company, and waiting in the outer office until she was finished. I chatted with the next applicant, a frightened girl wearing white gloves, about how scarce jobs were. She chewed at the fingertips of her gloves and stared at the closed door in front of us as though she could see what was happening on the other side.

"That job at Friesen's," Susan had said the day before, "they just called and said I was on the Short List."

"The Short List?"

Susan gave a bitter laugh. "It's the highest achievement of the capitalist system, didn't you know? They eliminate people one by one and then rank the remaining three or four. We get to come in again and compete against each other. One of us gets first prize and the others who got their hopes up for nothing get told to fuck off."

"It does seem a little . . . well . . ."

"Sadistic," Susan said, reaching across my table for another nanaimo bar. "But what can you do but play the goddamned game the way they set it up? So I'm on the Short List and I get to say, 'Oh, goody, goody,' and put myself through another stupid interview tomorrow. For a receptionist job, for Christ's sake, a lousy receptionist job."

Thursday, November 17, 1983: had my second interview with Friesen's but I could tell I blew it, I sounded too ambitious, when that asshole asked, "would someone with your education be satisfied with just being a receptionist?" the right answer was "yes, yes, yes," but how could I say that, how could I, how could I, and the way he looked at his greasy partner when I answered how I'd be interested in advancing in the company, right answer for a man, wrong answer for a woman, *yes,* I should have said, leaning earnestly across the desk, letting my skirt pull up just a little higher over my knees, *being a receptionist is all I've ever dreamed of.*

When the man I recognized as Harry Friesen, a round and unsmiling man with the smell of old perspiration and cigarettes about him, ushered her out of his office, saying, "Thank you, Susan," his eyes were already on the girl I had been talking to. "Jennifer?" he said. Susan walked across the reception area, where she probably would have had to work if she'd gotten the job, and without looking back she opened the door and walked out, leaving me to scurry along behind. The opening door caused a draft in the room that caught the long strand of hair that Harry Friesen had combed carefully across his bald spot and twirled it ludicrously in the air before dropping it on the other side of his head. I saw the girl called Jennifer looking at him with an expression of horror. It was something, at least, for me to tell Susan.

In the car on the way home she sat staring straight ahead, not saying anything. Finally, as I turned into Macken Avenue, she said quietly, "What am I going to do, Ellen?"

"Working for a living is much over-rated," I said, but she wouldn't laugh, only looked gloomily at the windshield wipers making their repetitive swirls across the windshield.

"I know how they feel," she said, not having to explain. "Back and forth, back and forth, and what good does it do?"

"Look," I said, "why don't you come to my reading group tonight? It'll cheer you up." I had asked her before to come, because the meeting tonight was at my place and we were discussing *Clan of the Cave Bear,* a novel I had lent her and thought she would enjoy.

She had refused then, but now she said, "I haven't finished the book yet," and I knew that meant she was changing her mind, so I said, "Oh, come on," and finally she agreed.

I was nervous, remembering the bank party. But that night Susan was surprisingly polite, nibbling at the croissants I had made and nodding at the other women's observations, even the most banal.

"At least Ayla never has to go to a job interview," was about all she said the whole evening.

"You were very restrained tonight," I said, after the others had all left.

"Restrained. What a good word. I sneaked one of Whitman's Valiums—they always make me mellow."

I was surprised, not that she would take a tranquilizer but that Whitman would. Perhaps it is because I think men have less need than women of such things, an attitude I realize is out-dated at the same time as I cannot relinquish it. "Well, anyway, you were very well-behaved."

"You bet your bloomers I was."

Monday, Nov. 21, 1983: insisted W. leave me the van today, so went to Vancouver, but Connie and everybody were at work, so just knocked around feeling like a tourist. a show at the Planetarium, all about black holes and entropy, how can you even imagine that, the Big Bang leading finally only up to the Big Hole, it all sounds like a sexual joke, well, I suppose it is. walked down Robson, the cold pulling at my face, people look so strange, a punk haircut makes me stare like a country bumpkin, well, that's what I am. finally drove up to SFU, walked around the AQ twice, looking in at all the kids taking notes (fantasy #82: I go back to university, study law). got all sentimental about Edmonton, what great days they were, but, tell the truth, all I wanted then was to get it over with, education just drudgery, memory the great romanticizer. late getting back to Chill. to pick up W., he was pissed-off, of course, will use it as an excuse not to let me have the van again.

Tues., Nov. 22, '83: on a chocolate binge today, god, I'm getting so fat, my hips look like chesterfield cushions. Ellen says I should go to her fitness class with her, but blech no thanks. Jane Fonda, you are no friend to aging women, parts of the female body have earned the right to sag, maybe I should have my fat surgically removed, transplant it in my boobs, cellulite instead of silicon, W. would like that, well, fuck him, if he likes big boobs so much he can grow his own.

Monday, November 28, 1983: ugly cold day. struggled with a poem, can't get it right, wadded it up and threw it on the floor and then picked it up and smoothed it out and tried again, what a bloody futile business, drank about a quart of coffee, got to stop that. in afternoon over to Ellen's (for coffee), and we sat and yakked and I whined about how I was going nuts in this town, and she told me she felt the same after her husband died and how she made this list of things she could do (a Short List? I said). well, I nearly shit myself when she told me about number six—

Oh, yes. Number six. When I remember the list, I stop at number five; number six is something I have tried to push out of my memory, something that should be forgotten. Like the pockets of the old sweater I found last week in the back of the closet, full of Kleenex, a spool of thread, credit card receipts, scraps of paper with unexplained phone numbers—things that come out in a linty lump and expect to be made sense of, things that are only clutter, that should be thrown away. So why had I told Susan about number six, I wonder. To entertain her, I suppose, and because she made me feel safe, telling her things like that. I emptied my secrets to her, I think, all but the ones she needed to know.

Number six on my list was "Casual Sexual Encounters." I approached it as methodically as I did the other items on the list, although that may be only the way I prefer to see it now.

My sexual relationship with Gordon had never been particularly passionate, which was, after my abandonment by Paul, for whom sex was too important, what I wanted. For some reason, Gordon would become aroused after watching, of all things, the Mary Tyler Moore Show, so every Wednesday night at 8:30 we would make love, and that was usually all until the next week. In the summer when the reruns were on we would go for a month or two at a time without any sexual contact. It was quite ridiculous, but we never talked about it. In our last years, he began to have trouble getting an erection (I always wanted, but never dared, to ask him if it was because the Mary Tyler Moore Show was no longer on the air), so our encounters became even less frequent. I pretended I didn't miss it, but I did, and after his death I was accosted by an even greater sexual restlessness, not the kind of itch I could masturbate away. I did not really want a husband, to marry again, but I wanted sex—it was nothing to be ashamed of, I told myself firmly. But I can see why, I said to Brenda sourly on the phone one night, other women are afraid of widows.

The next night I dressed carefully, drove down to the nearest hotel bar, ordered a beer and waited. Eventually an overweight man with almost no hair but probably younger than I was asked if he could join me. Well, I thought, I can't be choosey. An hour later we were up in his hotel room. It was not a great erotic adventure. The man had some numbers and an American flag tattooed on his right buttock. Afterwards, he said something about giving me taxi fare, and I realized that he may have thought I was a prostitute.

When I got home, I cried for Gordon as I hadn't since he died. When I told Susan about it, I did not tell her about the crying. It was like the anecdote about my uncle, I suppose, a few details omitted, that was all, to make a better story.

—I mean Ellen is just not the type, but she swore it was true. anyway, it was good for a laugh, and me saying maybe the tattoo said "666," except how would he be able to hoist his ass across the checkout stand when the time came. still can't imagine Ellen going out and picking up a guy in the Royal—she's too straight... no, not straight so much as controlled. maybe I just can't/don't want to imagine her out of control the way sex can do it to you. I've been thinking about her and that guy all evening—maybe that's what I should do, go pick up some guy, W. wouldn't even notice I was gone.

"Control." Is that what Susan thought I had? And "out of control." I think about that phrase. It is how you describe a car before an accident.

Tuesday, November 29, 1983: schlepped around all day, Ellen called and said let's go out for lunch so we went, to the Royal, of all places, but nobody picked us up, how disappointing. don't know what I would do without Ellen, she keeps me sane. I guess she's become my best friend.

Best friend. The words are like a pressed flower on the page, waiting for me to find it. A best friend is someone who will forgive you for things a stranger would hate you for. Or perhaps it is the other way around. I pick up the scribbler, press it, open at that page, against my chest. I can feel the faint declaration of my heart-beat pushing through that final page, through the cover, into my hand.

When at last I put the journal back down, I read the final two entries.

Thursday, December 8, 1983: Jim came over this morning with The Cat. Jesus. I'd forgotten all about it—

I look down at Dong sleeping in a lump of sunlight at my feet. "This is where you came in," I tell him, nudging him with my foot. He stirs, stretches a little without getting up, goes back to sleep.

I was over at Susan's when her friend from the city arrived with him. He was just a kitten, black with white paws, and a homely little face. When Susan reached up to take him, he crawled so far back into Jim's jacket he finally had to take it off to find him.

"He likes this stuff," said Jim, giving her the jar of vegemite. "Just put a dab on your finger, and he'll lick it off."

"Jesus," said Susan, after he'd gone. "Whitman will kill me. I totally forgot I promised Jim I'd take one of them." She stroked the kitten on her lap, where it had begun to mew in that pitiful way its genes had promised would bring help. "I always liked cats. More than dogs, anyway—they just bark at you and try to hump your leg—hell, I've got Whitman to do that. But cats, cats are okay."

"Will there be a problem toilet-training it, do you think?"

"Naw. Cats are easy. Maybe I can paper-train it to shit on Whitman's thesis. Did you hear the one that goes, 'What do you call that crumbly stuff that sometimes gets on ladies' panties?' "

"No, what?"

"Clitty litter."

"Susan. You are shameless."

"Yeah, I think so."

I reached out and touched the kitten, could feel it trembling under my fingers. "What are you going to call it?"

"Oh, something irreverent. I hate cats with cute names."

"It's a male?"

"Yeah. For now. Maybe I can call it Dink. Or Prick. Or Whang. Or Dong. Dong, yeah, that's good."

"Oh, Susan. Dong? What would Whitman say?"

"He'd say, 'Oh, for Pete's sake, you can't call a cat something like that.' Well, that settles it. Dong it is." She picked the kitten up by the scruff of the neck, dangled him like a Christmas tree ornament in the air.

I smile now, remembering it. I pick up the cat, put him on my lap, where he grunts like an old man and curls back into sleep.

—W., of course, was really p.o.ed. "can't you give it back?" he said. "nope," I said. when he finally stopped grumbling, he asked what we should call it. "its name is Dong," I said, and I got another lecture, you-can't-call-a-cat-something-like-that, and how would it sound if I had to call him outside, "here, Dong, here, Dong," and even as he says it, he has to smile, and he says, "just don't expect me to call it that," but he doesn't sound too mad any more.

Sat., Dec. 10: time for a new notebook, how time flies when you're having fun, etc. another argument/fight with W. today—god, what has happened to us, we never used to be this way, or is it like my Edmonton-university memories, something time makes better than it really was? I don't know, don't know, don't know. I still love him, I guess, maybe it's just me I don't love any more. but he drives me crazy, how I'll say something and he'll just sit there, I have to make everything into a question or he won't answer, what kind of conversation is that? so like I always do when I'm so mad at him I feel like hitting him, I start talking about Freddy, it's another way of hitting him, I suppose, but it makes me feel better because I know it gets to him. someday he'll find a way of hitting back, and I'll have to find another weapon.

The mysterious Freddy again. Not long after Whitman had first mentioned him to me, I asked her, casual, joking, if there had been any other great loves in her life before Whitman.

She was silent for a moment. Then she told me about Freddy. "We were both really young. And we were madly in love."

"And?" I prodded. It seemed strange to me then that she was reluctant to go on.

"Oh, I guess the usual thing. My parents didn't like him, and his parents thought we were both too young, which I guess we were." She sighed melodramatically. "It was all terribly, terribly romantic."

"Did you, uh, you know, make love?"

"Oh, yeah," she said quickly. "I Lost My Virginity To Him. We didn't fool around. I mean we *did* fool around. What a strange expression: 'fool,' 'to fool,' 'to fool, around.' "

"Have you ever told Whitman about him?" I knew, of course, that she had.

"Oh, yeah," she said, with a bitter little smile. "Oh, yeah." She threw the dishcloth, wadded up like an emphatic period, into the sink. "What about you and that first husband of yours?" It was, I think now, a good way of changing the subject.

"Paul," I said. It was hard to think about him, even after all this time. I had worked hard at cutting him out of my memory, if not out of my excuses. Ours was the kind of marriage provoked primarily by the yowling of hormones, the kind that is later written up in women's studies journals.

"I was quite mad about him, really, and I guess he was about me at first too. It was a very, you know, physical relationship.

Sometimes—oh, I can't believe now I ever did this—we would make love in public places, like the park, just because we couldn't wait to get home." I laughed, embarrassed. "Then he found someone else. That was it. He filed for divorce." I think of the day his lawyer, some relative of his, came over with the final papers. I was sitting in front of the fire reading, and when he handed them to me to sign I threw them into the fireplace. It astonishes me even now that I would do something so emotional, so useless. The lawyer sat there with me watching them burn, and then he stood up and said, quite softly, "You bitch," and then he left.

"And were you crushed?" Susan asked. "Broken on the wheel of love, etc.?"

"Absolutely," I said, lightly. "I carried around the standard illusions about how one day he would come pleading back, and I would either forgive him or not, depending on which fantasy it was. But of course he never did. Come back. One day years later I ran into him at Eaton's, and I asked him for coffee, thinking it should be okay now, surely we could be civilized, but he said, 'No,' no reason or excuse, just 'No.' It was humiliating."

"Maybe he was afraid of getting involved again."

"Another fantasy," I said, smiling. But it made me feel a bit better, that someone could see it that way.

"Remember that judge in the rape case in Vancouver, the one they rewarded by giving him a daily column in the paper, who said women don't get any brains until after they're thirty? Well, fuck, maybe he's right. Except men don't get any brains until then, either. If then."

"That's why young people say don't trust anyone over thirty. All those brains."

I have decided not to begin the second journal, not just yet, although I am not really sure why. I suppose I want to save it. But it is as though the whole house is turning around the box it is in, an axis, a centre. I am reminded of a poem by Wallace Stevens I studied at university, so long ago, something about a jar on a hill; how does it go? "It made the slovenly wilderness surround that hill. . . . It took dominion everywhere. . . ." I can't remember. Once I could repeat that poem whenever I wanted. I learned all of "Sunday Morning" by heart, I adored it so much. Now all I can pull back are a few phrases, "tipped by the consummation of the swallow's wings. . . .love whispered a little out of tenderness. . . . an old chaos of the sun." So little finally is left of intensity. The professor I had for freshman English was doing his Ph.D. on Stevens, and although it was supposed to be an introductory course we spent nearly half the year on Stevens. The other students grumbled about it, but because the professor was young and I was falling in love with him like most of the other girls in class, I would listen to him read the poetry, and tears would come to my eyes. My God, I think, yes, it's true: tears would come to my eyes. I have never since been so moved by words.

"It was just his power trip," Susan said, when I told her about it. "The classroom situation is all about control, and when you get male profs and female students, well."

"Well, what?" I was annoyed at her cynicism. It was my memory and she had no right to change it.

"Well, shit, Ellen. When I was at university I had a prof who made it pretty clear he had an *A's for lays* policy, at least for the prettier girls. One of my friends, she was really good-looking, well, her psych. prof called her up to his office to discuss her paper, which he hinted she plagiarized, and he tried to grab her breast. And there were worse stories—"

I did not want to hear. I did not have one instructor at the university whom I did not admire and respect, and I would not believe such things happened, not at a university, not even in Edmonton, where I conceded the long cold winters might drive people to deviance. Susan may not be lying, I told myself, but she is surely exaggerating. Now, I suppose, I see that we could both have been right, that the corrupt and the beautiful can live in the same place.

In any case, Stevens has sat unopened on my shelves for years. I have not wanted to open those volumes and find only words where I remember feelings. Tombstones, coffins: it is not the way to see books. I think of my mother, her careless love of them, the way the house was always full of half-finished novels, spatters of food on the pages from where she read them as she stirred the pots on the stove. They were all sturdy hardcovers, from before the days when paperbacks were common. "I will never read a book in paperback," one of my high school teachers had declared. I wonder if he says that today. He would be over eighty, if he is still alive, but I cannot imagine him anywhere else but in the Grade Ten classroom, making us memorize, why I still cannot imagine, the end rhymes of Shakespeare's sonnets: "Eyes, state, cries, fate," we would recite. "Shore, end, before, contend." If it had not been for my mother reading the poems aloud with reverence in her voice, that is probably all I would remember of them. But it was novels, not poetry, she loved most. I have some of her books still: Zane Grey, with his stoic characters soliloquizing to their horses; Margaret Mitchells' *Gone With the Wind;* Booth Tarkington; Dashiell Hammett; Dickens. I like the continuity they give to my life, the way Zane Grey fits in between Jean Genet on one side and Thomas Hardy on the other. If from my mother I have a love of reading, from my father I have a love of order, order that has filed Wallace Stevens, too, on this bookcase when I first moved here. I have dusted dutifully around him like an ornament and kept the covers closed.

Thinking of Stevens makes me remember suddenly the two folders of Susan's poetry in the box. I may have forbidden myself her journal for a while, but these are something else. Eagerly, I take them out, and with them comes a third folder, labelled "Letters from Editors." I open it first.

Inside are about thirty rejection slips. They are from literary magazines, I conclude, with names like *The Fiddlehead, Camrose Review, Waves, event, The Canadian Forum;* sometimes there are several from the same journal, apparently in response to different submissions. One or two have a note scrawled at the bottom: "not really the kind of poetry we're interested in," "try us again with new material," "work at tightening your language, heightening your ambiguities." I wonder what "heightening your ambiguities" means. How must she have felt, I think, as I pick up one after another; how must she have felt as she opened the envelopes with nervous fingers and found inside one of these clipped to her poems, and over and over again that same ugly message would slither through her mail slot? I do not understand why she would keep on with it. But then I have never had that passion to create, a passion that afflicts so unfairly both those with ability and those without. There are advantages to having a limited imagination, to being a reader rather than a writer.

I look at some of the poems themselves. Certainly they are not as good as Wallace Stevens, even I can see that, but they do not seem to be too bad, although they are all love poems, a subject I imagine gets overdone. Who are they written to, I wonder, Whitman or Freddy? I pick one up; it seems typical.

Outside,
the trees lift gnarled fingers
to the sky.
The rain steams down
my window.
I trace slowly the outline
of your face
in the glass.
Perhaps it will
pull you towards it,
an image that is
my face, too,
waiting behind the rain.

In the second folder the tone seems different, darker. They are
less love poems than anti-love poems. I read them over and over,
but they slide away from me at the point of understanding, like a
letter you decide not to mail just as your fingers release it into the
mail box.

what the dreams tell me
are nightmares, snakes
with your face in
rectangles on the walls,
almost like windows I try
to crawl through, but
you constrict around
my wrists with your
evil bracelets of ownership.
there is a knife somewhere
to free myself of you, but
it is in another dream.

Is this good poetry? I do not know. I go through them all,
slowly, but it is hard to see Susan behind the careful words, to see
whom she is writing about. I know I am not supposed to be doing
this, trying to peel back each line to uncover the truth about the
author, as though the poem were a price tag stuck over the list of
ingredients on a jar of jam, but I do not care. What can I do with
these poems that Susan has not already done? Perhaps the best they
can serve is to explain her life.

The phone rings. I go over, reach for the receiver, and then, as it
rings again, I draw my hand back. I am not logical about the
telephone. I will gallop in from outside, spilling groceries across

the floor, or leap from the bathtub to answer it; other times, expecting no more or less important a call, I will sit and watch it ring itself back to stillness, although of course as soon as it has stopped I will wonder who might have been calling. It rings now for the fourth time, and, even as I turn to walk away, I change my mind again and snatch it up.

It is Margaret. She wants to talk about Whitman. There must be something about another person's pain that drifts across town like a gossip column of smells, one that Margaret is skilled at reading. She tells me she wants to put Whitman's name on her prayer chain. I cannot imagine what she is talking about.

"Oh, you know. If someone is in trouble, is sick or suffering or in need of comfort, and one of us on the chain knows about him, that person will phone the person next to her on the line and she'll phone the next and so on, and we tell each other to pray for the person in need. There's eighteen people in my chain, and with all our prayers together for one person it's bound to help."

"It can't hurt, I suppose."

"Funny you haven't heard of prayer chains before," Margaret says, and I can tell what she is thinking now. "Why not join ours? There's still room, and every link helps."

"Well," I say, stalling. "What were you telling me about Whitman?"

"Oh, yes, Whitman. Well, I know how awful he must be feeling, poor man, and I wanted to do something to help. What I wanted to ask you was, you knowing him better than I do, I suppose, if you think I should ask him about this. I was thinking of going over to see him tonight."

"I don't know," I say. "I think he just wants to be left alone."

"Oh, is that right?" She is clearly disappointed.

"Maybe later," I say.

Perhaps she hears an abruptness in my voice and resents it, because she says suddenly, "I went to see Susan, you know, just a week or so before it happened."

I didn't know. Margaret must be aware of this; there is triumph in her voice. "Oh. What did you talk about?"

"This and that," she says casually. "Religion. Sin. Women. We had an interesting conversation."

She stops, waiting for me to ask her more. Suddenly I am furious at her, her meddling, her intrusion into Susan's life, and now into Whitman's. Perhaps I am afraid, I don't know; I only know I can't bear to talk to her now, to let her dole out to me in irritating little pieces her last conversation with Susan.

I tell her someone is at the door, that I have to go, and I hang up before she can reply.

I am too agitated to return to the poetry, so I gather it back into its files and put it back in the box. I suppose I will have to decide later what to do with it. Then I take my cup of coffee and go outside, sit on my front steps.

My next-door neighbour, Mrs. Schadel, a grim widowed woman whose head has always seemed too small for the rest of her body, comes home with a bag of groceries and is startled to see me sitting there. It is not something I do very often. As she rummages in her enormous white purse for her key, she gives me a nod and not quite a smile.

"Cool for this time of year," she says, spilling some linty Kleenex out of her purse.

"Yes," I say. "Cool."

At last she finds her key and goes inside, and I sigh with relief. Mrs. Schadel and I are not on the best of terms. When Gordon was alive she would be over almost every week, asking him to help her fix things, and Gordon, who was amused and flattered by her helplessness, would always go. She didn't particularly like me then, so now that Gordon is dead she has even less reason to do so. Fortunately, I care very little for what she thinks. Still, it is difficult living next door to someone who dislikes you. "It ain't neighbourly," Susan said once, referring to her own next-door neighbour, a man who kept borrowing things from Whitman and not returning them. Susan would have to go over and retrieve them, until finally she refused; I expect the man still has things of theirs, things that he will be able to keep forever because Whitman will never ask for them back.

I sit here, looking out at the street and sipping my coffee, although it is rather cold by now. It is dusk, that time of day that reminds me of old sepia photographs, the air grainy and heavy with exhaustion. Children are being pulled indoors like toys on the strings of their mother's voices. I have heard those voices for years, I think, but they still belong to strangers.

And I feel for a moment—but only for a moment—that sadness of a woman without children. It is something that has always made me different from everyone on this street, from every woman I have met in this town. Until Susan came.

"We decided not to have kids," she told me once, Hallowe'en, I think, yes—I can remember the children coming to the door in their witching costumes, and her saying that she hated the way witches were so misrepresented, that they were just healers, herbalists, persecuted by the church, and how we are still teaching children that they were evil, denying women their real histories. And I said, as I so often did to her, that I'd never thought of it that way. She closed the door, angrily, and told me then, as though it were part of the same story, how about five years ago she had panicked, "the biological clock stuff," and she and Whitman tried six or seven months for a child, but that nothing happened. "So we decided we didn't want kids after all, and I went back to shoving in the old diaphragm. Weird, eh?" She gave a laugh that sounded like the clatter of the cutlery she tossed into the sink. "We may not even be able to have kids, but I don't want to find out for sure."

Seven

I open the second journal. December 12, 1983, the first entry says. But my eyes push ahead, look for December 15, a day I remember well and am eager to compare with Susan's perception of it.

But there is no December 15. I turn the page, go over the dates and their terse entries.

> Tues., Dec. 13: just vegged out, watched the soaps all afternoon and ate cheezies, gawd, all this junk food, I should be more healthy, I could put filter tips on the cheezies.

> Saturday, December 17, 1983: went to see *Officer and a Gentleman*, something about it sucks, the wimmen in it, my god, simpering to the tune of Stand By Your Man, and how you treat a man like shit and it brings out the best in him, what barf, but W. liked it, so of course we got into an argument, and I said if only he'd wash his neck I'd wring it, which is hardly an original line but it ended the argument, oh, I'm bringing out the best in W., all right.

> Sunday, Dec. 18: rewrote three poems, feel good about that at least, good enough to refuse to cook supper, so we ordered a pizza, if I died tomorrow the man would starve rather than learn how to heat up a can of beans, he thinks if he doesn't learn he won't be expected to do it, he's no fool.

But there is no December 15. I remember Brenda telling me about her mother, who'd been in the concentration camps, how one day someone sent her an anti-Semitic pamphlet that said the holocaust was just propaganda, that nobody died in the camps, and how her mother kept saying over and over to Brenda, "It *did* happen, didn't it, didn't it?" This is not the same, of course, but I have something of that feeling, of having something important be denied, erased. I refuse to believe that it meant too little to Susan to mention. I suppose she just didn't know what to say, but still I feel cheated, that I have to remember for both of us.

I went over to her place that afternoon with a casserole I had made for their supper. It was something I did not mind doing, since I liked to cook and Susan would buy the groceries. Instead of our usual coffee, she brought out some home-made wine someone had given Whitman, and then she laid on the table in front of us two shrivelled cigarettes.

"I found them in the bottom of the tea cannister yesterday," she announced. "They must be five fucking years old."

"But . . . I didn't know you smoked." I had no idea why she was making such a fuss about two old cigarettes. She began to laugh, and suddenly I realized what they must be. "Oh—you mean they're *those* cigarettes."

"One for me and one for you. Merry Christmas."

"Oh, Susan, I don't think I—I've never smoked any before. I don't know how."

"Well, good grief, then it's about time." She lit up one, inhaled deeply, and handed it to me, saying in a strangled voice, "It's just like an ordinary cigarette. Inhale and then hold it."

I did my best, feeling absurd, remembering the faces in the *Woodstock* movie, how this is what they were doing. The smoke was harsh and bitter in my lungs, and I coughed it out. I had never learned to properly smoke a regular cigarette before. I remembered an alarming film called *Reefer Madness* we saw in Guidance class in high school, but years later I saw students at the university were watching it as a joke. I hoped it was. Susan was lighting the second cigarette.

"What are you supposed to feel?" I asked nervously.

"You probably won't notice anything. You'd need more than these. It just relaxes you. And makes you want to fuck trees."

"Oh, wonderful."

But she was right. Not about the trees, but about not feeling anything. A vague dizziness, perhaps, but nothing more. It was quite disappointing. I couldn't imagine tossing people in jail for this. I've felt more intoxicated cleaning my oven.

Susan took her final sip from the second cigarette, which she was holding with a bobby pin. "These are really roach clips," she said. "Bobby pin is just their cover story."

When she was finished, she brushed the two ends into the garbage and rinsed out the ashtray. "Ahhh," she sighed. "One of these days I'll have to be pulled kicking and scheming out of the 1960s." She made herself a peanut butter sandwich and poured us some more wine, and we argued about Margaret Thatcher.

"She *is* good for the women's movement," I insisted.

"Even though she's a fascist," Susan sneered.

"Well, maybe even because of that. She shows that women have gained the right to be as rotten as men."

"That's just my point." Susan leaned across the table, her hands parallel to each other, slicing the air earnestly in front of her. "Why should it be progress for the women's movement to produce and promote women like that, women who will cut the throats of other women?"

"But it liberates us from being seen as just 'nice,' always good and moral."

"But, shit, 'good and moral' is surely better than sinking to the level of the lowest common denominator."

"Even if that's where the power is?"

"Well—" I had tripped her on that one, I could see, gloating a little. Sometimes it was more important for me to win than to be right. "I just hate to see women so dependent on male standards," she grumbled.

"It's just how things are. We're all of us dependent on men. If it comes down to an impasse between a man and a woman, the woman has to give in." It was not exactly what I wanted to say, but I did not correct myself.

Susan looked at me in disbelief. "You're kidding. You really mean that the-man's-the-boss and that's that?"

"Well, in a way." I was not sure of myself, but I did not want to back down. I was not a feminist in the way that Susan was, but neither was I a Total Woman.

I had gone once with Margaret to a lecture called "Becoming a Total Woman," and it was very depressing. After the talk, by a young woman wearing too much make-up and decolletage, there was a testimonial period, where women were encouraged to stand up and tell their stories. It was like what I had heard AA meetings were like: "My name is ———, and I'm a feminist," and then others would get up and tell her how to be cured. One woman said her husband always beat her until she realized it was because she was not fulfilling him as a man, not being truly feminine, and now, well, he still would beat her but he said he liked her better. Margaret at that point leaned over to me and whispered, "That's a bit much." Margaret has always been a kind of shopper for philosophies, looking for bargains in strange places, but even she realized that one visit to this store was all she could afford. Susan had looked at me, amazed, when I told her about it, in somewhat the same way she was looking at me now, actually, and she had snorted, *"Totalled* woman is more like it."

"I'm just being realistic," I continued now, nervously, trying to sort through my own random experiences. "When Gordon and I moved here from Vancouver, for instance, I hated the idea, but I gave in. I had to . . . let him win, I guess."

"Had to? What do you mean, *had* to?"

I wished I had never gotten myself into this. "Well, men expect us to be that way, yielding, you know—"

"And so, bingo, because they expect it that's what we are?"

"Well, no, not necessarily. Maybe I gave in to Gordon," and the explanation came to me so easily I am still not sure if it was because it was true or if it was because I knew it would be hard for Susan to refute, "because I loved him."

I don't know what I expected Susan to say, perhaps to scoff, "Love! He just used it to pressure you into doing what he wanted," which would, after all, have been true enough, but she said nothing, only picked up her wine glass and drained it and poured herself another. The words *loved him* seemed to echo faintly off the walls, the white appliances, our own suddenly impenetrable lives. It does not seem strange to me now, I suppose, that Susan could make no more derisive an answer than she did. Susan respected love.

Finally, she said, "Yeah, well, love. I guess that'll do you in, all right."

I hated the way our mood had changed, the way I had somehow won the argument without knowing why, and as though I had played unfairly. I went back over it, picked it up at the point before I said I loved Gordon, nudging her back into it.

"Well, anyway," I said, "men do have expectations of us, to be the ones to give in first. It's always been that way."

"But just because that's how it's been historically—and actually I don't think it has—doesn't make it right, for God's sake!"

I smiled to myself. This was the way the Total Woman lecturer said we could get what we wanted: manipulation. Except that now I was losing the argument again.

"Well, yes, but total equality—I don't know if it's really possible," I said.

"Of course it is. Why would you think it isn't?"

"But men have these *expectations* of us, and if we want to live with them we have to, well, acknowledge that."

"Oh, okay—you're talking male ego, then, right?"

"Yes, I suppose." I was relieved. She had found a way to see it in acceptable terms.

"The male ego is so big it makes Mt. St. Helen's look like a little prick. Whitman, for instance. God. Once—oh, I shouldn't tell you this—well, once, after we'd slept together a couple of times—well, I'd been reading Plath's *The Bell Jar* and thought it was wonderful, and we had just finished making love and I was looking at his, you know, crotch, and I said, 'turkey neck and turkey gizzards,' because that's what Plath's character thinks the first time she sees a naked man. Well, it was just a joke, for fuck's sake, but Whitman got really upset."

"How do you know?" I asked, adding, when she looked at me oddly, "I mean, Whitman's emotions seem so . . . opaque to me, somehow." Like trying to pick up mercury with a fork, I remembered reading about someone.

"How do I *know?* Jesus, the man falls to the floor clutching his heart and whispering 'Rosebud,' of course I know he's upset."

"Did he really?"

"Oh, of course not, Ellen. Whitman has no sense of humour, that's the point, at least not one comprehensible to normal people. Once when we were grocery shopping and he wanted to buy some peanut brittle, I said, 'I can make your peanut brittle,' and he just looks at me like he doesn't understand, like he knows it's funny but not to him."

"Maybe it's just jokes about sex he doesn't like."

"No, no," she said impatiently. "It's everything. When people joke around, he's like a deaf person lip-reading."

By Susan's standards, I thought, perhaps nobody has a sense of humour. " 'It is dangerous to be sincere unless you are also stupid,' " I said, to show her I understood, that I could recognize humour, at least, if not create it. "Shaw, I think."

"That's good," she laughed. "I'll have to remember that for the next time Whitman gives me a sermon on something."

"Anyway," I said, "did you resolve it with him, after the, you know, the turkey business?"

"Well, it took a while. I mean, he was really pissed off. He told me he didn't make fun of *me*, and I still couldn't believe he was actually that upset so I just kept joking, and I said, 'Well, that's because I don't have anything that absurd to make fun of.' And he stormed out, after getting dressed, of course, and if I hadn't gone grovelling back to him to apologize, that would have been the end of things between us. Now that's the male ego, right?"

"Well," I said, although I was amused at the story, "I can see his point."

"His point?" Susan snorted. "What point? It was just a joke!"

"But it would upset you, too, if someone laughed at your, your, you know—"

"My you know?"

"Yes, your you know, said it was too small, or too loose, or something."

"But that would be a specific attack on me. I was just making a general remark on male equipment."

"Maybe he thought it was more specific."

Susan was getting annoyed. "Oh, maybe. But I still think he was over-reacting."

"I guess you're right," I said, giving in, not wanting her to think I had taken sides against her, although I suppose I had.

Susan had clothes in the dryer, and when she heard it click off she said, "Come talk to me while I hang up these fucking shirts."

I followed her into the bedroom, a large room with a queen-size bed and mirror panels on the sliding doors of the closet. I felt awkward being there, sitting on the bed Susan and Whitman slept in.

"Cold in here," I said.

"These will warm you up," she said, and she threw the pile of shirts in her arms at me. They fell on the floor, the bed, but mostly on me, their sweet warmth from the dryer hitting me the way a warm room hits you when you come in from the cold. It is such a sharp memory: I close my eyes and can still feel that sensual shower of shirts on my shoulders, my head, my arms, filling my lap with their extravagance.

Susan was laughing, picking up her wine glass again. "You look like that scene in *Gatsby* where Daisy is gushing over Gatsby's rich shirts."

"These are better," I said. "They're warm."

Susan began picking them up, slinging them onto hangers. "Remember irons? Jesus, I haven't ironed anything for years. One day historians will date the beginning of civilization from the discovery of permanent press."

One of the shirts had flung its arm around my neck; I reached up to pull it off, but Susan said, "No, leave it. It looks good on you."

"Oh, sure," I said, but I put my arm down and spread the shirt, a blue striped one, out across my chest.

"I like men's shirts," Susan said, holding up against herself the one she had just put on the hanger. She watched herself in the mirror. "They're so long and roomy."

Suddenly she tossed the shirt back on the bed, and in one casual motion she pulled the sweatshirt she was wearing up over her head and dropped it on the floor. Then she turned to the bed, picked up the shirt, and slipped it on. I'm sure it all happened very quickly, but I remember it slowly, her turning to me, her small, naked breasts close to my face, my tumble of feelings: embarrassment, curiosity, surprise. It is hard to name emotions when they overlap each other; they are like elements in chemistry that react when they meet, except that chemistry gives us new names for what happens.

"Pretty good, eh?" Susan buttoned the shirt, which hung almost to her knees. "Why do they put the damned buttons on the wrong side?" She pulled one of Whitman's ties from the closet, tried to knot it around her neck. "How on earth do they do this?"

I got up and did it for her, the fabric sliding in and out of the loops, my fingers surprising me with their long memory. I had learned to do this for Paul, and for a moment it was as if he were standing there again, impatient at his own ineptness, at having to wear a tie at all for whatever occasion it was he didn't want to go to.

"Now a belt, maybe," Susan said, and she reached into the closet and pulled one out, put it on. "If this were a designer belt it would be a Gloria Vanderbelt." She appraised herself in the mirror. "Not bad." And she did look nice, the tie and belt formalizing her somehow, making her look elegant in a way an evening gown probably would not. "Now you, come on."

"What?"

"You get to put on a shirt, too, come on."

I laughed. "I can't wear one of Whitman's shirts; don't be silly."

"Oh, come *on*. We can draw in moustaches and go out and see if anyone recognizes us."

She began unbuttoning my blouse. I tried to push her hands away, but she was determined, was already pulling my arms out of the sleeves. She stared at my chest. "A bra. Christ, I haven't worn one for eons."

"Some of us don't have any choice," I said, annoyed. "I read somewhere once that a woman needs to wear one if she can put a pencil under her breast and not have it fall down."

"A pencil—Jesus, you could carry a typewriter under yours. Take off your bra, come on."

"No," I said, a little frightened now.

"Come on, you saw my boobies, let me see yours."

"Susan—I'm embarrassed. Please stop."

"Come on, come on, I let you see mine."

I cannot remember who undid the clasp, both of us perhaps. I know that I did decide to give in, let the straps fall from my shoulders, the brassiere fall to my waist, where it snagged absurdly on the waistband of my slacks. I try to stand outside myself, see what Susan saw, a middle-aged woman, with large breasts capitulating to gravity.

"Jesus," she said. "They're beautiful."

"They're too big," I said. "It's like carrying two bags of groceries around everywhere."

She reached out a hand as though she were unaware of what she was doing. Her fingers brushed a slow half-circle on my left breast, paused on my nipple.

"I'm cold," I whispered. I crossed my arms over my chest. My nipples, erect from the cold, pushed into my forearms. I picked up my blouse and put it back on.

"Yeah," Susan said. "Let's get out of here." She flung the rest of Whitman's shirts onto the hangers, neither of us saying anything. I picked my brassiere off my waistband where it dangled like some unravelled white bandage and wadded it up, but I had no pocket I could put it into. I kept holding it in my hand, its buckles and clasps cutting into my palm.

"I should go," I said, when we were back in the kitchen.

"No, stay, please. I'll make coffee."

I sat down at the kitchen table, the brassiere still foolishly in my hand. I shoved it down the side of my chair, where I forgot it and where Susan must have found it later but never returned it to me, and I was too ashamed to ever ask for it back. Who knows where it is now, I think, brassiere heaven.

"I'm sorry if I embarrassed you," Susan said. "Too much grass and cheap wine. I was being childish." Still wearing Whitman's shirt and tie, she did look like a child now, dressed up in adult clothes.

"No, it's okay," I said. "There's nothing wrong with women

seeing each other's bodies." I wasn't sure about that. I thought of her fingers on my breast and how I did not pull away.

Susan poured the coffee. "When I was a student, I slept with a woman once." She paused, waiting.

"Oh," I said.

"I felt like a shit about it afterwards. It was the sixties, and everybody was into experimenting. You know. There was this girl in a couple of my classes and we got to be friends, and when eventually she told me she wanted to sleep with me I said sure, like it was one of those experiences you were expected to have before you grew up, and here was my chance."

"Why did you feel like a shit?"

"I just told you. For her it was . . . important, it was genuine. For me it was just using her, the way men use women who really care about them just to get sexual experience, another notch for the crotch, so to speak. Well, that's all she was for me, like okay, I've had my lesbian experience, now I can go on to having sex with a black man, a married man, a man with a tattoo on his ass—"

"Cheap shot." But it made us laugh, silly girlish giggles that warmed the room. "Did you enjoy it?" That was really all I wanted to know.

She hesitated. "It was . . . okay. Yeah, it was okay. But I never felt, oh, I don't know, right about it somehow. Politically correct, hormonally incorrect, that sort of thing. And I just like men too much. To sleep with, anyway. Did you ever, you know, feel that way about other women?"

I thought about it for a moment. "No," I said, finally. "I don't think so." I almost told her about visiting the gay club in San Francisco with Brenda, but I decided against it. I suppose I was afraid of having her know that about me. "I grew up earlier than you, when we didn't even know about such things."

"Well, I guess if you were gay you'd have found out by now."

"I guess so."

We were silent for a while, still not comfortable with each other. We sipped our coffee and looked out the window.

"But you know," Susan said suddenly, "there's something about women relating to women, even if it's not, well, explicitly sexual."

I waited for her to go on, but she didn't. "How do you mean?"

"Well, for instance. I see all these older women, widows, who are living alone and hating it, lonely, frightened, poor, desperate for a man, any old fart would do, to come along and save them. And most of the men, of course, have died off. So it seems to me that the women should get together, form some one-to-one relationships. Then they would have someone else around who cared, someone to love. It's just society telling them such an arrangement is weird. Well, it makes sense, doesn't it?"

"I guess so," I said, "if the two women were compatible. Perhaps they could . . . share the available men."

"Naw," she said, batting the air with her hand. "The point is to do without them entirely. I think it's a great vision of the future." She began to sing, in a ridiculously low key, "Thaaaanks for the mammaries," and we both laughed, laughter of dismissal, that declared, *this is not serious; see how easily we push it aside;* laughter like a snowplow after a blizzard clearing the road, making it safe, the dangerous snow all in the ditches where it would melt in spring, run off through culverts, into sloughs and rivers, out into the huge warehouse of ocean.

Eight

December. I had gone to spend Christmas, as I usually do, with my sister, Claudia, and her family in Lloydminster, a flat-faced town straddling the Alberta-Saskatchewan border, where my brother-in-law manages to make a living as a carpenter. They live on the Alberta side of the town, which they seem to feel is superior to the Saskatchewan one; it has something to do with politics or sales tax.

We have little in common, really, Claudia and I, but because we are sisters we feel we must keep the traditions. She is older than I and disapproves of me. Neither of us is sure why; it is one of those things that began when we were children, and now we are set into that pattern, both of us determined we have outgrown our childish animosities but feeling them packed between us still like the dead air trapped inside double-glazed windows.

Claudia has three children, all girls, and they were going through what she called "stages." The oldest is seventeen and involved with a boy who is part East Indian, and although he seemed nice, clearly her parents were not happy about it. He seemed preferable to me to the boyfriend she had last year, a sulky boy everyone called Fungus. The second daughter is fifteen and so addicted to television that even on Christmas Eve she left to watch it in her room as soon as all her presents were open. The youngest, Robin, is twelve, lingering before that descent into adolescence. She was the only one who did not make me feel I was taking too long in the bathroom in the mornings. I should not be disappointed, I suppose, that they resented me. When they were babies I saw them merely as wet, lumpy things that made loud, repetitive noises, and when they became ambulatory they seemed to be programmed the way I understand MX missiles are, to seek out and destroy. My response to them, logically, was avoidance. By the time they became recognizable as people and I became interested in them, they had lost interest in me, which is only fair.

I made an effort this visit to spend some time with Robin, who seemed not yet to see me as some annual obligation. We played cards, and one day she told me about Duran Duran, which I first thought was a motorcycle but then learned was her favourite rock group. Her language became frothy and incoherent as she attempted to tell me how she felt. I tried to remember what it was like for me when Elvis Presley first howled his way into my teen-age heart. One of my teachers, trying to understand, said she had felt something like that about horses, which made more sense to me then than it does now. Presley has been dead for most of Robin's life, I thought, my God.

I told Robin that I'd like to go for a walk, that snow was something special to me and I wanted to take advantage of it. She said she hated the snow, but she came with me. The air outside was crisp and dry, not like it is on the coast. Our breaths pushed grey clouds ahead of us as we walked to the edge of the town, where the sidewalks grated into dirt and the fields lay quiet and lathered with snow. On the way back, squinting into sun, I thought about Chilliwack, its dull winter rains, and I wondered where Susan and Whitman were now, what kind of Christmas they were having.

Whitman had two weeks off work, so he and Susan had gone to Seattle for a few days, then to spend a week with his mother in Victoria.

Fri., Dec. 23, 1983: Seattle. nice, staying in a hotel, always makes me feel like a real grown-up. just wandered around the city, watched TV in the evening. except they had this x-rated channel and W. insisted on watching and it got him all horny and then we had a fight because I said I didn't like it that he needed that crap to get him in the mood. oh, shit. we had sex, anyway, but it was the pits, we were both still mad, punishing each other. I was too dry and he just rammed on in anyway with his miserable bone. like getting fucked by a turnip. I didn't come, that's for sure, and maybe he didn't either, I hope not.

Saturday, December 24, 1983: Christmas Eve, whoop-de-do. W. tried hard to be nice, always asking me what I wanted to do now. and to some movies in the evening, didn't want to chance TV again, one was a French film with subtitles, and I missed most of what was going on because I kept trying to follow the French, not read the subtitles, all those fucking years in school studying French and I can't understand a gawddamned word. quelle piss-off.

Sunday, December 25, 1983: Victoria. loved the ferry trip through the Wanda Fuca Straight. W's mom looks so old. thank god she doesn't expect us to visit often. but I like the old bat, love it when she takes a strip off W. and he can't talk back to her because she's his sweet old mom.

Mon., Dec. 26, 1983: visited W.'s Uncle Allan and Aunt Joyce in the afternoon, god, how boring. played cards all evening at home, a crazy game W.'s mom knows called "shit on your neighbour." W. got so mad at me because I'd save my shit cards to play on him even if I had a chance to play them on his mom first. he's right, I know, Jesus, why do I want to pick on him like that?

Tues., Dec. 27: Whitman Is Getting Restless. Tomorrow, I just bet.

Wednesday: Yup. W. says he wants to get back, just can't leave that thesis alone. his mom just shrugged, said, okay, if you have to go, but she asked me to stay over New Year's as we'd planned. W. is annoyed, though, doesn't like the idea of his mom and me together without him, thinks we'll compare stories about him. when I'm home he ignores me but now he wants me to come back, of course it just makes me determined to stay. his back to me in the narrow bed is hard as a wall all night.

Thursday, December 29, 1983: W. left on the 1:00 ferry. "see you," he said tightly. feel lonely without him, but I won't go back until January, I won't.

Friday, December 30, 1983: W.'s mom must think I'm nuts. went for a long walk along the water, nearly froze, the wind was so cold, then on the way home, I got lost. Christ. I was sure I knew where I was, then the street names started sounding unfamiliar, I had no sense of direction, just got panicky, and it was getting dark. I started crying, just bloody wailing, and this old couple saw me standing there, took me into their house and called W.'s mom and she came and got me. Jesus. how humiliating.

Saturday, December 31, 1983: some people came over and everybody drank too much, mostly me, and it's almost 1984 I can see by my clock but don't think I'll make it. . . .

Sunday, January 1, 1984: nineteen eighty-four: Big Brother Is Watching and Bored Stiff. slept most of the day, watched some dreadful TV with W.'s mom, her taste is worse than mine, no, that's like modifying a superlative.

Mon., Jan. 2, 1984: think I'm getting a cold sore. wonderful. played Scrabble all afternoon, that old bitch beat me, made me make supper. I made an enormous pot of spaghetti, it was some kind that tripled in volume, how was I to know. she said we can have spaghetti sandwiches tomorrow, but I wonder what she really thinks, like Ellen, what do women who are good cooks really think of women who aren't.

Seeing my name here, unexpectedly, at that date, is unnerving. It was the last day before something moved in between us, scribbling its new address in my book and whispering, "Don't tell, don't tell."

January 3, 1984. Susan was in Victoria. Whitman was back in Chilliwack, working on his thesis. I was back from Lloydminster after making my usual excuses about having to get home, Claudia saying oh-you-don't-have-to-go-yet but glad as I was that it was over for another year. At the airport in Edmonton I said to Robin, "Come to the coast and see me sometime," and then I was immediately sorry, because she said eagerly, "Oh, wow," and I thought, what would I do with a twelve-year-old in Chilliwack? I would have to buy Duran Duran records and worry about drug traffickers. "Sometime, maybe," I said, giving Claudia a stiff hug good-bye.

January 3 was a grey Tuesday, the rain frail but continuous, and I was writing my annual letter to an old friend in Toronto, when the phone rang, and it was Whitman, asking if by any chance did I have in my famous library a copy of *The Brothers Karamazov;* he wanted to borrow it. Sure, I said, come on over.

I remember being calm. I think I must have been expecting this call for a long time.

"He just wants to borrow a book," I said out loud to myself in the mirror in the hallway as I went to meet him at the door. Maybe I believed it; I don't know any more. What matters finally are not your intentions, only what you do.

I took him to the study, his tall, nervous body close behind me, those long-fingered hands shoved into his pockets. He smelled like rain.

"I didn't even check," I said. "I just assumed I had it." My eyes slid over the familiar spines, found the novel on a bottom shelf. I knelt to get it, can still hear myself saying, "Are you using Dostoyevsky for your chapters on Skinner or on Humanism?"

He knelt down beside me, and I felt his hand, his hand trembling, on the back of my neck. "Ellen," he said, "oh, Ellen." I turned to him. What did I say, I try to remember now. Was it "No, we mustn't," or had I only whispered it to myself, quickly, something that was supposed to be necessary, a propriety?

His lips were on my hair, my throat, my mouth, his fingers running up and down my back, my sides, catching on the curve of my breasts. I could feel the throb of his penis against my thigh.

He pressed me back against the bookcase; the books on the upper level rocked on their shelves, and for one horrified moment I thought they would all come down on us, bury us in an avalanche of language. But only one book fell, and I still remember wondering which one it was, wanting to ask Whitman to stop, just for a moment, to see which author had hurled himself at us. A hardcover, too, I could see from the corner of my eye, dangerous.

Whitman was unbuttoning my blouse; I shut my eyes against the memory of Susan doing the same just a few days ago. Don't think, I told myself, don't think; it will be your only defense. And it was easy not to think, to let my mind numb itself to everything but the feel of Whitman's fingers, slow and marvelling, sliding the straps from my shoulders, pulling the brassiere down and touching my breasts, my nipples so dumbly contracted. I could feel my vagina moistening, wanting, wanting.

Whitman took off his shirt, his pants, his shorts, not hurrying, looking at my breasts, pausing once or twice to reach out and fill his hands with their heaviness. I remembered Susan's small breasts, knew mine were the kind men wanted, felt a lurch of guilt and then shoved it away, let myself see only the male figure before me, the penis asking its blunt question.

Whitman's body, I could see, was aging the way a woman's did, the waist thickening a little, the thigh muscles softening. His upper body was surprisingly well-developed, his skin pulling taut across his chest and biceps. It seemed out of proportion to his body type, with the long thin arms and legs; I wondered if he might work out sometimes, could suddenly visualize barbells beside his typewriter in his study. His feet were full of thin, intricate bones, his toes almost as long as some of my fingers. I noticed the way his calves and ankles were still corrugated from the socks that lay in two brown puddles beside his shoes.

I started to say something, what I don't know, but Whitman put his fingers against my lips. Then he pressed me to the floor, onto my back; I could feel my breasts slide in their foolish way into my armpits. He pulled me towards him, parting my legs with a kind of expertise that made me go tense; I did not want to think this was something he did with the same efficiency as putting in a new typewriter ribbon. He leaned over me, his elbows braced on either side of my head, and his penis nudging, nudging, against me. His eyes were closed. I would have to help him, I realized, and I reached down and guided him. I remember holding my breath as he slid into me, in an old adolescent panic that I would not have enough room, that it would be like trying to swallow a cucumber whole. But all it felt like was good, a present I had been promised. We moved together in that rhythmic trance until I could feel his contractions.

I hadn't come, although I was close and did not expect any more, but when Whitman withdrew, he reached into me with those wonderful fingers and rubbed me to orgasm. It was something Gordon had never done willingly, and because I knew it repelled him I stopped asking. With Whitman it was different. Already I was feeling the fear of knowing I would want this again. "If you find a man who really knows how to make love to a woman," I could hear a friend's voice from an old conversation, "don't thank him; thank his last girlfriend." As we lay there, gathering back the lives we had tossed off, it was as though Susan were in the room with us.

We dressed quickly, not speaking, keeping our backs turned to each other. I remember pulling up the zipper of my skirt and hearing at the same time the sound of Whitman zipping up his pants, and wanting to say something about it, about how co-ordinated we were, anything to blot up the silence, reaching for language like a towel. But I stopped myself, thinking, he will have to speak first, as though that were the proper etiquette.

When Whitman had finished dressing, he reached down and pulled *The Brothers Karamazov* from the shelf. "Mustn't forget this," he said.

"Yes," I said. "That's what you came for, after all."

He looked down at the book, twisting it in his hands. "Yes," he said at last, as though he'd had to think that over.

We stood there, stranger to each other now than we had ever been.

"Do you think we should talk about it?" I said finally. "I mean, well, there's Susan."

"I know," he said. "I know. I don't want to hurt her." He paused, his eyes flicking miserably around the room, settling at last on a picture on the wall behind me. It was a portrait of myself when I was a child, but he probably didn't realize that. "Maybe I should just think about it for a while. I don't . . . I don't really know what happened."

"All right," I said. "All right."

Don't-know-what-happened, I thought. Yes, that was the best excuse. Swept-away-with-passion, not in control, not ourselves. It was easier than admitting that this day had been hunching toward us for a long time and that we both knew it.

When Whitman had gone I sat at the kitchen table and cried. It was for all the decent reasons. Susan was my friend and I had just made love to her husband. I covet my neighbour's husband, I thought bitterly. Oh, I was severe with myself, I think now; I made myself suffer, no doubt about it, but not suffer enough to swear not to do it again.

Even now I can hardly bear thinking about it, for what it makes my body feel. "Made my body sing," it says in a novel somewhere, and, yes, that is what Whitman did. He made my body sing, and such beautiful songs. It is absurd to want this, I think, leaping up and pacing around my kitchen, feeling that wetness between my legs that makes me think that if Whitman walked through the door this moment I would not, in spite of all that has happened, be able to stop myself. "Sadistic bastard," I shout at the ceiling, where God is supposed to be, somewhere up there under the shingles, giving us lust and marriage but not at the same time, with the same people.

I almost go into the bedroom and masturbate but decide not to, know that it would be a release but a disappointment, that I would only feel foolish afterwards. I make myself another cup of coffee instead. Something in the caffeine must act as a sexual suppressant, I think; that's why all the housewives in North America drink so much, to keep from attacking the husbands across the street, suburban kaffee-klatsches only group insurance.

I pick up the journal. January 3, 1984. I know already what happened to Susan that day, but I let her tell me again.

Monday, January 3, 1984: please, please, please, don't let it happen again, please God no. shopping with W.'s mom this afternoon, and coming down the escalator at Eaton's right at 5:00, closing time, people everywhere, it just zapped me, zap, like that, I get to the bottom and I can't move, people have to push me to the side, W.'s mom finally looks back and there I am stapled to a display stand, she has to come back and pry my fingers off, and I'm just hysterical all the way home, wailing no, no, not again, and I phone Ellen and tell her to come and get me at the ferry tomorrow, if I wait I may never be able to leave this house, W.'s poor horrified mom stuck with me forever. jesus, fuck, shit, piss, cunt, prick, why should it come back now, it's not fair, god *damn* it.

Five o'clock, January 3, 1984. I stare and stare at that time. At five o'clock January 3, 1984, Whitman and I were in the study, making love. At five o'clock January 3, 1984, Susan was transfixed with a panic so desperate her mother-in-law had to pry her fingers off a display stand in Eaton's in Victoria. It is only a strange coincidence, I think, but I feel my hair crawling on my neck, the way they describe it in horror novels, and I look up uneasily, as though a stranger had suddenly come into the house.

"Agoraphobia?"

I had just picked Susan up at the ferry terminal, and we were driving back to Chilliwack. It took me over two hours to get to the ferry, and now it would be at least that back, in rush hour, but I could not tell her no. Pick me up, she had said on the phone, please pick me up, and yes, I said, yes, of course, I'll be there. As I'd watched the ferry pull up, the turmoil of water as it maneuvered in to dock, I felt like turning and running, thought I could not face her, that I would see her and shout, "Susan, I'm sorry." But then I went back inside the terminal building and bought a cup of something that smelled like gasoline but that was supposed to be coffee from the vending machine and told myself not to be foolish. *Pull yourself together,* said some voice in my head, the voice of my father, who could not stand tears, especially his own, and whom I learned to please by being contemptuous of emotions expressed in public. *Pull yourself together,* I whispered to myself, my lips actually moving, as I sat on one of the cold metal chairs by the windows and pulled my coat tidily over my legs and waited for Susan.

And when I saw her coming down the escalator, looking wildly for me, her relief as she saw my wave, I knew it would not be as difficult as I had thought. Susan saw the person she expected to see, needed to see, and I would be for her whatever she wanted. I may even have believed it was what was best for her.

She leaned back in her seat, her face swollen and splotchy and pebbled with sweat. I had never seen her looking so awful. "Yeah. Agoraphobia. You know what it is, don't you?"

I nodded.

"I first got it, oh, maybe five years ago. It just moved in on me slowly, nothing to worry about, really, little anxiety attacks as I'd be driving, then pretty soon I found even going grocery shopping was a major trauma. Sometimes I'd get the cart half filled and I'd just freak out and run out of the store, people probably thinking I was nuts and they were right. Once in a line-up at the bank I could feel it starting, as though I couldn't breathe, my heart slamming around in my chest like it wanted out, my knees shaking, but I could control it until it was my turn at the wicket, and then, handing my bankbook over, that did it somehow, as though now I were trapped, I'd surrendered my choice about staying or leaving. Jesus." She banged her head angrily against the head rest. "I just grabbed my passbook out of the teller's hands, the poor woman, and ran out."

"Did you know what was happening?"

"Hell, no. And I couldn't tell anyone, I was sure they'd only laugh, so I started saying I felt sick whenever I had to go out anywhere, all the time just hating myself for not being able to control it, you can't imagine."

"Did you tell Whitman?" Just saying his name felt dangerous.

She gave a bitter snort of laughter. "Sure, finally I had to, and he just didn't have a clue what I was talking about. He kept saying, 'But it's so easy, see, you just open the door, step outside, walk down the street,' and he'd show me how, as though that were all there were to it, some motor skill I'd forgotten."

"But you found out it was . . . an illness, didn't you? And it was better then?"

"Yeah, eventually. Finally a doctor Whitman dragged me to—and I do mean physically *dragged,* I was screaming and holding on to the door frame, he just threw me into the car and locked the doors and I cowered on the floor like some animal—oh, Jesus, I can't stand to think about it, that grim look on his face, like he would just force me no matter what—anyway, this doctor recommended a therapist who came to see me at home, and she was okay, she explained that I wasn't the only one this ever happened to, and that alone was worth a lot, that I could say, look, I've got this bona fide illness, with a fancy name and articles in the medical journals."

"And you got better." I didn't dare make this a question. Of course she got better, I told myself, and she'll get better again. This is not a punishment.

"I guess so. I'm not sure how. The therapist went with me the first few times, and then I got so I could go out alone, and after a while it was just gone. I've been trying to remember what changed, what made it go away, but I can't remember, can't fucking remember."

"Well, it will go away again," I said, reaching out and stroking her shoulder. "Don't worry."

She grabbed my hand, pulled it so desperately to her cheek that I lost my balance behind the wheel, and the car swerved to the left. An oncoming truck honked at me; I felt the driver's angry glare slap at my face as he hurtled past.

"Oh, Jesus, sorry," Susan said, taking my hand and setting it back on the wheel.

"No wonder you're agoraphobic," I said, laughing, but of course it had frightened me, too. "It really *isn't* safe out here."

"Yeah." We were silent for a moment. A police car with its lights flashing passed us. Susan put her hand up over her eyes, as though she might only be shading them, until it was out of sight. "Ellen, really, thank you for coming to get me. I don't know what I would have done without you."

I blinked and blinked, guilt like a small hemorrhage behind my eyes. I gripped the wheel until my fingernails were cutting into my palms.

"Oh, Whitman would have come for you if I hadn't," I said. Ahead I could see the freeway entrance at last; it would be easier driving now, I thought. I took my right hand from the wheel and rubbed it on my slacks. The cold dampness pulled through the fabric onto my thigh.

"He's not off work until five, and if he *had* come, he'd have been pissed off. I can just see him—he'd be sitting there not saying a word, driving fifteen miles over the speed limit, not looking at me, wanting me to feel guilty, guilty, guilty."

I started to say something to reassure her, the kind of clumsy and expected contradiction that oh, no, he wouldn't be that bad, but I stopped myself. Probably it was true. What did I know of Whitman? To me he was something from a novel, not as he was to Susan, a husband, someone you have to live with, day after day. Instead, I said, alarmed as I heard the question, the way it filled up the car like a new passenger, "Do you love him?"

She was silent for a moment. "Oh, I suppose so." It was the kind of reluctant acquiescence you would give to someone asking if you were going to a dentist to get a cavity filled. "It's just that it's not like it was at first, and I don't just mean the romantic stuff, I know that's supposed to drizzle away, it's that we have no . . . patience with each other, we always seem to blame each other, seem to think our lives could have been more exciting or something if we weren't tied to each other. Oh, fuck, I don't know." She was starting to cry, began wiping angrily at her eyes and nose with the back of her hand. I kept staring at the road, couldn't stand to look at her unhappy face. "I don't think it's like what you and Gordon had."

I thought about that. "Maybe not. But then Gordon was old when I married him; he'd worked a lot of things out. And I was, well, I was looking for a place to hide." I was surprised to hear myself articulate it like that, but it did not sound untrue.

Then Susan was saying, "I'm going to throw up," and I twisted the car quickly onto the shoulder, and she half-fell out the door and vomited again and again, me sitting helplessly behind the wheel, my forehead on the backs of my hands, until she pulled herself back inside, pale and shaking, saying, "Take me home, please hurry, I just want to get home."

There is nothing, to my relief, of that day in her journal, and nothing for the whole next week. I did what I thought would help. I bought groceries for her and cooked her meals, listened to her tell me what she felt like whenever she went to the door and stepped out, that hysteria rising around her like black water. I talked to Human Resources and to a counsellor at the college, but no one was very helpful; everyone kept talking about The Cutbacks and Restraint and how such programs and specialists had been cancelled.

My doctor suggested that a support group might help, and he thought there might be one meeting regularly in town, but when I told him that most agoraphobics had trouble even leaving their own houses he agreed that would be a problem. He dug a pamphlet out of his files called "Agoraphobia: What It Is" and told me to give it to Susan, but this seemed about as useful as suggesting to her she go out to meetings.

"Just be a good friend to her," he advised finally. "Don't push her; try to be understanding."

A good friend, I thought. I've been a very good friend. At least, I told myself, stepping out of his office and feeling the sun, the cool air, on my face as though they weren't things I deserved, nothing more has happened with me and Whitman. When we saw each other we would nod and say hello, like good neighbours, turning away too quickly, perhaps, so that someone watching might think, *they have quarrelled,* and someone else, a little wiser, might think, *they are afraid.*

On the way home I stopped at the library. The librarian, I was relieved to see, was occupied somewhere else. She was a loud and large woman, with muscular arms that always looked too big for the sleeves of her blouses, which were tight as tourniquets. Susan called her Conan the Librarian. No matter which books I checked out, she would exclaim, "Oh, *that's* a good read!" as she plunged her date-due stamp in the direction of the flyleaf. The counter was blue with ink from when she missed the page entirely. I slid past her desk to the card index.

There was no subject listing for "agoraphobia," so I browsed through the shelves and finally pulled out a number of books with titles like *The Psychoanalytic Theory of Neurosis* and *Schizophrenia and Functional Neuroses,* all of which had agoraphobia listed in the index. I sat down behind the stacks and opened one of the books. A medicinal smell seemed to rise from it.

"Fear of open streets is often a defense against exhibitionism or scoptophilia," I read. What on earth was scoptophilia? I read on:

> The anxiety attacks of a female patient with agoraphobia and crowd phobia had the unconscious definite purpose of making her appear weak and helpless to all passers-by. Analysis showed that the unconscious motive of her exhibitionism was a deep hostility, originally directed toward her mother, then deflected onto herself. "Everybody, look!" her anxiety seemed to proclaim, "my mother let me come into the world in this helpless condition, without a penis." Originally the attack represented an attempt to exhibit a fantasied penis; the knowledge that this object was fictitious produced the transformation from perversion to anxiety hysteria.

I sighed and closed the book. It seemed quite absurd. Was this really state-of-the-art psychiatry? Perhaps it is an out-of-date publication, I thought, opening the cover again. "Copyright, 1972," it said. Hardly archaic. I opened another book, this one smelling vaguely of urine. Agoraphobia, it said, is a regression into childhood, a search for a primal, usually oral, satisfaction. Another book said it was the quintessential escape both from the self and the other. None of them said, "If your friend has it, this is what you should do." None of them said, "If you don't sleep with your friend's husband again, it will go away."

There is a journal entry, finally, for Wednesday, January 11, 1984:

> decided I just *have* to make myself go out, I can't stand feeling like this, W. looking at me with pity/scorn/hate, god knows what, saying every time he comes home, "did you go out today?" as though I could just decide to do it, whenever I wanted. so I phoned Ellen, told her to get the coffee ready, I'm coming over, and I *did*, I *did*, not for long, not even a half hour, but it's a start, makes me feel great.

But the next day she phoned me, crying, saying she started to come over but couldn't even get half way down the walk before it hit her, and she had to run back inside. "They call it housewife's disease," she said bitterly. "Well, that's me. A house wife, married to the goddamned house."

"Get a lawyer," I said. "File for divorce."

"Sure. It can get custody of the appliances."

"I'll come over," I said. "I'll bring a book."

Sometimes in the grey afternoons, when we had tired of playing cards and our conversation had drifted into little dusty piles in the corners, I would read to her, poetry usually. I liked the way she would close her eyes, cup her chin with one hand and listen. "Jesus," she would always say afterwards, "that was nice." I had asked her once to show me some of her poems, but she was evasive and said, "No, not yet. I'm too self-conscious about them. When they get published, then." I did not mention them again, and neither did she.

I thought today I would try the new Atwood book on her, the one with the funny poems that were really short paragraphs of prose. I paused at the door into the study. It was not easy coming in here, but it was just a room, I told myself firmly, just a room full of my books; I would not have to fall for memory's sleazy tricks if I didn't want to. I found the Atwood volume and took one of her earlier ones, too, but as I turned to leave my foot touched something on the floor, a book. I picked it up, puzzled, couldn't for a moment recall why I would ever have bought it or why it was on the floor. It had fallen, I could see, because it must have been just set horizontally on top of some other books and wasn't part of my collection in its alphabetized rows. It was called *Satan's Mark Exposed,* and at the same instant I remembered both that Margaret had lent it to me and why it was on the floor. It was the kind of absurd juxtapositioning that I would have enjoyed telling Susan about, and suddenly I was furious at Whitman for giving me such secrets. Still angry, I put the book on top of the Atwoods and took it over to Susan, who shrieked on seeing it, "Get the priest, get the priest," and held up in a cross two carrots she had started peeling, and I thought, how could I choose any man over this woman?

Nine

Monday, January 23, 1984: Ellen brought some novels over, but I just can't get into them, read the same page over and over, there's a lead plate behind my eyes, nothing can penetrate. discovered, though, that if I'm slow and careful I can go into the back yard, actually walk as far as the fence, today the fence, tomorrow the world, there's no stopping her now, I am woman, hear me whimper.

Tuesday, January 24, 1984: that crazy friend of Ellen's came over today, Margaret—

I am surprised, am sure Susan never mentioned Margaret coming to see her in January. And Margaret said nothing to me either; I expect she knew I wouldn't like it.

—oh, maybe she's not as crazy as she seems, I mean, she's found something that works for her, who am I to sneer? too bad I didn't tell her about the agoraphobia, maybe Pastor Bob would have a cure, maybe he'd recommend an exorcist, what fun. wouldn't it drive W. wild if I told him I was going to get religion, get born again, maybe the second time will turn out better? he'd just freak, it would be a better weapon than Freddy, oh, god, why am I such an asshole, trying to get to him all the time, he doesn't do that to me.

Wed, Jan 25: today W. said he was thinking of getting a word processor, that it would make writing his thesis a lot easier. "you just punch in *Skinner* and it'll do it all for you, I suppose," I said nastily, and he didn't get mad, he just sighed and said calmly, "I wish you understood, Susan, I really do," and what kind of answer can you make to that, shit.

Thursday, Jan. 26, 1984: the back yard closed itself off to me again, I got down the back steps and then someone came out of the house next door and it was panic-city, I would have screamed but my lips were afraid to part, I was back inside so fast my feet didn't have time to turn around. called Connie, let the phone ring 100 times before remembering B.C. Tel., the bastards, are charging people for calls like that. so here I sit, in the offal of afternoon television. "People's Court": now that's TV at its best, a half hour of real people hating each other, the microcosm, the judge perfectly cast as God, capricious and rude, I love how he calls women "feisty," imagine calling a man that. wonder how Ellen's making out with her case.

For a moment I cannot think what she is talking about, and then I remember. When the summons first appeared in my mailbox, ordering me to report for jury duty, I was angry and resentful, but then I thought, well, it might be interesting. I drove in to the city on Tuesday, nervous around the huge new court-house, but finally I found my way to the room full of other people who had been ordered there. We were each assigned a number, and then our numbers were all put in a box and the woman in charge drew them out one after another.

"It's like a bingo game," hissed the man sitting beside me. I nodded. It did seem like a strange way to handle things.

Then my number was drawn. I still needed to be approved by the lawyers for each side, but they both accepted me with barely a glance. I felt pleased, as though I had passed a test, but I wonder now how they decided, what it was they knew about me that made them take me and reject the woman whose number had been drawn just before mine. What did it say on their papers beside my name? *Grey, Ellen: widow, 45, unemployed, has no noticeable opinions on anything.*

When I got home, Susan, of course, was eager to hear what happened.

"What kind of case is it?" she asked.

"I'm not sure if I'm allowed to talk about it," I said dubiously.

"Oh, hell, the trial hasn't even begun yet. You can tell me what the case is *about,* for heaven's sake."

"Well," I said, knowing I would have to give in to her eventually, "it doesn't sound all that interesting, actually. It's a robbery of a corner grocery store in Vancouver. Not murder or anything."

"Aw, shucks. Well, it could be worse. It could be a traffic violation. Well, when do you go back?"

"Two days," I said.

And the next Thursday the trial began, early in the morning; I had to get up at 5:00 a.m. to be there on time. The courtroom was the way I'd always seen it on television: the twelve of us jurors slotted tidily into our seats; the defendant, a young man of about twenty wearing a suit and tie and stiff new haircut; the lawyers, shuffling their papers and having last-minute consultations; the judge, looking bored already.

The trial itself was actually over very quickly. The prosecutor called only three witnesses: the store owner, an East Indian man who told us through an interpreter that the defendant probably was the man but he wasn't absolutely sure; the policeman who investigated the case and who told us that, yes, there did seem to have been a robbery; and finally, the most interesting witness, a young woman wearing a yellow dress and sandals, who said the defendant was her boyfriend and that she had been out in the car waiting for him as he robbed the store. The defense attorney did what he could to shake her story, but he succeeded only in making her cry.

"I'd hate to have to go through that," the woman in the seat beside me whispered as the girl finally stepped down. I nodded.

The defense had no one to call except a character witness, a man who said that he had been the defendant's phys. ed. teacher in junior high school and that Tommy had always seemed like a nice boy and a good athlete.

And then the judge told us to go away and deliberate and make a decision. It wasn't until then that I fully realized what was expected of me. I was expected to sit in a room with eleven other people and decide whether a man was guilty or innocent. Even though it did not seem like a difficult case, I was suddenly appalled at what I would have to do, pass judgement. Guilty. Innocent. A jury of one's peers, I thought, only other sinners casting their votes like stones.

"So? What was the verdict?" Susan asked later that evening.

"Guilty," I said, taking another sip from my coffee. I could hear the faint sound of Whitman's typewriter, could imagine the letters hammering onto paper, making judgements too, but ones you could change, as easily as winding the sheet out of the typewriter and throwing it away and starting again.

"You couldn't have deliberated very long," Susan said.

"About two hours," I said. "All but one of us voted *guilty* the first time around, so it was really just a matter of convincing this one man to change his mind. He was a surly kind of guy—I think he was annoyed at us all because he wanted to be foreman but we chose someone else. He ran a clothing store on Robson, and he complained about having to take the time off. I suppose he wanted to impress us with how important he was. Anyway, he was the only one who voted *not guilty.*"

"What was his argument?"

"Well, he just didn't believe the girl, that's all."

"Why not?"

"Well, he said she might just be wanting to get back at her boyfriend for some reason, like maybe they'd quarrelled about something else, and this was her way of getting even. Like crying rape when it wasn't."

"Jesus!" Susan knotted her two hands into fists and slammed them onto the table so hard our cups bounced. The typewriter in the study was silent for a few minutes, as though it too had been jarred by the noise, by Susan's shout that was so full of anger it made the whole house around us tremble. "What a bastard, eh? When it's a woman's word against a man's she's the one who's lying. 'Like crying rape.' Jesus. So how did you finally convince him?"

"It took a while. Someone else pointed out that she could be just protecting herself with a story like that, that maybe the police had offered her some sort of deal, and that sounded plausible, so we discussed it for a while, but nobody else changed their votes, so it was still just him."

"Well, what changed his mind?"

I hesitated. "I think it was . . . well, I heard him say to the man beside him, 'If we give our verdict before 4:00 we won't have to come back tomorrow, will we?' Anyway, about fifteen minutes later he said, 'Oh, okay, then. I change my vote. Guilty.' We were all relieved, but I don't think he really cared, one way or the other. He just didn't want to come back again tomorrow."

"Ain't justice grand?" Susan said.

"Yes," I said. "Of course, I was glad, too. Not to have to go back again tomorrow."

We were quiet for a moment, and then Susan said, "Well, I read somewhere that in the early days of the jury system if the jury couldn't reach a unanimous verdict fairly quickly, they would be tied in a cart and whipped and pulled through the streets of the town."

"That's incentive to agree, all right. Well, we didn't need that today."

"You know, I wanted to be a lawyer, once," Susan sighed. "Really?" I said. "I think it's the kind of job that would make you very cynical."

"I'm cynical anyway," Susan said.

We were quiet again, sipping our coffees and staring past each other into space. Then Susan began to laugh, and because something, perhaps the same thing, suddenly seemed funny to me too, I joined in.

"See what I mean?" she said, still laughing. "Cynical."

That night I dreamed of Susan, wearing a bright yellow dress, the dress the girl in the trial had been wearing. It was such a vivid dream that I told Susan about it the next day, and she grinned and said, "Was I driving a get-away car?"

"No," I said, trying hard to remember, "But you were standing on a road, hitchhiking, and a truck stopped for you, a blue truck, and I was in it and got out and took pictures of you, in your yellow dress, beside the blue truck."

"Very symbolic," Susan said. "Weren't there any horses in it?"

"Horses? No. Why?"

"Oh, I dunno. I just like dreams with horses in them."

Friday, January 27, 1984: the TV went on—I love the passive/impassive voice—at 10:30 a.m. and stayed on until midnight, I watched everything, everything, nothing too insulting, my mind is turning to muskeg.

Friday: that might have been the day Whitman came over, the day he told Susan casually—I can hear him saying it, the casualness—that he wanted to come look at my books, that I might have something he needed.

I look up from the journal, at the door, as though he were there again, his hands nervous in his pockets, his eyes looking past me, saying, "Can I come in?" and me saying, "Of course." And me saying, when he reaches out to touch me, "No, we can't. You're married to Susan, and she's my friend, and we can't," pushing his hand away, mine trembling from its own desire to close over his, but pushing it away, pushing it away.

I look down again at the journal. January 27, 1984. Susan is watching TV, has been watching TV since 10:30 a.m. I want her to look up as Whitman comes back a few minutes after he has left, his hands empty, saying, "No, she didn't have the books"; I want her to look up and not see a man who has just made love to me.

But what is the point now of trying to fool memory, slide in a nicer version? I did not push his hand away. I did not. We went to my bedroom, and our hands touched each other as though they had never felt nakedness before, and our wavy voices filled the room with sounds that had nothing to do with the careful syllables of conversation.

After, as he lay there, eyes closed, he said, "You must think I'm a real bastard."

"It's my fault, too."

"Yeah. Well. But it's worse for me." He sighed. "I did try, you know. Not to come over. I just couldn't stop thinking about it."

"I know," I said. "I couldn't, either."

We were silent then, in that sombre way of people finding it hard to believe they could have felt such passion, anything so absurd. I remembered, for some reason, a saying of my mother's: "By his silence, man refuses; by her silence, woman consents."

"I should ask you," Whitman said at last, awkwardly, "if you, you know, take anything. Birth control."

"You don't have to worry," I said. "I won't get pregnant."

I thought he would ask me more about it, but perhaps he concluded that my answer meant I had reached menopause, because he only nodded, and then we were silent again.

"I hear you had jury duty yesterday," he said finally. "How did it go?"

"Oh, it was interesting. Not that hard a case, I suppose."

"What was the verdict?"

"Innocent," I said. I am not sure why I said that, perhaps because I could not bear to say the other word, to have it float into the air over our heads. I could not even say, the way you are supposed to, *not guilty,* a phrase which seems to pick up guilt by association, which does not mean the same as *innocent* even though it should. If Susan has told him about the case he will know I am lying, I thought, but it is too late now.

But Whitman only nodded and looked up at the ceiling. "Can I smoke?" he asked. He reached for his shirt and his cigarettes without waiting for my answer.

"If you need to," I said. I disliked smoking, the way the smell would burrow into my clothes and carpets and drapes and stay there for days, and I was determined not to pretend otherwise, but when he didn't answer I said, "I'll get an ashtray."

I blinked at the brightness of the living room, the kitchen, angry at myself for not putting on a robe and for forgetting to close the curtains, for having to scuttle around like a thief and for having to go back naked into the bedroom. Whitman watched me as I opened the bedroom door, extending the ashtray before me like something I was afraid of. "Jesus," he said. "You are a beautiful woman. You must have really been something—" He broke off.

"—when I was younger," I finished for him. I stood unmoving at the door. Let him look, I thought, refusing to let myself feel humiliated, refusing to feel the drag of age at my breasts, buttocks, hips. I am forty-five years old, I thought, and I will not be ashamed. The cornered light from the hallway pressed against my back, edged into the room. I did not flinch. It would be only later, after he had left, that I would stand in front of the mirror and cry, and I would hate the snivelling tears of a middle-aged woman wanting to be young again.

"I didn't mean that." Whitman sat up, his eyes shifting nervously about the room. "We all get older, hell; I just meant that if you look so good now you must have looked even better once. . . ."

I let him stumble on, and I said nothing, hoping it was a kind of revenge. I walked slowly to the bed, set the ashtray on the sheet where I could see the soft mound of his genitals. Before I could pull back, he grabbed my arm, hard, and pulled me down onto the bed; the ashtray thudded onto the floor. He began kissing my breasts, sucking the nipples. I could feel his erection growing again under the sheet.

"You should go home," I said. "Susan will be wondering what's happened." I wanted to hurt us both, I suppose, saying that.

He fell back against the pillows. "All right," he said. He lay there for a moment longer, with his eyes closed, and then he began getting dressed, not looking at me. He laced his shoes with such exactness it was as if he expected to wear them for a day at work, not just to walk across the street.

"What did you use Dostoyevsky for, by the way?" I asked. "For your chapters on Skinner or on Humanism?"

He looked blank for a moment, then gave a little laugh of remembrance. "I used him as an excuse to come over," he said.

Before he left he took another book from the library. I never did find out which one it was, as if it mattered.

"I told her I had to work late," Whitman said, standing under my porch light. It was the next Tuesday, the last day of January. I remember because I had just come back from a birthday party for one of the women in my reading group, and I was turning the calendar leaf over to February, thinking something to myself about starting a new month, a new page, when I heard his knock on the door. When I opened it I could see behind him the rectangles of light from his own house. The moon was set in the sky like a huge white stone.

"Come in," I said. "You're rather taking a chance."

He stepped inside, not hurrying, and quickly I closed the door. "I know. Maybe that makes it more . . . exciting, that there's a chance we might be found out."

The thought made me cold. "Are you serious?"

"No, no, not really." He gave a brittle laugh and dropped into a chair in the kitchen, splaying his hands on the table for support, like an old man. He looked tired, fatigue scribbling new lines around his eyes.

"Would you like something, coffee, a drink, heroin?"

There was a softening of his face, which I took to be a smile. "Heroin would be nice," he said.

"I'm all out of syringes." I was feeling foolish, standing at the sink pushing around my unwashed supper dishes like some nervous hostess, making coy conversation.

"A coffee would be good, too," he said.

While the water heated, I came to the table, sat across from him. "Well," I said, "how are you?"

"Susan said you haven't been by for the last few days."

"I guess I haven't," I said.

"Is it, you know, because of us?"

"Probably. How do you think I feel?"

He picked up a paper napkin from the table, twisted it in his fingers, tore a piece off and pushed it under his thumbnail. Suddenly he said, "If I were a decent husband I wouldn't do this to Susan."

"Am I just something you're doing to Susan?" The words were in my mouth before I could stop them.

He kept twisting the napkin. "That's a good question," he said finally, as though I were a clever student. "No, I *did* want—*do* want—you, God knows, but it's—I'm married, that should mean something. I'm married to Susan."

"Maybe," I said coldly, wanting to show him I could be analytical too, "you want to punish her for having had Freddy. You want to get even." *Get even:* it was the term the man in the jury had used, talking about the girl and her testimony and why he did not believe it. *Get even:* such a misleading phrase, sounding as though it has something to do with balance or fairness when it almost always means the opposite.

Whitman looked up at me, startled. "I suppose that could be part of it," he said.

The kettle had been boiling so long the room was steamy. I made the coffee, brought it back to the table. When I sat down he continued as though there had been no interruption, "It's not so much that she had this idyllic youthful affair with him, but that she keeps throwing it up at me. It infuriates me, which is why she does it, of course. I'm always the wrong choice, the poorer lover—"

He stopped, wanting, I am sure, my contradiction. But why should I? I thought. I said instead, "It all seems so—"

"What?"

"Well, so childish, somehow." I felt myself tensing against his anger. "I mean, it all happened so long ago, and why should it matter now, anyway?"

He stared down into his coffee cup which he was gripping with both hands, as though he were looking for an answer there. Then, to my surprise, he laughed. "Of course it's childish. There's no excuse. It's just conditioned response. Susan brings up Freddy. I get mad."

"But you must have had affairs before you met Susan, too."

"Yes, sure, but I don't throw them up in her face. I don't make her feel she's some awful mistake."

"And after you were married?"

"After?" I could see he knew what I meant, was pretending he didn't.

"After. Affairs."

He lifted his cup to his lips and then set it back down without taking a drink. "Just one," he said after a moment. "About five years ago. It was a kind of silly business, another student in my department. She wanted me to leave Susan and got very demanding. . . . well, she had a right to, I suppose. Oh, it was just a silly business. I was under a lot of stress, and Susan had that agoraphobia—"

I wanted to ask which came first, her agoraphobia or his affair, but he went on, "In the end, though, I chose Susan. I guess that's important."

"Are you warning me?" I said.

He looked up. There may have been tears in his eyes—no, I must be firm with myself. There were no tears. He was distressed, but there were no tears, of course not.

"Oh, God," he said then, covering his eyes with one hand, his thumb anchoring on one side of his head and the other fingers drooping across his face. "I'm not a very nice person."

He was so mournful I almost laughed. "Don't worry," I said, offering at last the soothing female words. "None of us are very nice."

I took his hand from his face and led him to the bedroom, where we smoothed the tension between us away with forgiving hands, our bodies beneath them like landscapes rippling with small mountains of bones, slopes and concavities of skin, everything fitting together so easily, making nothing matter but this. Passion, it is called, passion. I looked the word up once. The first meaning given is "suffering or agony;" only the last definitions mention the emotions, desire.

"You left the ashtray here," Whitman said, after, picking it up from the night table.

"In case I had company," I said.

He smiled. "Yeah, well." He fumbled a cigarette from his shirt, lit it. We watched the smoke dangle in long grey streaks in the air.

"How's work going on the thesis?" I asked at last, a safe question, a polite question.

"Oh, yes," he said, "old Burrhus Frederic." He sank back against the pillow, relaxing.

"Who?"

"Skinner, B.F. Burrhus to his friends. If he has any."

"Why wouldn't he?" This is what a wife does, I thought: how-was-your-day-dear? I remembered a handbook they gave to all the girls our first year at university. It said never to talk about ourselves on a date, but to ask lots of questions, to encourage the boys to talk about themselves. This would make them feel important. I thought even then that this meant that the boys must be basically stupid, to be manipulated so easily.

"Oh, his theories, you know, telling people freedom and dignity are illusions, that we're all just products of conditioning."

"You look a bit like him, you know. There's a picture of him in my old psychology text, taken in the thirties sometime." I realized too late that now he would know I must have looked it up recently. *B.F. Skinner*, it had said under his picture, *originator of the Skinner box*. In the photograph he is looking away from the camera, at an experiment he is doing, and his eyes, totally black in the picture, draw you to them immediately, because they do not look at you, because you are less important than the experiment.

Whitman was pleased at the comparison. "You think so? Well, he wasn't a bad-looking man, for a behaviorist." He was actually grinning.

" 'Wasn't'? Is he dead?"

"No, no. Just, well, older, you know."

"It happens to people." I hoped he was remembering the last time he had said something to me about getting older. "Does he write anything about sex, about people, you know, in our circumstances?" It was a brassy question, but I thought I might as well make this interesting.

"About sex." He was quiet for a moment, rubbing the back of his hand absently along my upper arm. "Well, that's just the basic stimulus-response stuff, isn't it?" He smiled at me, confident. This was what he knew about.

I noticed what a clean profile he had, a nose so straight you could lay a pencil along it, a jaw that curved back so sharply the skin stretching over it looked almost painful, taut as cloth over an embroidery hoop. The careful part in his hair lay like a straight white strand along his scalp. The hair on the crown of his head was thinning; a pale glow of skin reflected back the bedside lamp. "In a few years," Susan's words were in my head, "he'll be wearing a bald spot like a yarmulke. My husband the rabbi." I reached up and ran my fingers through the hair on his chest, which was thick and brown and curly, looking out of place on his lean body.

"Is it?" I said. I had forgotten the question. Oh, yes. Sex.

"Feelings, Skinner would say, appear to us to be the dominant thing, but it's all just survival value, conditioning, reinforcing power."

"Is this. . . ," I struggled for the words, old textbook terms, "determinism what you agree with? I mean, do you think Skinner is right?"

"Well, that's the question, isn't it? I guess I'd like him to be; I mean, it would be so convenient, making it all into a science, taking away so much of our guilt and responsibility. But, damn it, the more I read him the more I see free will sneaking into his equations—" I had never seen him so animated, his hands talking into the air. He would make a good teacher. "If an operant is an emitted act, for instance, which we can reinforce and condition only *after* it has appeared spontaneously, we still haven't accounted for its appearance the *first* time. And to say that the environment is responsible, that it has nothing to do with freedom and dignity and autonomy is to ignore that *we* make our environment—" He stopped abruptly. "This must seem tedious to you."

"Oh, no," I said, although he was partly right. I suppose I was flattered that he would want to talk to me about this at all, that he would think me capable of understanding.

"I get, you know, preoccupied with it. Susan gets pretty frustrated with me." He stubbed out his cigarette more firmly than was necessary and immediately took out another and lit it, inhaling so deeply it almost made my own lungs ache to watch.

"Well," I said, "you just have to keep things in balance, the thesis, the job, Susan. They each have to have a place and be given attention."

And myself, I thought, I also want to have a place, attention. But I cannot ask for it; I can only wait and take what is left after the others have had their turn. Those are the rules. They are probably written down somewhere, some etiquette book on How To Have A Successful Affair. There would be a whole chapter called "Leftovers."

"Yes, balance. Balance." He sighed, looked at his watch. "Jesus. I should go. Susan will wonder where I am."

"Do you think maybe she knows?"

He had his back to me; I wanted to see his face as he answered, but all I heard were the neutral words, "No, I'm sure she doesn't."

"How would Skinner explain her agoraphobia?"

He stopped buttoning his shirt. I could see him sorting through answers, deciding which one to give me. "Just as an inappropriate response, I suppose," he said finally, "behaviour that could be unlearned. They're treating depression like that now."

"Does it work?"

He didn't seem to have heard me. "But maybe Skinner wouldn't really understand it any better than I do. I've tried everything, every argument, every trick—I try to be patient about it, but there's something in me that thinks she could leave the house if she just *wanted* to, that this is just some way of punishing me. I don't know, Jesus, I just don't know."

"Free will or determinism?" I said, showing how well I understood, what a good student I was, the only girl in high school biology who could dissect the frog without being squeamish.

Ten

There are so few entries left. Only a month. It is like the end of a novel when you don't have a new one you are eager to begin; you go slowly, don't want it to be over, not yet, even though you know how the story ends.

Suddenly I remember the short stories. I am procrastinating, I know, but I will have to look at them sometime; it is, after all, what I am supposed to be doing, looking at her literary work, not rummaging through her thoughts like a vandal. I close the scribbler gently, set it on the kitchen table, and dig out of the cardboard box the three file folders with the short stories. "Short Story: The Way Home" the first one says. I begin to read.

It is a disappointment. The style is all right, a bit jerky, with too many short sentences, but something you can get used to. It is the story itself that seems sentimental. It is about a young woman from a small town who moves to the city and works as a secretary. She feels lonely there, and when her parents come one day to visit her, she goes back with them, realizing her mistake was to have left home in the first place. It is too easy, I think; the woman is not believable.

The story is in the third person, but of course I wonder (and I know I shouldn't) how much of the woman is Susan. She seldom spoke to me about her parents, her conversation curving around them somehow, like a car avoiding something dead or dangerous on the road. What really had she told me? Only that her father died and that she and her mother did not get along. Perhaps this story was just an apology, the kind all children want to make to their parents for growing up.

I think for a moment of my own parents, my mother dead when I was fifteen from the ugly cancer that kept her screaming for morphine for months until the end, my father so incapable of believing it that I would hear him talking to her sometimes late at night, angry, and turning away from Claudia and me as though he had died, too, or we had. Once, walking into his bedroom without knocking, I saw him standing by the bed and he was wearing my mother's dressing gown. When he saw me he shouted, "What the hell do you want?" and he must have thrown something at me; I heard it thud against the door as I ran down the hall, into my room, shoving my fist into my mouth to keep the hysteria from screaming out. When I was old enough to leave home, he married again, a woman much younger, and moved to Toronto, where I visited once and felt like an intruder and visited again for his funeral five years later. "Orphan," I said to the figure in black in the mirror. Then I pulled on the gloves my step-mother had lent me and joined the others downstairs. I was determined not to cry at the service, but when I saw Claudia give in, I did, too, letting the tears run all the way to my chin before I wiped them away. Gordon, Brenda told me years later, wanting to make sense of me, was simply my surrogate father, and, who knows, perhaps she was right. We understand so little why we do things.

I page again through Susan's short story. "The Way Home"— she never found the way, I think. I might have helped her, given her the knowledge I had, but I didn't, and now it is too late. I put the story aside, the way you do with a letter you know you should answer but probably won't, and I pick up the second file.

This story is called "Choices." It is written in the same terse style as the other one, but it seems to be more interesting, although very short. It is about a man who is writing an important philosophy exam at a university, and he has to write an essay on "situational ethics." If he fails the exam he will lose his scholarship. The exam is not closely supervised, and he cheats, copies from a paper that he has brought with him. The idea is good, although I wish she had taken it a bit further. I have read worse stories. Perhaps this one could be published.

The last story is called "Foxtail and Freddy." Freddy. My heart suddenly begins to beat faster; I feel a dampness on my palms. Fear feels like this, I think. Am I afraid? I remember seeing the title before, when I first took things out of the box, but for some reason it did not mean anything then. Surely Susan would not choose that name for her character unless there were autobiographical connections. This may be my last chance to find out about the Freddy Susan remembers. I open the folder.

It is, I can see then, not a short story after all, but a play for radio. Radio play: what an archaic form to choose. I think of episodes of "The Lone Ranger" and "The Shadow." Eagerly I begin to read.

Fox-tail and Freddy
a play for radio

Characters:

Carol, 24 (and 16)
Robert, 24
Freddy, 16 (and 21)

Sound: Car motor a steady drone, fading into background.

Carol: What do you think about when you drive, Robert?

Robert: Oh . . . not much.

Carol: Don't you ever, you know, fantasize? The Walter Mitty stuff? Maybe write different endings for some things in your life?

Robert: No, not really.

Carol: Oh. *(pause)* I think about my past. It's like, when you're moving, in a car, you're . . . nowhere, nobody, just moving between two fixed points, and it's the best time to consider your past because you can see things more clearly, see what you really are and were and did. . . . You know what I mean?

Robert: Mmmm. It's hardly a new idea.

Carol: *(hurt)* I guess not.

Robert: Now I've hurt your feelings.

Carol: *(airily)* No, no—I realize the unlikelihood of a mere nurse having an Original Idea. You're the scholar.

Robert: *(patiently)* There may be no such thing as an original idea, Carol. And I wish you wouldn't put this "I'm just a nurse" business onto me.

Carol: Well, you . . . patronize me.

Robert: I'm sorry if it seems that way. *(pause)* How far are we now from Peace River?

Carol: Not far. We should be seeing the river banks any time now.

Robert: Is that them up there?

Carol: *(excited)* Yes, I think it is.

Robert: And how much farther to the homestead after that?

Carol: Oh, a hundred miles or so. . . . Things are beginning to feel familiar. It starts with seeing the Peace, I guess. Our farm was right on its banks, you know.

Robert: Mmmm.

Carol: Look, you can see the river down there now. And there's the new bridge.

Robert: This is quite the hill. . . .

Sound: Car noises become more prominent; the engine whines to indicate car may have been geared down.

Carol: (*in a far-away voice*) And there's Peace River, all hunched down in the valley. There's the main street, and the hotel. . . . I stayed there once. . . . (*her voice fades*)

Sound: Car hum up slightly, then abruptly cut off by:

Music: One or two distinctive notes of music, which will henceforth introduce and end all flashbacks.

Freddy: Well, here we are.

Carol: (*sounding sixteen and frightened*) Oh, Freddy, what if Dad's called the police—they might be watching for us at the hotels. . . .

Freddy: I'm sure they won't. Maybe they don't even know we're gone yet.

Carol: I just can't go in there, hiding my hand, looking guilty. What if they ask for a marriage certificate or a birth certificate or something?

Freddy: They can't do that, Carol. *Please* don't worry. Look, I'll go in alone, and get us a room, okay. You can just wait here.

Sound: Car door opening.

Carol: Oh, Freddy, wait. I just keep thinking, is this the right thing to do, to start out by running away, hiding, stealing your Dad's car. . . . And even if we get to the city, we'll have no money, you'll have to get a job, and without even your Grade Ten—oh, maybe we should go back!

Sound: Car door closing, slowly. Pause.

Freddy: (*slowly*) Go back, you really want to go back, to those small-minded people, to your father, and the way he treats you?

Carol: Maybe he won't, maybe Mom can stop him—

Freddy: *(passionately)* And what about us, you just want to throw all that away? They won't let us see each other again, let alone get married. Don't you know that?

Carol: We could wait, until we're . . . older, and you could finish school meanwhile—

Freddy: You sound like my mother—wait, wait, wait!

Carol: *(crying)* I just want to go home, please just take me home.

Freddy: Oh, Carol. . . . Look, let's take the hotel room anyway; if you still want to, we can go back tomorrow. But just once let's be like married people, you know?

Carol: All right. All right. . . . *(her voice fades)*

Music: *Same bars as introduced the flashback*

Sound: *Car humming in background*

Robert: . . . someplace later?

Carol: What? What did you say?

Robert: I said, do you want to stop for coffee at this next place, Grimvale or whatever—

Carol: Grimshaw—

Robert: —or do you want to stop someplace later?

Carol: Oh, later, okay? Grimshaw already. I must have day-dreamed my way right through Peace River. How did you like the town?

Robert: Nothing special. A nice setting, that's all. Didn't you say you and that boy—what was his name, Eddy?—

Carol: *(softly)* Freddy—

Robert: —ran away to there once when you were kids?

Carol: *(with an uneasy laugh)* Yeah, we did, once, a long time ago. And the next day we went back home again. Does it . . . bother you, to think of me, with him?

Robert: *(calmly)* No. . . . Why should it? If your past were that important to me, I wouldn't have married you.

Carol: *(in a low voice)* No, I guess not. But it's . . . natural to be, well, a bit jealous. Like, it hurts me to think of your affairs before I met you, with Donna, for instance, of you making love to her. . . .

Robert: Then maybe you just shouldn't think about it.

Carol: *(sighing)* I suppose so. *(pause)*

Robert: What kind of radio stations do you get around here?

Carol: Country-and-western, mostly.

Sound: *Radio being turned on, static until a station is tuned in and country-and-western plays faintly in background.*

Carol: I remember as a teenager, how late at night you could pull in Vancouver, or Seattle, or even California sometimes, and I would almost shove my head into the radio to hear, hating being stuck up here in the north, so far away from where everything was happening. . . .

Radio announcer: . . . and now here's a big Johnny Cash flashback. . . .

Music: *"Ring of Fire" begins to play.*

Sound: *Motor hum up slightly from background, abruptly cut off as—*

Music: *"Flashback notes" cut across the song, which fades, then revives, sounding slightly different, as though played on a cheaper radio. Fades into background.*

Freddy: Gee, that's a great song. . . . *(hums to music)* "Down, down, down . . . burning ring of fire. . . ."

Carol: Freddy . . . *(her voice almost lost in the music)* I'm pregnant.

Music: *abruptly turned off.*

Freddy: What?

Carol: I'm pregnant.

Freddy: *(slowly)* Are you sure?

Carol: *(impatiently)* Yes, yes, I'm sure.

Freddy: Well, what . . . what are we going to do?

Carol: *(angrily)* Why ask *me* what we're going to do? All *I* can do is let . . . it . . . keep on growing inside of me. But you, well—you can just take off and pretend you never knew me—it's *me* that's going to be the scandal, and my father, oh God, he'll kill me, he'll—

Freddy: *(interrupting)* Do you think I'd desert you now? You know me better than that, for heaven's sake. We'll get married, that's all. It'll just be sooner than we thought. We'll quit school—

Carol: You can't do that! You've got to get your Grade Twelve at least, and what about university—

Freddy: We don't need university, not even high school, to farm, and that's all I really want to do. Isn't that what you want, too?

Carol: I suppose so. . . .

Freddy: Look, we can live with my folks for a while, and . . . and I'm sure Dad will let us have the old Miller place, the house, we can still live in it, we can fix it up—it'll all work out.

Carol: My dad will never let us get married, and we'd need his consent.

Freddy: *(bitterly)* That's right. Your dad.

Carol: *(softly)* What'll we do, Freddy? What'll we do?

Freddy: *(beginning in jest but becoming more serious)* We could kill ourselves. I could turn the car on and roll up the windows, and we could just sit there until the exhaust . . . exhausted us, and they'd find us here tomorrow, dead in each other's arms. . . .

Carol: *(continuing in same tone)* And they would all be sorry for how they mistreated and misunderstood us. . . . *(pause)* We can't let ourselves think like that.

Freddy: You're so practical.

Carol: *(ironically)* Not always. *(pause)*

Freddy: *(excited)* We'll run away together! Like Don Elchuck and that Melnyk girl—they were just sixteen, too, and they went all the way to Vancouver. My cousin Ken lives in Calgary, and if we could get that far we could stay with him at first, he's got an apartment of his own, we could stay there until the baby came, and people would forgive us eventually and we could come back—

Carol: Or not come back— *(shivers)* Oh, I'm cold, Freddy.

Freddy: I'll turn the car on.

Carol: *(with a bitter laugh)* Just to be sure to open the windows a bit.

Sound: Car engine starting.

Music: "Flashback notes" are played.

Carol: What?

Robert: I said, I hope you don't mind my turning the radio off; that C & W stuff irritates me after a while.

Carol: No, it's okay. I suppose my tastes have changed too. . . . There's Fairview up ahead. Only another ten miles from there to the homestead.

Robert: Do you want to stop in town for coffee?

Carol: Okay. There used to be a café on Main Street. . . . There it is.

Robert: They still have angle parking everywhere—how quaint.

Carol: Quaint. I guess so. . . .

Sound: Car doors opening, slamming shut. Footsteps, café door opening, closing, as a bell tinkles.

Carol: (calling) Just two coffees please. *(sighing)* It was really a big deal for us to come here when we were in school, especially for us farm kids. We'd forge our parents' names to notes giving us permission to go uptown at noon, and then we'd sit here and drink Cokes, or coffees if we really wanted to be sophisticated, and imagine how adult we were. . . . *(her voice drifts off)* I'm sorry—daydreaming again. Does it . . . annoy you to know my mind is off somewhere else?

Robert: Not particularly.

Carol: Not even if . . . you know I'm thinking about . . . about Freddy, about when we were together here?

Robert: (patiently) Carol, I have told you—I am not jealous of Freddy. Do you *want* me to be?

Carol: (frustrated) Oh, I guess not. It's just that nothing ever seems to *touch* you. You're so . . . civilized.

Robert: That's hardly a major character flaw, choosing to be reasonable instead of immature.

Carol: Maybe being unreasonable sometimes *is* being mature.

Robert: (with a little laugh) I doubt that.

Carol: (sighing) All right. I can't argue with you. *(pause)* Well, I guess we should go.

Sound: Footsteps, door opening, closing. Car starting; motor noise up for an instant, then fading into background.

Robert: How much further?

Carol: Only about five miles. Turn left at the next corner.

Robert: How often have you been back here since you left?

Carol: Christmas, once, I think. Dad didn't exactly make me feel welcome. And Mom, oh, I don't know, I guess I never forgave either of them for, well, for anything. They had wanted me to leave, and I did, and there didn't seem much point in my coming back and pretending we were all a big happy family. The last time was for Dad's funeral—that's, what, four years ago now? The cemetery's off the road just a mile or so from here, that direction. It was such a nice, warm day, the funeral. . . .

Sound: *Car noise rises slightly, then stops abruptly as—*

Music: *"Flashback notes" sound*

Sound: *Murmur of voices in background, occasional phrases like "lovely sermon," "taking it well," "a good man" are heard; voices fade as Carol and Freddy speak.*

Freddy: It's been a long time.

Carol: Years.

Freddy: I'm . . . I'm sorry about your dad.

Carol: Are you really?

Freddy: *(uncomfortable)* Well, things worked themselves out. He was never, well, nasty to me, you know, your dad, after.

Carol: *(bitterly)* I guess he saved it all for me.

Freddy: I'm sorry. . . .

Carol: Well, it's all over with now, isn't it?

Freddy: *(relieved)* Yes, it's all past. *(pause)* You must be almost finished your nurse's training, are you?

Carol: Another year. I'll probably have a job at the Royal Alex.

Freddy: That's great. You've really done . . . very well, Carol.

Carol: Yeah. . . . I hear you've bought the Miller land.

Freddy: Yeah, it's a good section. And I'm doing most of Dad's farming now, too—he's pretty well given it up. I usually have to get a hired man every fall.

Carol: Well. You're happy, then?

Freddy: *(hesitating)* Happy enough, I guess. And you?

Carol: I get by.

Freddy: You're . . . not married?

Carol: *(coldly)* No. I see you and Gail are expecting another addition.

Freddy: *(embarrassed)* Yeah. About September, I guess. I, uh, see Gail's talking to your mom now. Do you . . . want to say hi to her? I'll ask her to come over—

Carol: No, no, please—please don't—

Freddy: *(softly)* Carol . . . if you knew, if you knew how often I've looked at Gail and wished it were you, how I've looked at our baby and thought about the child *we* had that I'll never know—

Carol: *(a bit frightened)* That's over with, Freddy. Past.

Freddy: I still wonder why you left—

Carol: My dad made me—

Freddy: And you didn't wait for me—

Carol: *(raising her voice)* I didn't wait! *You're*— *(lowering her voice)* you're the one who got married—

Freddy: You never answered my letters—

Carol: You wouldn't leave the farm—

Freddy: *You* didn't want to come back—

Carol: *You* got married—

Freddy: After *you* gave up the baby! *(pause)*

Carol: I have to go, Freddy. *(softly)* It's getting cold. Time to turn on the car and roll the windows up— *(her voice breaks)*

Freddy: Oh, Carol—

Carol: *(with a little laugh)* Yes, and oh, Freddy, too. . . .

Music: "Flashback notes."

Sound: Car motor humming in background.

Robert: Do I go right or left here?

Carol: Oh, right. The farm's just over there, see? The barn roof has caved in, I can see that from here.

Robert: Isn't there anyone who looks after the place?

Carol: Not really. The neighbours have the quarter rented, but Mom still owns the buildings. I don't know why she doesn't want to sell. She comes out from the city in the summer sometimes with my brother.

Robert: No one's been here for a long time. The grass is so deep I can hardly see the tracks. Odd stuff. What is it?

Carol: Fox-tail, we'd call it. It grows everywhere here. The weed inspector came down to our farm once when I was just little and called it a "noxious weed," and I said to him, very seriously, "No, it's fox-tail." My mom used to like to tell that story.

Sound: Car motor being turned off. Pause.

Robert: Well, let's get out.

Sound: Car doors opening, slamming shut. Bird singing in distance, then complete silence for a moment.

Carol: *(with a little laugh)* Now that I'm here, I don't really know what I want. I never thought beyond just coming here. Funny, how it's all so familiar, the house, the barns, the spruce tree outside my window there. Yet it almost seems I've never been here before.

Robert: Eliot—the poet, T.S. Eliot—

Carol: *(annoyed)* I know who T.S. Eliot is.

Robert: —says that the end of all our explorations will be, quote, "to arrive where we started and know the place for the first time."

Carol: That would mean your past is something that happened to a stranger.

Robert: Or to a friend.

Carol: No. . . To a stranger is right; to a stranger.

Robert: Can we get into the house?

Carol: Sure, you don't need a key. But it'll be so . . . empty. We sold everything at the auction, everything. I don't really want to see it. Let's just walk. In the pasture over there there's a little rise and you can see the river.

Robert: All right.

Carol: The fences are all down now. We rolled up the barbed wire and sold it at the auction. *(with a sad laugh)* Whenever anyone greeted Dad with "Wie geht's, Henry?" he'd answer, "Oh, the gates are fine but the fences are down!" What would he say now, now when they really are? *(sighing)* Sometimes I think I come close to understanding him, my father, come close even to . . . forgiving.

Sound: Footsteps through swishing grass.

Robert: This is that—what did you call it? Fox-tail?

Carol: Yeah. By fall, it gets all bristly and spikey, but now, before it goes to seed, it's so soft, nice to lie down in. . . . There—can you see the river?

Robert: Quite a view.

Carol: This was sort of my favourite place. So private—the bush screened you from the house, and only the river banks were on the other side. I used to come here a lot. . . .

Music: *"Flashback notes."*

Freddy: You're sure nobody can see us from here?

Carol: Just the cows. And God. Who do you think He is, God?

Freddy: Those poets we read had the right idea. God is nature.

Carol: That's . . . heresy.

Freddy: Why?

Carol: It just doesn't sound like all the stuff I learned at church. There's Heaven and Hell and Sin—

Freddy: Especially Sin—that's the best part.

Carol: *(laughing)* You're awful!

Freddy: I know. . . .

Music: *"Flashback notes."*

Carol: Robert?

Robert: Yes?

Carol: Let's make love, now, here?

Robert: What? Don't be silly, Carol.

Carol: Why not?

Robert: We're too old for that kind of thing.

Carol: Too *old?* Good grief, at our age?

Robert: We're so exposed out here; anyone could wander by.

Carol: No one will. There's not even any cows any more. Just God. Maybe.

Robert: I'm sure God would be titillated.

Carol: Oh, Robert, come on; don't be such a prude! The fox-tail is so soft, see. . . .

Robert: *(sighing)* Carol, I'm sorry—but I'd just rather make love in a comfortable bed in a comfortable room, and pass up the thrill of mosquito bites on my butt and ants crawling up my orifices. Besides, I didn't . . . bring anything.

Carol: I'm at a safe time. Just this once—I won't get pregnant.

Robert: Like you "didn't" with Freddy?

Carol: What?

Robert: Freddy. Isn't he what this is all about? I'm supposed to take his place in this romantic little skit.

Carol: That's not true!

Robert: No? Didn't you come here with him? Maybe this is even where you conceived his child. That would make our . . . copulating here now so much more symbolic.

Carol: You don't understand—

Robert: I understand that I do not want to be a prop in your fantasies. And I do not want to be responsible for another unwanted pregnancy. That's assuming the first one really *was* unwanted. Maybe it's just *my* child you have a revulsion about bearing.

Carol: I don't! I mean, sometime I want to have your child—just, not yet—I thought we talked all this over; we decided to wait, to leave ourselves free for a while. It's what you wanted, too—you agreed—

Robert: Because it was what you wanted.

Carol: Well, why didn't you *tell* me you felt differently?

Robert: I didn't want you to feel obligated.

Carol: So you wait and toss it all up at me now, and blame it on what happened with Freddy! You almost sound . . . jealous.

Robert: Well, you should be happy then. It's what you kept wanting.

Carol: Well, are you then—jealous of what happened with him?

Robert: I just resent your comparing us all the time.

Carol: I don't—

Robert: Then deny that you made love to him here.

Carol: *(pause)* Okay, it's true! It's true! I did! But maybe I've been . . . comparing you just to try to provoke some response from you, jealousy, *anything*. I'm so sick of the way you can be so damned uninvolved!

Robert: Carol, you knew when you married me that I don't like to discuss my feelings. That doesn't mean you have the right to throw Freddy up at me the way you do, trying to make me feel you wish you'd married him.

Carol: I don't wish that. *(softly)* I don't. I didn't marry him then and I wouldn't marry him now.

Robert: Because he married someone else.

Carol: No. Because . . . because I didn't love him enough. But I loved you enough, and I married you. *(pause)*

Robert: Oh.

Carol: "Oh." Is that all you can say?

Robert: Yes! Damn it, try to understand, okay? You have to learn to compromise, Carol. Don't always be trying to change me. I have the right to be . . . my way. *(pause)*

Carol: *(sighing)* I suppose you have. *(pause)* Well, shall we go back now?

Robert: *(awkwardly)* If . . . uh . . . you still want to, we . . . could make love. . . .

Carol: *(surprise)* Why? Why would you want to, now?

Robert: Well, I thought . . . you might still want to.

Carol: *(hesitating)* No . . . I guess you're right. It's sort of silly.

Robert: *(relieved)* Well. Let's go back then.

Carol: *(gently)* I'm glad you would have, though.

Music: *"Flashback notes."*

Carol: I have to go, Freddy. It's getting dark.

Freddy: Can I meet you here tomorrow?

Carol: I don't know. . . .

Freddy: Please, Carol.

Carol: Well, maybe, then . . . I've *got* to go. 'Bye, Freddy—

Freddy: *(his voice fading)* Carol. . . .

Sound: Bird singing.

Music: *"Flashback notes."*

Sound: Same birdsong.

Robert: Well, shall we drive on, or did you want to stay here any longer?

Carol: No, we can go. I'm . . . finished here.

Music: *Up and out.*

I gather the pages carefully together, bounce them gently on the table until all the edges are straight, tidy. Is it a good play, I ask myself dutifully. As with the poems, I really have no way of knowing; I am no literary judge. The story is rather predictable, perhaps, the characters one-dimensional. But performed, read out loud, it might be better.

And then I let myself think about what I have read in the only way I care about, the way it tells me about Susan. It is a bewildering play. Is Freddy here the real Freddy, as she wants to remember him? And Robert: is that how she sees Whitman? There is much of Whitman in the character, but Robert's lack of response to Freddy—that is not Whitman, no. Then there is Carol. I smile a little to myself. Carol is not Susan. She does not say "fuck" once in the whole play, for one thing. But is Carol an aspect of Susan, perhaps, a way she wants to see herself? Then there are the two Carols, one remembering the other; that may be significant.

And the baby. Could there have been a baby? No, I think, there was no child. That is surely something I would know.

My head aches from trying to put it all together. Perhaps I am simply superimposing one story on another, like the police do with their acetate sheets, trying to construct a real face out of fragments.

Then I notice something I should have seen at the start. The play is typed on a manual typewriter, and the top pages have a brown and brittle look that the other manuscripts in the box do not have. I lift the pages to my nose, and yes, there is that musty smell of old paper. Susan and Whitman have been together about fifteen years—the play may well be that old. Perhaps it is true then in the sense I am looking for; perhaps Carol and Robert are the people from whom Susan and Whitman have evolved. Still, I think, that does not help me a great deal, does not tell me what I really want to hear. The play has disappointed me, I suppose, raising my hopes that it would exonerate me, perhaps.

It is late, I decide; I will go to bed and think about nothing, and sleep will let me fall through its sudden trapdoor into dream, where what is true does not have to be real.

Eleven

I am awakened by the slither of something falling from my lap, and I sit up, startled. I am in the armchair, I realize, and it is Susan's journal that has fallen. A dream, I think, trying to tug it back quickly, but it is too late. There are only a few tendrils, something about Freddy—but no, it is gone.

I get up, stretch. My back aches; my right arm feels numb. Like an old lady, I think, falling asleep in her chair, sedentary with arthritis. The thought always frightens me, that I will be old and sick, and I will have no one. I think of Gordon, of how easy it was for him, never having to be afraid of age and illness because he had me, so much younger. I remember a movie I saw long ago where the hero says, "I love you so much I want to die before you do," and how even then I thought that there was something fraudulent in such a testament, that he was speaking more of selfishness than of love. Surviving is harder than dying, if only because it takes so much longer. That is why women have children, I think, so someone will be there to push their wheelchairs. Even if it doesn't happen that way, if the children neglect you, you have the myth along the way, like believing in an after-life; it doesn't matter if it exists or not, but it makes life more tolerable.

It is raining a little, the sky a heavy hood of cloud, but I need the fresh air, so I go out for a walk, to the store on the corner where I buy milk and some tomatoes, even though they are not very good. As I go up to the counter to pay, someone behind me says, "Well, hello stranger."

When I turn around and look at the chubby, balding man smiling at me, I think for a moment he is indeed a stranger, and then I recognize Gordon's oldest son, Gerald. It must be two years since I have seen him. I smile back and ask him how the wife and kids are, although I have forgotten their names. His wife is Margaret's daughter, and Margaret refers to her often enough; I feel foolish forgetting her name. Linda: suddenly it comes to me, but I have already said, "the wife," a phrase I hated when Gordon used it about me. Gerald assures me the wife is fine, and the kids are growing up, and I say that's good, and tell him when he asks that I am fine, too.

When we leave the store and he sees I do not have my car he offers me a lift, but I tell him I like walking in the rain. He shouts something about how we should all get together sometime, and I say, "Yes, that would be nice," and wave and walk on. It is raining quite hard, and I am immediately sorry I did not take the ride. Even if I did like walking in the rain, and I don't particularly, I would not like getting wet. By the time I get home I am soaked to the skin. As I turn into my driveway, thready rain sewing across my vision, I look up quickly at the house across the street. The van is gone, of course, but the lights are on in the house. Whitman is at home.

The cat is glad to see me and rubs so insistently around my legs that it is hard for me to walk. He hates the rain, keeps wanting to go outside, then sits on the step and yowls accusingly to get back in, as though I have played some nasty joke on him. After I change into my robe I find the vegemite jar and dig out a black glob on my finger. He licks and licks at it, trying to purr at the same time. It is soothing, that little rough tongue on my finger, the cat so easy to please. I wonder how he knows not to bite, how he knows my finger is not to be eaten, too.

Suddenly there is a sound at the door, someone knocking, and my first thought is of Whitman. My whole body responds, knowing what it wants, before I can tell it to calm down. Even if this is Whitman, I lecture it, things have changed now; get yourself under control, for heaven's sake. I take a deep breath.

When I open the door, it is not Whitman standing there. It is Gerald.

"I hope you don't mind," he says. "Seeing you in the store, like, and since I was in the neighbourhood, drop by for a drink, I thought."

I do not want to let him in, but what choice do I have, the way he is standing so clumsily on my porch with the rain hitting the back of his head? He is my step-son. I remember how after Gordon's death he made all the funeral and legal arrangements. "He's good at that sort of thing," his wife kept reassuring me, and I suppose he was. I have a blurred memory of him bringing some papers over for me to sign and my starting to cry and him patting me awkwardly on the shoulder and saying the rain made everyone depressed.

A moth begins to putter around his face. I have to let him in. "All right," I say, hoping he will hear the reluctance in my voice.

He comes in and brushes the rain from himself, takes off his coat and hangs it carefully in the closet, then pulls off his cowboy boots and leaves them by the door. I remember he wears them to make himself look taller; he is actually an inch or two shorter than I am. Noel Coward's jibe about never trusting men with short legs because their brains are too near their bottoms comes into my mind, and I am instantly ashamed; Gerald cannot help being short. I give him an apologetic smile and ask him what he would like to drink.

"Whatever you got," he answers. I get him a beer. He looks out the kitchen window, nods at the house across the street. "That's where that Mrs. Jervis lived, isn't it?" he asks. "Did you know her?"

"Yes," I say tersely. I do not want to encourage him to talk about what happened.

"Well, that's how it goes, eh?" He jerks down a swallow of beer and, without waiting for an invitation, goes into the living room and sits down on the chesterfield, putting his feet with their thick grey socks up on the coffee table. "Nothing much has changed, eh?" He looks around the room as though it once belonged to him. There is a brassy confidence in him I do not remember.

"Not much," I say, sitting down across the room.

"Well, *you* have," he says. "You look damned good. You look ten years younger."

"Oh, sure," I say, but in spite of myself I am pleased. I am aware that I am only wearing my robe, and even as I look down to pull it more tightly closed around my throat, I can hear the sound—thud, thud—of Gerald's feet hitting the floor, and I know without any doubt at all why he is here.

"Your father—" I start to say, warding him off with the only words I can think of that might work, but he has crossed the room already and is standing beside my chair, and his thick fingers are on my neck, moving one by one like beetles under the collar of my robe.

"You must get lonely," he is saying in a husky voice. "A shame, a good-looking woman like you."

"Gerald, I'm flattered, really I am, but I'm not, I really don't want. . . ." Stupid, polite phrases, and meanwhile his hand is

moving down onto my right breast. I reach up and clutch it
through the robe, and we have a ridiculous struggle, him trying to
shove it further down, me trying to hold it where it is. Even if I win
I will not have gained anything, I realize. I decide to stand up,
confront him; I am a few inches taller, after all.

But it is a mistake. As I stand up he gains the advantage because
I am off balance, and his hand slides as far into my robe as it wants
to go. He is suddenly holding my whole breast, and the foolish
robe splits itself open for him so the other breast dangles naked in
front of him, too. The sight seems to be too much for him, and as
he gapes I step quickly back and slap the robe together, tying a
knot at my waist so tight it should be impervious to the most
determined locksmith.

"You'd better go home now," I say, backing behind the chesterfield.

"Hey, come on," he says, coming after me, his cupped hand
held out as though he expects me to drop my breast into it again.
"You know you want it. It's nothing to be ashamed of."

He moves around the chesterfield, slowly, murmuring things I
do not want to hear, reminding me of the way you approach a
horse, the way you think the horse is greedy and gullible, the way
your voice is gentle and your outstretched hand promises something more than a trick.

"Gerald," I say, my voice firm and reasonable, "look, let's talk
this over."

"Sure," he says, "all right." And he drops his hand and shrugs,
as though talking it over were perfectly fine with him.

I turn to go back to my chair, but it is the wrong thing to do. He
moves quickly behind me, crossing his arms over my stomach and
pushing his groin against my buttocks. I try to twist away, but I
trip on the robe and fall to my knees. Gerald falls with me, a
boulder on my back, knocking me breathless. He turns me to face
him and then presses me against the back of the chesterfield, his
moony grin dangling over my face.

"Come on," he says. "You need a man, you can't let it go to
waste." He bends down to kiss me; I can see his huge moist mouth,
like an airplane with the bomb bay opening, a lumpy tongue ready
to drop.

He takes my hand and pushes it against his crotch; there is
probably a penis lumbering awake behind the denim, but I don't
want to stay there long enough to say good morning. He tries to
make my fingers unzip his fly.

"Help me," he is whispering into my neck. "Please. You can take it in your mouth if you want to." Oh, yes, there is a name for that, although, not surprisingly, I cannot remember it now. I tried it once with Paul. It was like trying to make love to a tongue depressor.

His other hand is trying to shove itself between my legs, and when I feel his fingers fumbling through my pubic hair for my vagina I feel real anger for the first time.

"If you don't leave this minute," I say loudly, "I'll tell Margaret."

It is the perfect thing to say. It stops him the way his father's name did not. Margaret: the warder-off-of-evil; Margaret: better than calling on God.

Gerald pulls back, staring at me. "Hey, now," he says, fear twitching at his face. "I was just trying to do you a favour."

"Do yourself a favour, you mean."

"Well, okay, that too. You're a good-looking woman. I thought you wanted it, that look you gave me in the store."

And immediately I feel guilty. What look? Is it my fault? "I didn't mean to give you any such look."

"Well," he pouts, "you did." Then he slides his foolish grin onto his face again and says, giving it one last try, "You're sure? We'd be good together, you know. It's not healthy to go without."

"I don't go without," I say. I cannot believe I would tell him that. I must get him out of here before I say something else I will be sorry for, give him other weapons against me. I pull myself in panic to my feet, and as I am scrambling up, my knee catches him in the groin. He gives a little girlish scream and rolls over onto his side, curling himself around his genitals. At first I think he is having a fit of some kind, and then I remember that men have this peculiar sensitivity.

"I'm sorry," I say. "I didn't mean to do that." I nudge him a little with my foot, the way I do with the cat when I want him to move. "Are you okay?"

He staggers up and doesn't look at me, walks to the door like a man who has been in an accident. After several stumbling tries he puts on his boots. He grabs his coat from the closet, sending the hanger skittering across the kitchen floor, and then he puts his hand on the doorknob and looks up.

"Say hello to Linda and the kids from me," I say. Of course it sounds sarcastic, but I had not meant it to; it was one of those formulas that gathers on your tongue when someone is standing with his hand on a doorknob trying to leave. He gives me a look of such hate that my hand clenches on the chesterfield arm as though something were flying across the room at me and I have to duck.

"You're a C.T., you know that? You lead men on and then you can't deliver."

I start to protest, "That's not true—," but he has already turned and gone out. He slams the door behind him, but not too hard; there is still Margaret to consider. I wait until I hear his car start, and then I run to the door and bolt it. I lean against it and take some deep breaths. After a while my heartbeat returns to normal, and I go into the kitchen and pour myself a glass of rum. I sit down at the kitchen table and try to make sense of what has just happened.

The whole episode is just too bizarre. "Gerald," I say out loud. "For God's sake." I remember him in this house years ago, shy and inarticulate, letting his wife repeat and explain whatever he said. And now here he is, telling me he is what I want, shoving his hand under my robe. I take a big swallow of rum.

The cat comes out from where he has been sleeping and yawns widely.

"You were a big help," I say. "I hope you behave better when you go visiting."

He called me a C.T. I may have heard the phrase before, but I cannot remember what it means. I will phone Susan; she will know. I can already hear her howls of laughter as I tell her what happened—"and then he sort of rummaged around under my robe as though he'd lost something there—." I am putting the story together for her as I reach for the phone.

And then of course I remember. Susan is no longer here. I cannot tell her. I feel what it means to be without her in a way that suddenly terrifies me. There is no one for me to talk to. The story about Gerald grates like chalk in my mouth, and I finish the glass of rum in two deep swallows, almost gagging. I begin to cry a little, over Susan, over Gerald, but then I wipe my eyes and blow my nose and tell myself to stop being self-indulgent.

"Doing you a favour," he said. My God. All I had felt, from the moment his fingers touched my neck, was distaste. I go over it all again, carefully, to make sure: did he excite me here, here? No, I conclude, there was nothing; I felt as aroused as a sack of potatoes being loaded onto a truck. I think of Whitman, the first time with him in my study, how he had pushed me back against the book-case. Why was that so different; why was I so eager for him that my mind stopped like a radio being turned off and my body sang yes, opening itself to him as though it were perfectly right, my desire so intense the whole room seemed to tremble and disappear? If it is only sex with Whitman, why shouldn't another man do just as well? Of course it is more complicated than that, I sigh, and I look out my window at the light across the street. A choice has been made for me, whether I like it or not.

I decide to have a shower before I go to bed. I make sure the doors are all locked, and then I step into the tub, let the water smash around me. I usually prefer baths, but there is violence to a shower that seems necessary now. When finally I turn the tap off, Gerald is just a soapy scum burping into the drain. I look at myself in the mirror as I step out of the tub. " 'A good-looking woman,' he said. Well, that's true, anyway," I tell Dong, the voyeur, who always comes into the bathroom with me. I go into the kitchen to turn out the lights, and I see Whitman's are already out. He must be in bed. Perhaps he reaches out for Susan, absently, the way I did, and finds emptiness, nothing at the ends of his fingers but the cheat of memory.

When I go to bed I cannot sleep, and I reach down and rub myself slowly toward orgasm. I have a few standard fantasies which I can plug in like cassettes when I am not feeling imaginative; they involve embarrassing images like myself in a jail cell with naked, aggressive men wearing masks, but I have decided that if they work I will not feel ashamed, even if they are not, as Susan would put it, politically correct.

The man in the mask pushes me down onto the bunk in the cell. Two others wait outside, keys to the cell in chains around their waists. The man orders me to undress, and I do, trembling. He reaches out for me. And suddenly his mask is gone and he has Gerald's round white face. My orgasm retreats in disbelief. *What the hell is going on*, it says; *get serious or you can kiss me good-bye.* I clench my teeth, squeeze my legs together so tightly my fingers hurt, but I get the mask back on and Gerald disappears.

The man reaches out to me, his thick penis sliding in, in, and I twist into my orgasm, not a very good one, but it is enough to release me, open the doors into sleep, a beige room at the top of the stairs.

The next morning it is warm and sunny, and if it weren't for the beer bottle I find in the living room I might think last night was just a dream, the kind where people you know do absurd sexual things and then the next day is a non sequitur where you have to pretend when you meet them that nothing happened. Well, I cannot see what good it will do to go over it all again, to think of things I should have done or said; *esprit d'escalier* it is called, retrospective cleverness. Gerald will not be back, I am sure of that. He is like the man in the bar, something to be forgotten.

Dong is waiting on the front steps to be let in, and he pushes inside as soon as I open the door. He still has food left from yesterday, but he only glances at it, wanting something fresh, and then winds himself around my legs with such apparent adoration that I have to laugh. It is amazing behaviour, really; how does he know that such fawning is more likely to pay off than yowling or urinating on the carpet? But I do not give in. "Eat what you have," I say. "Think of the starving kitties in China."

I make myself waffles for breakfast, something I have not done for a long time, but they stick to the waffle iron and I have to dig the dough out of the little squares with a knife. I used to make good waffles, and it is upsetting that I seem to have forgotten how. At last I give up and put the bowl with the remaining batter away in the fridge, where it will stay until it is old enough to be thrown out, and I make myself some toast and ham and eggs instead. But I can hardly eat anything, so I give most of the slab of ham to Dong, who gallops eagerly to his dish and then only sniffs at it and looks up at me, disappointed. "Don't be so *fussy*," I say, annoyed, and I open the door and shove him out, although he goes stiff-legged with resistance and it is like trying to push a stalled car.

I take my coffee into the living room, and I see Susan's journal is still on the floor, lying face down with some of the pages scrunched up. Of course it fell by accident, but still I feel responsible, as though this is some indication of how I treated Susan, carelessly. I go and pick it up, straighten the crumpled pages. My hand goes over and over them, smoothing, soothing, but the wrinkles do not go away.

Finally I decide that I must continue reading. I try to find the place I was at when the journal fell, but I cannot remember, so I go back until I am rereading familiar entries. I am less afraid now, I realize, than I was at the beginning. Perhaps it is because Susan cannot tell me anything worse about myself than I already know. Suddenly there is this:

Thursday, Feb. 2, 1984: Ellen over, brought grocs and helped me make supper. it occurs to me that maybe I depend on her too much, maybe it really doesn't do me any good, her doing so much for me, she makes it too easy for me to stay sick.

I lean my head back and close my eyes. *She makes it too easy for me to stay sick.* Oh, yes, I think. I wondered if she felt this. I had gone over it too, over and over. When I was most angry with myself I would think, what better husband to have an affair with than one whose wife could not leave her house? What better friend to have than one who was always at home to your visits and grateful? But then I would tell myself, no, it is not that sinister. I am not that evil. It was as though I needed to look at the ugliest possible explanation, and then I would feel better, knowing things are rarely as bad as our worst imaginings.

I touch my fingers to Susan's words. "I didn't want it that way," I whisper. "I swear." Finally I take my hand away and go on.

Friday, February 3, 1984: I seem in the last week or so to have become, at least, a good housekeeper, that's the secret agenda of afternoon television, to drive women back to housework. well, my home is my castle, Rapunzel, Rapunzel, let down your golden dink, we said in school, someday my prince will come, not on my clean floor he better not, the house is spotless, I vacuum every day, not just the easy middle of rooms, but in the square corners of things, I have a special nozzle for that, the one that looks like long, thin lips, I wash the windows and my cloth squeezes into every right angle, sucks up the last smudge. have washed the walls, too, even W. mentioned it, my hands are so rough from all the water they've been in I could grate carrots on them. houseproud, my mother called it. houseproud, housebound, housebroken, household, housekeep: words of possession, all of them, ownership, by houses, you are what you live in, Christ, I'm a split-level in Chilliwack.

Saturday, February 4, 1984: decided not to waste this clean house so had Ellen over for supper, W. so goddamned uncommunicative, it's like watching someone with brain damage relearning speech, how does he survive at work, how does he talk to people there. or is it just when I'm here that he gets that shellacked look on his face and won't even try to have a normal conversation.

I can see us sitting around the table that night, Whitman and I looking down at our plates and smoothing our napkins on our laps as though we were trying to cover ourselves. It is hard to recall the words we spoke, or even the silences between us like something inedible.

But I do remember what we ate, spaghetti and meat sauce, and the way we ate it, my thinking that it must indicate something about who we were. I ate mine by cutting the spaghetti into small pieces, manageable and tidy. Whitman ate his the way you are supposed to, the way they do in Italy, turning his fork in a tablespoon. Susan did not use a spoon, rolled the long threads on her fork and then bit off the few long strands that dangled down. A red dab of meat sauce spotted her cheek.

I can still see it there on her face, like a large blemish, and then I have to remember something we talked about, or rather something Susan tried to talk about. Pornography. I don't know how the subject came up, probably because the bombing of the porno video stores in Vancouver was in the news again that day.

"Well, I'm glad they did it; I really am," she said defiantly, as though she expected an argument. "I mean, those places rent out goddamned *snuff* movies."

"Really?" I said. I did not know what a snuff movie was and I was too embarrassed to ask, with Whitman there. I cut my spaghetti into even smaller pieces.

"Really," she said emphatically. "I'm sick of seeing violence against women dismissed as 'erotic.' I mean, you do agree, don't you, Ellen?"

"Yes, of course," I said. And then, polite, I asked, "What do you think, Whitman?"

He didn't say anything, just kept rolling and rolling his spaghetti in his spoon, shaping it until there were no loose ends. Perhaps he was just preparing his response, the way he did sometimes, but the silence swelled around us, and finally Susan, impatient, jabbed at it with her fork and said, "Oh, he thinks it means you advocate censorship and book-burning and prudery then. He thinks my attitude is a violation of free speech and all that."

Whitman keep rolling his fork, as though it took all his concentration.

"Remember that movie we saw in Seattle?" Susan continued, turning to him. He nodded, but did not look up. She turned back to me. "It was a Dutch film; I think it was called *The Girl with the Red Hair,* and she was a resistance fighter against the Nazis.

Anyway, after, I said to Whitman that it's only history that has made her heroic, a martyr, only because of who won the war, and maybe history will also judge those who bombed the video stores as heroic—like, who decides when it's terrorism and when it's freedom fighting? One of the Nazis in the film called the woman there a terrorist, too. Anyway, Whitman said it's not the same, that Holland was an occupied country, but I mean, shit, for women *this* is an occupied country; the pornographers are just the Ministry of Propaganda. There's not one woman in this country who's free, really free, to walk alone at night. When the rapes get too blatant the police put a curfew on the *women*, for Christ's sake, really, they've done that, some American city—"

I was alarmed at her intensity, a little frightened, too, because perhaps she was right. Perhaps there really was a war; perhaps history would judge me as a collaborator. What did I know of the brutal things men could do to women? I read the statistics—wife-battering, rape, incest—but like most people who want to get through life the simplest way possible, I did not want to generalize beyond my own experience: if it does not happen to me it does not happen.

Susan sat back in her chair. "Well, anyway," she said, her voice calmer. "But you see what I mean, Whitman," she added, not really making it a question but still, wanting some answer. We both looked at him, waiting.

He reached across the table for a slice of bread, spread the butter on it slowly, carefully, his knife prodding into the corners. Then he looked up and said to Susan, in a voice that I visualize now as one that has been squeezed flat, the normal peaks and valleys of sound compressed into a thin dense line, "You have meat sauce on your chin, Susan."

Susan stared at him, as though she did not understand, and Whitman reached across the table with his napkin and wiped it off.

"Thanks," she said, and then she got up abruptly from the table and brought in the coffee. The cups rattled in their saucers as she set them down on the table. I can still feel the coffee burn my mouth as I drank it hot, too hot, wanting so much to finish and leave, not to be here between them, to be a part of so much failure.

Sunday, February 5, 1984: Connie down to see me today, we gabbed until our mouths were sore, but it's not the same as it was, she's got her job and everything, just makes me more aware of what I'm missing. she said my house was too clean, and, fuck, she's right. cleanliness is next to mindlessness, if I'm going to be neurotic there are more interesting ways than becoming a dustcloth, a dustsloth, that's more my style, I'll grit (!) my teeth and let the dirty-minded dust collect, I'm sick of Playing House. I bet young houses have a game called Playing People.

Monday, February 6, 1984: Ellen was over, we played 66. put on some Simon and Garfunkel and got all sentimental about the good-old-days: Jesus, music can do it to you.

I turn the page, and see something that startles me, that I have not seen in the journal before. Dates are written down the pages, with about ten lines left under each, but that is all, as though Susan had intended to come back later and fill them in.

Tuesday, February 7, 1984:

Wednesday, February 8, 1984:

Thursday, February 9, 1984:

Friday, February 10, 1984:

I turn to the next page. It is the same, the dates carefully listed, and nothing beside them. February 11, 12, 13, 14, 15. It is not until Wednesday, February 22 that there is an entry, and it says only

must start writing in here again, maybe it will help.

I start to read on:

Thursday, February 23, 1984: if it would just stop raining. but they say that melancholy personalities feel better if—

Then I stop. I am so close to the end, and there is too much left out. I turn back to those blank days, the pale blue lines underneath them still waiting to be filled in. It is as though Susan has given them to me, said, "Here, you do it; write down what happened."

I pick up a pencil. Under February 6, although it could be any of these days, I write, "Ellen came over for lunch, brought me more books which she knows I won't read. in the afternoon my husband gets off work early, parks down the street where I won't see the van, and goes over to Ellen's where they fuck themselves silly."

I read this over. It does not sound bizarre. Then I flip the pencil over and erase and erase, until the paper has begun to wear through, until there is no trace of any words, until the page is clean again.

I lean back in my chair. Remembering, not remembering: it all seems pointless. But there are philosophers who say reality is just a construct, so maybe recalling it differently could change the past. How should I remember then, February 8, for instance? A Wednesday, let me think. I would remember Whitman coming over, us deciding it would have to stop, kissing each other good-bye with great sadness. February 9 Susan would come to my door crying, "My God, I'm cured, I can leave the house, it feels so wonderful, let's go for a drive somewhere like we used to." Revisionism: seeing a different vision.

Twelve

It is the next afternoon. I am trying to figure out what happened to me this morning, whatever possessed me.

I spent the early morning keeping busy, not wanting to finish the journal. After my aerobics class, I vacuumed the house and did a large wash, hanging my clothes outside in the spring air, although I know Mrs. Schadel disapproves and thinks it looks lower-class and messy. She told me once I owed it to the neighbourhood to get a dryer. I have one, of course, which I use when it is too wet to hang things outside, but I didn't tell her that; I don't know why.

When I finished the laundry, left the sheets undulating like huge white wings on the line, I decided there were letters I should be writing; I had fallen behind. I owed Claudia one. Perhaps I would ask if Robin could come stay with me for a while this summer; I would be lonely, and if it was not for too long we shouldn't get bored with each other. I got out my stationery, with my name and address at the top in the frilly script the boy at the drugstore had talked me into ordering, and I began, *Dear Claudia.* I wrote quickly, not stopping to think about wording things just right, and in fifteen minutes I was finished. When I stuck on the stamp, on a sudden impulse I put it upside down, standing the Queen on her crown. Let them open a file on me if they want, I thought.

Because it gave me an excuse to go out, I drove down to the post office and mailed the letter, and then I went to the shopping centre outside of town, where I wandered listlessly from one end to the other, trying on a few clothes in brittle colours that I knew did not suit me.

In one store, leafing through dresses, I noticed a woman on the other side of the rack doing the same. She had with her a small child restrained in a kind of harness to which was attached a long strap held by the mother. It was a practical invention, allowing the child freedom to wander, but not too far. I smiled. The mother smiled back. But it was not she, nor the child, at whom I was smiling; it was at the memory of Susan and me in this same shopping centre once, seeing perhaps this same woman, perhaps this same child tugging at the strap which the mother held like a leash. "Oh, look," Susan had said. "A seeing-eye baby."

I turned abruptly and left the store, shoving my hands into my pockets as though they belonged to a shoplifter and needed to be protected from temptation. Susan, Susan, Susan—there was no place free of her.

I bought a paper cup of orange juice and sat down on a bench in a corner of the mall, and I watched the people passing, their shopping carts full of packages and children. For a moment I closed my eyes, letting the noise thicken, coagulate around me. Finally I began to wander again through a few more stores, telling myself that perhaps I would buy something, that I was not just wasting time.

I was browsing in the bookstore when I heard a voice say, "Well, hello, stranger."

When I turned I saw it was Linda, Gerald's wife, her thin earnest face curling its features upwards into a smile. "So how *are* you?" she said. "Gee, it's been ages since we've seen you."

I cannot remember now what I answered, and what she answered to that—the usual obligatory small talk that women who meet in shopping centres must exchange in order to get the meeting over with. I had run into her in this same shopping centre before, but to see her again now, so soon after Gerald—my palms began to prickle with sweat. But it seemed clear that Gerald had not told her anything about us, so I was safe. Safe, I thought. Safe.

And suddenly the insanity of it all—all the stupid, ugly secrets—cracked out of me like an egg into a bowl, and I wanted simply to scream, to scream and scream until I was rid of them all.

And I suppose that is more or less what I did, not scream exactly, but shout, loudly, something with words in it, although I cannot exactly remember them. I think it was something like, "That's enough," or "Make it stop," nothing that made a great deal of sense, and nothing that really had much to do with either Linda or Gerald.

"What? What?" Linda jerked back, wondering in horror whatever she could have said that must have been so wrong.

The clerk in the store dropped what she was holding, and it clattered onto the floor in the sudden silence. She looked at us, alarmed and excited, thinking we must be having a fight. There was no one else in the store, but two teen-age boys passing outside stopped and stared at us, then walked on, thinking probably they must have been mistaken, that middle-aged ladies like us do not suddenly shout in bookstores.

"I'm sorry," I murmured, and I was, wondering how I could possibly explain myself. I clutched my stomach with one hand and the bookcase beside me—*Religion and Philosophy*, the sign above it said—with the other, and I said, with a slight grimace in my voice, "Just a sudden stomach cramp. It's better now."

The clerk looked at me in clear disbelief, but Linda said, "You're sick," in blatant relief that it had nothing to do with her. "Do you want me to drive you home, or to the doctor?"

"No, no," I said, straightening up and taking my hand down from the bookshelf. "I'm fine, really. Just a little spell." I smiled at her, confident and sincere.

"Well, if you're sure," she said, already backing away. "I'll tell Mom I saw you," she added, giving me over to Margaret, someone who would know what to do.

"Fine," I said, turning a little to the bookcase and pulling out a book to look at, to show her how rational I was again. A book with *Sin* in the title. No wonder I shouted, I thought, but the laughter that rose in my throat was not hysterical, only bitter, the kind people respect.

Back at home I poured myself a drink and sat down on the chesterfield in the living room. I am sitting here still, feeling ashamed of what I have done to poor Linda, suddenly yelling at her like a madwoman in a shopping centre. You are supposed to feel better after such an outburst, they say, but I feel more ridiculous than relieved. I can imagine Linda telling Gerald about me over the supper table tonight, and Gerald with his cheeks stuffed with mashed potatoes unable to swallow for a moment as he thinks, *My God, and I wanted to sleep with her.* Then there will be Margaret, phoning me later, asking, "What happened to *you?*" Well, it serves me right.

Control, Susan said of me once, that it was what she thought I had. It is what I thought I had, too. Yet today I stood in a bookstore and babbled, feeling something firm and closed in me suddenly shiver open. I remember Susan describing the way she stood in the

Eaton's store in Victoria, and I wonder if that is what she felt then too, some circuit jamming open and all the wrong messages getting through, getting out. It this the beginning of something? What cathartic thing will I be doing tomorrow? Running naked down Young Street shouting, "Repent, repent"? The cat comes and rubs against my leg, and I reach down and scratch his head. "You're living with a loony-tune," I tell him. He walks away indifferently and squats in that impossible position cats have, with their hind legs at ninety degrees, and licks his anus. "Taking your picture," my mother used to call it, and it makes me suddenly sad, thinking of her lost to me so long ago when I needed her so much, and now Susan, the two women I will probably always remember most for the things they never told me. And the things I never told them.

I have decided that I am back to normal. Whatever abyss opened for me yesterday in the bookstore has sealed shut again. I managed to go shopping this morning, to chat with people in an agreeable way; I am not going mad after all. *Going mad:* we have so many ways of saying it, usually prefaced with *going*, as though it is a trip somewhere; well, I suppose it is. Going nuts/bananas/berzerk/bonkers/strange/off the deep end/around the bend/off your rocker/out of your tree/off your head. Anything that requires so many euphemisms must, like sex, be much more popular than society would like us to believe.

But I am not going mad. I am back to normal. I remember a record cover I saw at Claudia's, one of the children's, I imagine; there was a song title or line that went, "The trouble with normal is it always gets worse." Well, I suppose that's true. Nothing in life stays stable for long; madness is not something you can will away indefinitely. At any rate, I have decided that today is a perfectly nice day, sunny and warm, and I will not waste it going mad.

After lunch I go back to the journal. I am determined to finish everything today, put everything finally together. As I pick up the scribbler, something falls from it, a card that must have been tucked inside somewhere. On the cover is a rough line drawing of a person lying down and three turkeys sitting on him. Inside, the greeting says, "Don't let the turkeys get you down." There is a handwritten message that says, "Yeah. Don't, okay? Remember that I love you and care about you a whole lot, and that things will sort themselves out for you. Love, Connie." Connie, I think. It must be her friend in Vancouver. What had Susan told her, I wonder. I feel suddenly excluded, as though I should have been the only one with a right to Susan's confidences. It is a childish jealousy, but I hold the card for some time reading over and over this intimate note from a stranger, this friend of Susan's who loved her more than I did.

Finally I open the journal again where I had left off.

Thursday, February 23, 1984: if it would just stop raining. but they say melancholy personalities feel better if the weather outside matches their natures. that's no help, just means I'd be feeling worse if the sun were shining. sat for an hour just staring out the window, started picking at the kitchen wallpaper, realized later I'd peeled off strips of the stuff, it lay in little balls all over the floor. what is the *matter* with me, I used to do that as a kid after they locked me in my room after Freddy, am I regressing, will I wake up tomorrow as an amoeba? I moved the big vase in front of the spot, if W. notices I'll say somebody with a dog came over—

At least it wasn't the living room wallpaper, I think with a sad smile; that would have been too symbolic even for Susan. They had put up new paper shortly after they moved in, a sunny yellow colour with green leaves falling through it. But something went wrong; the edges didn't quite match, the pattern leaning a little more with each panel, so that by the end the whole wall seemed to slant.

"It must be a metaphor," Susan said, "for Whitman and me."

—my period started today, yuck, aren't I old enough for menopause yet. Ellen over with some fancy new recipe, I sat here like a plant, watching her make supper, the ivy moves more in one day than I do. I don't dare tell W. how much of the cooking Ellen does around here. he started drinking tonight, was in such a foul mood, something about work, I suppose. I hate it when he drinks, how he uses it as an excuse to get hostile. (it's easier for me, I don't need an excuse.) well, in vino veritas, etc.

Whitman, drinking. I remember the time. He had come over late, the smell of brandy on his breath. "Hostile," Susan says. Perhaps that is the right word. It is not the one I had wanted to use. *He is very confident tonight,* I told myself.

"Love bites," he whispered, and his teeth pressed into my shoulder until I squirmed, and then bit my nipple until I said, a little frightened, "Don't, it hurts."

He laughed, a tense, gritty sound, then flicked his tongue along the inside bend of my elbow the way he knew I liked and breathed, "I'm into S and M tonight. I'm the S. You're the M. Wait until I tie you to the bed and get out my belt."

"You're very macho today," I said.

"Does it turn you on?" And he pushed into me so suddenly and fully I gasped. "I guess so," his voice blurred in my hair. "You were all wet and waiting."

And it was true, yes. But I was afraid of it, too, that tough assurance that needed me to be weak. I wanted back the man who came to me with a different need than this, who came to me a few nights later and did not look into my eyes and mumbled, "I'm sorry about the other night. I get stupid when I drink." When we made love we were gentle with each other, like people with sunburn, people with bruises.

Fri., Feb. 24: I am getting addicted to *One Life to Live*. Brad is trying to stop Jenny's and David's wedding, and Becky has finally outsmarted Lucinda, well, good for her, I never liked Lucinda, that sleazy business last week with what's-his-name. haven't touched my writing for weeks, seems so pointless, rejection after rejection, and maybe this is as good as I get. the potatoes for supper burned dry on the stove, what a mess, the house stank, W. came home and said, "what are you burning?" "my bridges," I said, I wish it were true.

Saturday, February 25, 1984: Ellen off somewhere for a few days with that friend of hers, came over and left me her house key in case there was an emergency, in case I felt like going for a walk, well, that was good for a laugh, but, god, wouldn't I love to, I'm so sick of this house, can a person be claustrophobic and agoraphobic both, hell, why not, the best of no worlds. W. rented a movie and one of those VTR machines for the evening, it was kind of fun, no commercials, no kids throwing popcorn, no having to leave your very own house.

When Brenda called and said she had to do some kind of teacher exchange project with a school in Dawson Creek and did I feel like driving up there with her, staying for a couple of days, just for the hell of it, I said yes, yes, I'd love to, what a great idea, forgetting about the church bake sale I had promised to go to, the lunch with Margaret I would have to cancel. It was one of those mornings when I was feeling most trapped, wandering like an amnesiac around the house the way I thought Susan must do, picking something up and setting it down somewhere else. So, yes, I said to Brenda, when do we leave, excited at getting away from it, from Whitman. It was like starting a diet; it is always easiest to swear you will be good and stay away from the calories right after you have eaten, before you are hungry again.

But when we loaded our suitcases into Brenda's car early on Saturday and I waved at Susan and Whitman, the couple next door, as we pulled away, there was nothing I wanted to do less than go.

> Sunday, February 26, 1984: nice sunny day, W. tried to coax me out into the back yard saying he'd put up the croquet set, he knows I used to like playing, well, I tried, I really tried, was out there for ten minutes helping him pound in the hoops and then and then, my stomach climbing up into my throat looking for a way out. "it's all right," he said, going around and pulling the hoops up, one by one, looping them over his fingers like long stiff earthworms, putting everything back in the garage. I'm sorry, sorry, sorry, how long will I have to keep saying that.

> Monday, February 27, 1984: wrote about a ten-page letter to Connie, took me all afternoon, what a lot of whining, what I really need is a friend who's as miserable as I am. W. came home from work with two roses and handed them to me. "what are these for?" I said graciously. it's worse for me when he tries to be nice, I've got nobody to blame. "they're a gift," he said, tersely, and I said, "well, aren't you sweet," trying to make it up, but he was hurt, who can blame him, I'm such a bitch. "A Gift," I thought, putting them in water, in German "Gift" means poison. God, I'm such a cynic. a cynic, I remember reading somewhere, is someone who, when she smells flowers, looks around for a coffin.

> Tuesday, February 28, 1984: I do miss Ellen, they must be in Dawson Creek by now. wonder how she's doing—

I push the journal abruptly away, as though an insect had suddenly flown up from it into my face. *Wonder how she's doing.* I will go for a walk, I decide, getting up, quickly. But at the door I see it is raining too hard, not the usual grey rain, but a real storm, clouds like black lungs breathing in the sky, raindrops the size of marbles. Lightning slices the air. One, two, three, four, five, I count, and then I hear the grunt of thunder. It is like the storm Brenda and I were in as we were driving north, past Prince George somewhere. The trip. I have tried so hard not to remember it. Perhaps I thought that I could fool myself even now, as I see those days in Susan's journal, thought that I could edit them from the chronology she set up for me, could define them simply as the week I was not here. But now they are my memory like the storm, and I cannot make it stop. I turn away from the sink, then back again, like a person who has found something she does not know how to dispose of.

Lightning slashes across my window again. One, two, three, four, I count, and then the thunder smashes itself against the house. It is getting closer, I think, finally curling myself into my chair. *What if you can't even get to one?* I ask my mother, who was as afraid as I was. *Then it will be too late,* she says.

Thirteen

We stayed overnight in Prince George, both of us like old people telling each other how long it was since we had last been up here, where we had stayed, how clean the air was then.

We left early the next day, driving north, north, the air turning crisp and pure again as we left the pulp mills behind and wound through the Pine Pass. We were cautious on the corners, watched out for the logging trucks. Sometimes we stopped and took pictures, tourists on a holiday.

Brenda was easy to travel with, someone who knew how to be quiet when she had nothing to say. By mid-afternoon we broke out of the mountains at Chetwynd, into the rich fields of the Peace River country, and by suppertime we were in Dawson Creek.

The school board had reserved a room for Brenda at a hotel downtown, and when we found it was a double she insisted we share, save some money, so I agreed. We ordered up a pizza from the restaurant downstairs, something that turned out to be a slab of bread with tomato sauce and grated cheese, but it made us laugh and feel worldly and reminisce about the pizzas Brenda used to make.

When Brenda was very depressed she would make pizzas. "Brenda's depressed," someone would say, and it was like Pavlov's bell, making us salivate. Her pizza was not just famous for its quality but for its quantity. She had four pizza pans, and while two were in the oven she would be filling the others, and then she would start all over again. Her record was fourteen pizzas. "That was the time the principal transferred the kid who kept biting the other Grade Two teacher into my class," she explained. Since Brenda did not even particularly like pizza, it was her friends and the other teachers at her school who would benefit most from her gloomy moods, carrying home huge cheesy wedges wrapped in tinfoil that she distributed as though we were kind to take them. "I'll miss Brenda's pizza," Gordon had said, when we moved. It was the only thing about Vancouver he ever admitted he would miss.

The next day Brenda left early for her work at the school, and I had the day to myself. I walked around town, although I was not really prepared for the cold, the thin snow that whirled up into my face, the patches of ice on the sidewalk. It was as though the weather had changed its mind, had melted the snow but left everything underneath still frozen, spring trying to claw up through ice, straining for green, for sky. The streets looked matted and messy, like animals caught changing from their winter coats to their summer ones.

The town was a depressing place, full of shops with closing-out signs, a few nervy enough to say "bankruptcy sale," using a word I can still remember my parents explaining meant something like *out-of-wedlock,* something good people never got involved with. I wandered through a Woolworth's store and bought a pair of gloves and a newspaper, which I read over lunch. "Tumbler Ridge," a headline said, "The New Boom Town of the North." I read the story, wondering what it would be like to live there, a frontier. Finally I went back to the hotel, read the book I had brought with me, and waited for Brenda. Two more days here, I thought, and already I am bored.

Brenda came back late, tired and gloomy about her work at the school. "I'm supposed to introduce the new social studies curriculum, and would you believe they didn't have the *books* yet, not one? And I expected to have whole class sets to work from. I had to put up so much board work my fingers are turning to chalk."

I offered her the selfish sympathy of someone who does not have to work and at times like this was especially glad of it.

"What did you do all day?" she asked me over supper.

"Oh, just wandered around. There wasn't really a lot to see."

"Look, why don't you take the car tomorrow? You can drop me at school, drive around. It's nice country out here."

So the next morning I left Brenda at the little elementary school east of town, waving apologetically to her as she trudged across the gravelly yard, her arms drooping with books and papers.

The rest of the day is mine, I thought, pulling back onto the highway. I considered driving up to Tumbler Ridge, although I supposed the road would be too poor, and it *was* Brenda's car; I had to remember that.

I reached the traffic circle just outside of town and turned into it, still not sure where I would go. Fort St. John, said the arrow pointing at one of the exits. Spirit River, said another, pointing east. Spirit River: why did that sound so familiar? I went around the circle twice, nearly getting hit by a car in the wrong lane, and then I turned onto the Spirit River road. The name nagged at me, as though I should remember it. Such a strange name: where would it have come from, I wondered.

Finally I stopped, pulled out the road map. There it was, I saw, just across the border in Alberta, and gust of memory blew through me. Spirit River, Alberta: it was where Susan was from. I tried to remember what her name had been; I knew she had told me. Germanic, I thought, something ending in "man," Susan —man.

Still trying to prod the name from my memory, I turned back onto the highway, continued east, the road pulling me along in easy meanders. *Welcome to Alberta*, a sign said suddenly. According to my map, the road from here on would be gravel. I considered going back, a little ashamed of my dependence on pavement, but it was Brenda's car, I told myself; how could I justify a stone in her windshield? I looked at the map again. It didn't seem far, and there was hardtop further on. If it got bad I could always turn around and come back.

So I kept going, waiting for the road to crumble into gravel, but there was only the black shine of new pavement ahead. It seemed a good omen. I smiled to myself, remembering Susan's wonderful snorting laugh when I told her about a news report I'd seen on TV somewhere. A reporter was interviewing a not-too-bright motor-cyclist who had just driven over a new road which had been improperly built and was very rough. A knob had fallen off the motorcycle as it went over this road. "Do you consider it an omen?" asked the reporter. The cyclist answered, "Oh, no, it's a new one." Susan, shrieking, "a *new* one?"

About an hour later, the car lapping up smooth new pavement all the way, I saw the sign for Spirit River. It was a small town, but the elevators stood like huge houses along the side of the road: *Alberta Wheat Pool, UGG*, the new green shape of *Cargill*. Behind them and to the west the real houses spilled, most of them looking old and stubborn but some of them new, a town insisting it had a future. But I was more interested in its past. Somewhere here, I thought, Susan was born. Susan —man. I tried to surprise the name, the way you can with a word that resists you but that will later sit up casually as though it had never been away, saying, *yes, you wanted me?* But Susan's name wouldn't come back, wouldn't jump the synapse into consciousness.

I found the local hotel restaurant and had breakfast, which was enough for about three people. I watched the waitress, her casual flirtation with two men in overalls. How much easier it all is when you are younger, I thought, knowing that it probably wasn't true, was just another of memory's convenient alterations.

As I paid the bill, I noticed a phone book on the counter. Perhaps, I thought suddenly, if I saw the name I would recognize it. Eagerly, without waiting for permission from the waitress, I began flipping through the book. There were only a few pages of listings for Spirit River. My finger fled up and down the columns.

"Can I help you with that?" the waitress asked, curious.

"No, thank you," I said. "I've found it." And there it was. Weissman, Esther, Box 213, and a phone number. I could feel my heart thudding. I felt as though I had discovered insulin.

"You can use this phone here if you want to call her," said the waitress, her eyes on the name my finger still pointed to, like an accusation.

"Well," I said, "I'm not sure. . . . I don't really know her. . . ."

"Mrs. Weissman? Oh, she's a neat old lady. She'd probably like a visitor."

"You know her then?"

"Oh, sure. This isn't New York, you know." She was enjoying my unease, smiling with one half of her mouth in a way that made me think she might have had a stroke, except that she was so young. She picked up the phone, set it firmly in front of me. "Feel free," she said, and moved off to clear the dishes from my table.

Esther Weissman. I cannot think of her even now as *Esther* or *Mrs. Weissman,* but only as *Esther Weissman,* two names. She lived on a farm a few miles outside of town. "Turn left at the old barn with the caved-in roof, and then another mile, and left again at the Weremchucks—they got a little blue house and an ugly yellow dog always laying on the road—I don't know how many times I've said one day I'm just going to drive over him—well, and then just maybe half a mile and there I am, a white house with red trim. Better park on the road. If it thaws today my yard is going to be nothing but a mudhole."

And there it was just as she had said, left at the old barn, left again at the ugly yellow dog: a white house with red trim. I had been half-hoping I wouldn't find it, that my city-sense for directions would first get me lost and then expel me, something that didn't belong here, back onto the highway. But there was the house, and Esther Weissman expecting me.

I walked up the driveway, watching the open fields receding. To the north I must have been able to see fifty miles, the view not even then crumbly with distance or the grainy yellow haze I was used to from the city. I remembered from the map that I could be looking past the last farm, the last road, how there might be nothing beyond my vision but wilderness. I felt a moment of dizziness, as though the air were too thin to support me, were pulling away with the landscape. Fear of open spaces, I thought; is that what this is?

"Hello!" The woman standing on the porch was a short, square woman wearing a paisley dress and a brown sweater. Her hair was a firm grey, frizzy on the ends from a permanent that was growing out. Her face was unmistakably that of Susan's mother, the same deep-set eyes with heavy eyebrows like two arched roofs, the chin that was larger than usual. "Well," she said, holding the screen door open with one hand, pressing herself back to give me room, "come in, come in. I have coffee ready. You'll have a cup, sure."

We sat down in her kitchen, a small room whose bright yellow walls were almost totally covered with framed pictures, handicrafts, calendars. I could see her living room was the same, the walls pushing back declaratively with picture after picture against the emptiness outside. In one corner stood a table filled with African violets; a shelf underneath held about a dozen more, the flowers like purple moths crouching on the leaves. What am I doing here, I thought desperately, what right do I have?

"You live here alone?" I asked. The coffee was so strong I could feel every sip shudder up my spine, jerk the hair on my arms to alarmed attention.

"Oh, yeah. The winters are hard, but I couldn't stand to be in town, people living on your doorstep. I have the truck, I can drive, and Howard, he's my son, he comes by to help out."

Her son. Susan's brother. I don't know why I had assumed she was an only child.

"So." Esther Weissman settled back in her chair. "Tell me about Susan." She watched me, an unapologetic stare, but I did not sense suspicion as much as ordinary curiosity.

"Well," I said. A nerve began tugging at my eyelid, little flutters that I used to think must be contorting my whole face but that I knew were barely visible. "She's a friend of mine. We live across the street from each other in Chilliwack."

"Where's that?"

"A town maybe a hundred miles from Vancouver—"

"Last I heard she was still in Vancouver. She doesn't keep in touch with me much." Perhaps I had expected accusation or self-pity when she talked about her daughter, but I heard none of it in her voice; when she told me about Susan it was the same way she spoke about the hard winters, about whether I took cream for my coffee. She had a way of stressing the verbs in her speech that made her sound practical and determined, but it might just have been the remains of an accent, some European history still asserting itself.

"She never talks about . . . her childhood very much, no."

"I'm not surprised. After her father died I hoped she'd kind of get over it, you know, but no, she still doesn't want anything to do with me. Such a shame, a mother and a grown-up daughter not getting along, but that's just how it is."

"Did something . . . something happen, something in particular?" I already know the answer to that, I thought.

She hesitated for just a moment, dropped her eyes to her coffee cup which she rolled lightly between her thick, short fingers. "There was a boy. . . ."

"Freddy?"

She looked up, surprised, intent. "She talks about him, then?"

"Yes, a little."

"And what does she say?"

"Oh, I guess she just wonders what might have happened if they'd got married."

"And she blames me and Henry for not letting them?" Henry, I assumed, was Susan's father.

"Maybe. I guess so. She doesn't talk about it much. . . ." I looked numbly at the door, wanting to stand up quickly, to say, *I must go. I don't want to hear, to say, anything more.*

"It's too bad. I mean, that she still thinks that." She looked out the window, as though she heard something, but there was only silence.

"You mean you would have let them get married?"

"No, no—" She was quiet for a moment, staring down at her hands. Then she looked up, as though she had decided something, and said, "It doesn't matter now, I guess."

"What?"

"Doesn't matter. If you know." She stood up suddenly, grabbed my arm and pulled me to my feet. My chair skittered back, almost fell. "I'll show you," she said.

"Show me—"

"I'll take you to meet Freddy."

And she was pulling me out of the house, to the old blue truck in the yard, making me get in, and me starting to say over and over, *I must go*, and the words disappearing in my gauzy breath.

"We won't stay long," Esther Weissman said, twisting the truck expertly along the frozen roads. I tried to remember the turns we took, how to get back to Brenda's car. I felt as though I were being kidnapped, hysteria pushing at my lungs. The fields, without winter snow or summer crops, had a blank, exhausted look, like refugees, as they moved slowly past the truck windows. I was shivering from the cold.

It was probably only a few miles, although it seemed like ten, before Esther Weissman pointed to a group of trees, a vertical relief, ahead. I could see fences threading between them, a house, a barn.

"That's the Schwartz place," she said. "That's where Freddy lives."

She pulled into the yard, full of rusting farm machinery, large chunks of metal whose functions I could not even guess at.

Then Esther Weissman was opening the truck door, reaching up to help me out, an awkward chivalry. We walked up to the house, our shoes grating on the frozen dirt. A dog barked nervously at us, then hid under the porch as we came up the steps. Esther Weissman knocked on the door, loudly, a knock that would have to be heard. When no one answered, she knocked again, louder.

Finally, the door opened, and a very stooped, wrinkled woman looked at us. "Hello," she said, her voice not much above a whisper, her smile a worried twitch. She pulled the door open a little wider, almost wide enough for us to come inside without having to push the door further open ourselves. She stepped back uneasily as Esther Weissman propelled me ahead of her into the house, her hand like a weapon on my back.

"This is . . . what was your name again?"

"Ellen," I said, "Ellen Grey."

"Ellen is from the city, Clara. She's a friend of Susan's."

The woman cowered back from me, reminding me absurdly of her dog hiding under the porch. She rubbed her hands up and down, up and down, on her apron, as though she were trying to calm them. I could see she had just been cleaning a chicken, could smell the wet feathers.

"Come in," she said, not looking at us.

"We won't stay," said Esther Weissman, and for a second her voice was softer, kind, perhaps. It was hard to tell; when she went on that inflection was gone. "I just wanted her to meet Freddy. If you don't mind. She says Susan still talks about him, about how we wouldn't let them get married."

The other woman had backed against her kitchen counter, as though we were intruders come to take from her the things she valued most.

"I'm sorry," she said in her whispering voice. "Yes, I'll call him. He's out back. He heard the truck coming."

She moved into the living room. We could hear her opening a door, the mumble of voices, words we could not quite understand. The kitchen was hot, but I was still shaking, felt as though the cold had found a place inside of me that would never get warm.

The woman came back. She was holding the arm of a man in his late thirties. He was medium height, a bit paunchy, but his blond hair was still thick, curling slightly where it touched his collar. His eyes were a beautiful, clear blue, looking shyly at us now. His mouth was delicate, with the slackness, the touch of drool at the corners, that identified him immediately as retarded.

Back in the truck, Esther Weissman said, "There was nothing between them. Nothing. I mean you can see that. Freddy's got the brains of a three-year-old."

She backed out onto the road, the truck slamming over frozen chunks of earth. I could hear some of them grating on the undercarriage. I watched her thick hands on the wheel, her forearms with the tough muscles of a man's. She shifted into first gear with greater force than necessary.

I was too dazed to say anything. My head was thick with voices: *we were madly in love; it infuriates me, the way she throws him up at me; I'll show you.* They were like pieces of broken pottery that the archaeologist can never fit together because the fragments are from different pots, all mixed together now in the silt of history.

We rode the rest of the way back without speaking. The noise of the truck packed itself into my ears. At last I saw Brenda's car ahead on the road, like something I barely remembered. It was only noon, I realized, but it felt as though several days had passed.

"Come into the house," Esther Weissman said as she pulled into the yard. "I'll make us some lunch."

"Well, I don't know—" My voice was a breath sucked away by the cold air. It sounded like that other woman's, Clara's.

"You'll have some lunch, sure."

Back in her kitchen, she put on more coffee. I stared at the brown water drizzling from the filter as though I didn't know what it was. Then she began making sandwiches, cutting thick slices of brown bread that looked home-made. On one slice she put two pieces of Velveeta and on the other several large slices of cheddar. She pressed the two together, flattening the bread almost to dough, and with a quick *thunk* of the butcher knife cut them in half. She made four sandwiches this way, set them on a plate in the middle of the kitchen table.

"I'm no fancy cook," she said. "Bread and cheese, that's my favourite lunch. But there's pie for dessert, save some room."

She watched as I began to eat, then took a sandwich herself, finished it before I was even half through mine.

"Now you tell me," she said, "what it's like with Susan."

"Well," I said, not sure what to say, what she wanted to hear. "The way she talks about Freddy, well, it's as though they had a nice romantic relationship, and her parents and his came between them."

"Yeah," she said, taking another sandwich. "She said something like that the first Christmas she came home and then again in one of her letters. I just didn't know what to say, what to think."

"But why would she make up something like that?"

She shrugged, looking past me out the window. "She and Freddy played together when they were kids. She felt sorry for him, like, when the others would pick on him and make jokes, she'd stick up for him. And Henry—that was her dad—well, he didn't like her doing that either. They'd get into awful fights. He was so strict with her, so strict, you don't know. And me, well, I had to go along with him, he was the boss, that's how it was in them days. I guess it's better today, eh, in the city?"

I started to answer, something vague and noncommital, but she waved her hand in the air as though I were interrupting, as though her story were something she had to tell quickly, while it was all clear to her.

"But the teachers said she was smart, she should go to university, and Henry, he was glad to get rid of her, she was just a girl, so he paid the money. The first two years she came home for Christmas, then that was it. Not for when Henry died, even, or when her brother got married. A letter once every two or three years maybe, that's it. But I think, well, she's got a right to make her own life, so if she wants to make up this story about Freddy it's not up to me to interfere. So I never said anything. I thought that, well, she must have her reasons."

"Maybe that was the best."

She smiled at my approval, the bread bulging her cheek out in a way that made her look wholesome, natural, like the women in *National Geographic.*

"You think so?" she said.

"I think so."

"It's been nearly twenty years since I've seen her, but I want her to be happy, you know what I mean? I mean, if it helps that she should want to forget about her past, well, that's how it has to be."

It took me a moment to understand what Esther Weissman was saying. She was, I thought, a remarkable woman. You have to care for someone more than most people are capable of, to sacrifice so much.

"Are you going to tell her you came to see me?" she asked.

"Well, I . . . don't know. What do you think?"

She shrugged, but she was watching me carefully. "You know her better than I do now. You decide what's best."

"I just don't know . . . what's best."

"Well, anyways, she's married now and everything. Somebody from the university, with a funny name."

"Whitman," I said.

"Yeah, that's it. His first name is John or Jack or something simple like that, but he uses this other name, Susan said, his middle one, I guess." It was something else about Whitman I didn't know. "Do you know him?"

"Oh, yes," I said. "Not well, but he seems okay." *Not well.* I clenched my teeth against the lie. But, thinking of it now, I suppose it might have been true enough.

"Well, anyways, she's happy, sure?"

"Oh yes," I said, giving her finally what I knew she wanted to hear, what she had earned the right to. "She's happy. She and Whitman."

When Brenda asked me that night where I had gone, I said, "Oh, I drove out east, into Alberta, to Spirit River." I couldn't explain to her what had happened. I couldn't even explain it to myself.

When she asked me if I wanted the car the next day, I said, "No, that's okay; I'll just stay here and read." I was afraid to go out again, as though things I didn't want to know would be floating in the air, like asbestos fibres, and I would breathe them in, knowledge a disease there was no cure for.

I spent most of the day in the room looking out my window, which overlooked the highway we had come in on. I watched the cars passing and passing, playing the old child's game with myself where I would make up stories about the people in the cars, where they were going and why, how sometimes the people they were going to see were passing them going the other direction and their lives would be changed because they had not been able to meet.

Mostly, of course, I was trying not to think about Susan, about yesterday. It was just so hard to believe, her making up this absurd story about a retarded boy. Why? Just to torment Whitman? And cutting her mother out of her life so completely—it seemed like a needless cruelty. *You don't know*, Esther Weissman had said. That was true, I suppose—to me Esther Weissman seemed like a simple and generous person, but what did I know of what it had been like between them, what wounds had been inflicted so deep they could not heal?

"You decide," Esther Weissman had said, meaning, *If she's happy why interfere? If*, I thought bitterly. *If.* I was a priest in a confessional who has learned something dangerous; neither keeping silent nor telling someone else is the right answer, but there are no other choices. Should I tell Susan? Should I tell Whitman? Should I pretend it never happened?

And there was another question, the one I try even now to think I did not ask myself: What will it mean for me, for me and Whitman?

The cars passed and passed. The sun slid into the horizon, a flat message into an envelope, the fields sealing it shut, too late to see what it said. Tomorrow I will be gone, I thought desperately, as I watched the last purple bruise the sky, and I have made no decision. Brenda will open the door any minute; we will go out for supper, go to bed early, and tomorrow we will be gone.

We climbed back into the hills. Behind us the fields watched with expressionless faces. I was glad when we got deep into the mountains, the unpeopled landscape, rocks and fir trees and rivers, the kind of ambiguities I was not expected to understand.

Brenda was tired from the three days at school, but relieved to be away. She drove faster than she usually did, passing the logging trucks and the occasional trailers instead of dawdling behind, as we'd done on the way up. I was nervous about her driving, the way she would nose out over the solid line eager for an opening, the way she wouldn't want to stop because then the line-up we'd passed would get ahead of us again. It was as though we were trying to run from something.

In Prince George we stayed at the same hotel as we had before, both of us a little ashamed at not being more adventurous, but wanting already the comfort of the predictable.

"The best surprise is no surprise," said Brenda in a prissy falsetto.

We had supper at a Chinese restaurant across the street, and Brenda, in a celebratory mood, ordered a carafe of wine for each of us.

"So what have you been doing for a love life lately in Chilliwack, anyway?" she said, pouring out the last of the carafes.

"Well," I said. "I'm having an affair with a married man."

I blame the wine, of course; I had not intended to say any such thing. But it was the kind of question to which you know you have a wonderful answer, and before your censors can snip it out, it rolls onto the screen. There are no slips of the tongue, Freud says. Nothing is accidental; everything is chosen at some level. I remembered how it was with Gerald: *I don't go without,* the braggart words speaking themselves from my mouth.

"Really?" Brenda said, pretending not to be surprised.

Too late now, I thought. I might as well tell her.

"Foolish, eh? But it just happened, and now I seem to have become addicted." I smiled, trying to look cavalier.

Brenda shrugged, as though she had heard worse stories. "Does his wife know?"

"No, I don't think so. She's actually, sort of, a friend of mine. Disgusting, isn't it?"

" 'Nothing human disgusts me.' That's from Tennessee Williams, I think."

"Well, that's big of you," I said nastily.

"I don't mean it that way. We all have . . . needs, that's all. We do what seems necessary."

"The guilt is really awful. She's a *friend* of mine, for God's sake. I know we can't keep on like this."

"Do you want him to leave his wife for you?"

I considered that for a while. "No," I said finally. "But I don't know what I want. I'm afraid to think about it."

"Not that you need my advice," said Brenda, with that deliberate casualness in her voice that meant she was being especially serious, "but my sister went through this for years, and my mother, of all people, found out about it and made her see that she would never be enough for a man like that. He would always want his wife, too. And my sister would just have to accept that."

"Or she could decide not to. She could end it."

"Of course," said Brenda calmly, as if I had given a reply she had maneuvered me into. Last year Brenda's principal told her she was the best teacher in her school.

"So what did your sister do?" I asked.

Brenda smiled. "Well, she decided to end it. And she started an affair with another married man."

I began to laugh, to laugh and laugh, until tears were falling out of my eyes.

Fourteen

The last entries. The last week.

Friday, March 2, 1984: think I'm getting a cold or something, good
excuse to schlepp around and eat ice cream all day (when depresst—
ingest, ingest), food is all that lies between me and comatose. took
the quilt (that's "guilt" with a subtle twist) into the living room and
lathered myself onto the couch and watched TV. (idea for a short
story: agoraphobic woman with writers' block strangles self with
typewriter ribbon, not funny.)

That Friday night I came back from Dawson Creek. It was late,
but Brenda wanted to drive on to the city, not stay over, so she
dropped me off and went on. Coming back into my house, its
faintly stale smell that I never notice when I'm here, I felt the tired
relief of being home, but something else too, a wanting just to
drop my bags there and leave, taking nothing with me, starting
over somewhere else. It was a house full of a history I did not want.
But you can't do that, I told myself, turning on the heat, the lights,
hanging up my coat, my fingers already doing the automatic
things the house expected because it had waited and now must be
paid attention, given explanations.

As I ran a bath I flipped through the mail, only a few bills and
two letters from the NDP, probably wanting money. I have sent
them cheques twice this year already, I thought; that is enough.
The handful of mail reminded me suddenly of being at Susan's a
few weeks ago when her mail had come, rustling at her door like an
eavesdropper on our conversation.

"*Look* at it," she shouted, slamming the thick letters one by one
onto the table in front of me. "Unicef. The El Salvador Relief
Commission. CARAL. Amnesty International. I send money to
one and they get me on a mailing list for a dozen others. Jesus
Christ, how much white middle class guilt do they think I *have?*"

She grabbed her hair in two fistfuls at the side of her head, and it looked so theatrical I started to laugh.

"You think it's funny?" she said, angry, dropping her hands.

"No, no, of course I don't," I said, contrite, trying not to smile at the way her hair stuck out from the sides of her head. She looked like a dandelion.

"The worst of it is," she said, dropping back into her chair and pulling the letters toward her, letting her hand fall heavily on the pile, "is that it makes me feel I don't have any right to feel personally unhappy. You know what I mean?"

I nodded, not sure I did understand. "Worthy causes," I said, knowing it was no answer.

I turned off the bath, turned off the memory, and undressed quickly. I did not want to think about Susan, about anything. I slid into the hot water like a letter into an envelope, down, down, my knees bending as the water folded to my neck, my chin, covered my mouth, my nose, floated my hair out in front of me like long dark seaweed. I could feel myself beginning to float, my buttocks lifting gently from the bottom of the tub. *Don't get in over your head:* my mother's words, used for practically any occasion, an all-purpose warning. Yes. Don't get in over your head.

The doorbell. I sat up, water slurring out of the tub onto the floor. I stood, dizzy from the sudden movement, grabbing the shower head to keep from falling. Wrapping a towel around me, I went to the door and said, "Who is it?" although I must have known already; of course I must have known.

"Whitman."

I opened the door. Water was running down my back from my wet hair, running down between my breasts, gathering coldly on my stomach, my groin, running down my legs, dripping onto the carpet.

"It's so late," I said in a whisper, as though the house were full of sleeping people.

"I saw your lights on. I had to come."

I had to come. It was what I wanted to hear, *had to,* a compulsion driving us, *had to.*

"Susan's gone to bed. She's got a cold or something. I told her I was going to McDonald's for a Big Mac."

"Well," I said, "welcome to the golden arches."

He reached for the towel, pulled it from me. It makes me tremble even now to think of how he looked at me, how his breath caught for a moment, how it made me feel so purely desired.

We made love as though we had been waiting for it for months, and I whimpered from the pleasure of his hands on me, and from knowing my going away had solved nothing at all, only made it worse, made me want him more. Our voices were wild, something escaped from cages, and they filled the room with ambiguous phrases, may even have said, "I love you." I tried not to listen, to hear such punishments.

Later, he said, "How was the trip?"

"The one to Dawson Creek?" I asked, trying to be clever. "It was fine, too." My knowledge welled up in me: *Tell him.* But I didn't, excuses rushing in like eager coagulants: *It won't help anything, it's not up to me,* and finally, the one I believed, *I'd have to tell Susan first.*

"Good," he said, lighting a cigarette, inhaling, pulling back into himself.

"And how was your week?" I asked, polite.

"Oh, it passed." He lifted his hand slightly into the air, then let it fall back to the bed as though he were too tired to complete the gesture. "The senior loans officer at head office rejected a second mortgage application for these people that I'd already approved. It really infuriated me. What do they want me for, if some ass at head office is just going to overrule my evaluations? He hasn't seen those people, talked to them, even, or done the credit checks—" The smoke jabbed in angry spurts from his nose and mouth as he spoke.

"What about the thesis? Did you get anything more done on it?" It was the way you divert a child who is unhappy, showing him something that will make him smile. But this time it didn't work; Whitman simply lay there, looking up at the ceiling where I could see a large spider squatting upside-down.

Finally he said, "Oh, sometimes it just seems so pointless, all the bloody work I've done on Skinner, like who am I trying to kid, I'm a goddamned loans officer in a bank in Chilliwack and I'll never be anything else. But I have to fight that, just grit my teeth against it, not let my mind get swallowed up by—it's a struggle against the banal—do you see what I mean?"

His voice was filled with such sudden desperation I couldn't say anything except, "Yes, of course, of course." I remembered the party he had had for the bank people, the way he had left them to go into his study, and Susan, annoyed, saying, *I see that look on his face often enough.*

As though he knew what I was thinking, Whitman said, "Susan thinks it's an escape, and, oh, maybe she's right. But if I give it up I give up hope for anything better. Education—" He gave a derisive little laugh, made his right hand a fist that he pounded lightly into the air in front of him. "It gives us illusions about what's important, ideas and all that rubbish, and then it tells us to go out and work in a bank."

"Have you applied to the junior colleges? You might be able to get on there without the Ph.D. finished."

"Last month I sent out one hundred and eighty applications, Ellen. One hundred and eighty. Most places don't even bother to answer any more."

I think now of Susan's file, "Letters from Editors," and I realize Whitman has one like that somewhere, too, full of paper saying *no no no* to what he wants most. It makes me suddenly see them both in the same way, people with an intellectual fire that persists no matter how cold a world they face; they simply button up against the pain and try again, and again. I don't know whether they are to be pitied or envied by people like me, the realists, the consumers, the ones who may be no more or less clever but whose intelligence can be satisfied by what the world allows them.

"Well, you just can't give up," I said brightly. "Times will change."

"Sure," he said. "They'll get worse. Work hard and you will be succeeded."

"What?"

"Oh, that's something a foreign student I had once wrote on an essay. Of course it was just a grammar error, but I thought it was pretty profound."

"Work hard and you will be succeeded." I began to laugh, and then Whitman did too, as though this were the first time he thought it was funny. We lay in bed together, laughing, and all I could see was Freddy's blank white face in the air above us, like the worst kind of ghost, the kind only one of us could see.

I'd have to tell Susan first. It was the first thought in my head the next morning. But when I phoned her she said she was feeling too sick for me to come over, "something contagious, I hope." Sunday was the same. I went to church instead, something I hadn't done for weeks. The service was delayed because there was a funeral in the morning, and then we had to rush because there was a wedding in the afternoon. When the collection plate came zooming around, I put in $20, more than twice what I usually give—oh, it is almost comic, seeing myself now so transparently, trying to buy an answer.

So it wasn't until Monday that I went over to Susan's, after my aerobics class, where I had been so uncoordinated that instead of kicking to the right with all the others I kicked to the left, catching the woman beside me in the groin.

I open the journal to that day, my fingers cold.

> Mon., Mar. 5, 84: still kinda fluey, my head feels like a glass is balanced on it, every time I move something slops out. Ellen over, we played some cards.

That is all, no mention of what we talked about. I don't know whether I am relieved or not.

"Welcome back," Susan said. "How was the trip?"

"Fine. But it's good to be home."

"Easy for you to say," she snorted.

We played her favourite game, 66, Susan as usual taking absurd risks as soon as she was a point or two ahead. Between games, as she was shuffling, I said, watching her fingers slice the cards expertly together, "Susan, you know, I was thinking about your Freddy the other day."

Her fingers did not pause. She completed the shuffle, then passed the deck to me and said, "Cut." When I did, she said, "Oh, why?"

I tried to keep my voice casual. "I was just wondering if, well, you say you and Whitman argue about him so much. But it was such a long time ago. Was he, is he, really that important to you?"

I could feel her eyes on me. "Yes, he is," she said, her voice calm, like mine.

"Oh," I said. "Well, it's just that it's easy to, you know, romanticize things that happened long ago. Maybe, maybe Freddy wasn't as perfect as you think." I had almost said *as you pretend*, but caught myself.

She was quiet for a moment, still watching me. I picked up a card from the pile we weren't using and turned it around and around in my fingers.

"Freddy is just, you know, something I need," she said finally. And it occurred to me then that Susan might have begun to believe the story she had invented, repeated it so many times that for her it had become truth, like misspelling a word over and over, each time reinforcing the error. It is something we all do, after all, to some degree.

"Well," I said, "it's just that I thought it might be worth, well, re-evaluating." And I knew then—perhaps had known all along—that I couldn't tell her, that I could push her only this far, and that if she wouldn't take it farther this was where it would stay.

I close my eyes and play the scene to myself again and again, thinking, there is the moment I should have said, *I know the truth about him, Susan—you have to face it*. There, or there. But I only looked up at her, relieved that I wouldn't have to go through with it, and Susan dealt us the next hand, and as soon as it was her play she grinned and said, "Aha! Ich will zudecken!"

"What?"

"It means this!" And she took the card lying face up and turned it over, covering up the pile from which we could draw, restricting the play to what we each held. "I've a hand you can't beat, lady."

"I didn't know you spoke German," I said.

She shrugged. "I don't really. A phrase here and there. Your play."

But she barely made fifty points, so I won again, and Susan laughed and said, "Aw, I just let you win."

"I'll bet," I said.

> Tues., Mar. 6, 84: Margaret over today. god, last time when she phoned, only about a week ago, asking to come over, I said I was too busy flossing my teeth. yet here she was at the door. amazing. well, I'd invite a tree in for some conversation, my life lately is as exciting as a yeast infection. she had all this religious stuff with her, but then I just let my mind go open, let it think what-if-she's-right, and it was pretty scary. I think she could see she was really getting through to me. but I mean what if there is some force, god, whatever, and what if this agoraphobia is something he can cure—tried to talk to W. about it, and he just acted appalled, said something subtle about how my brain must be rotting.

So Margaret had not been exaggerating, I think; she *had* been over to see Susan recently. It explains things. I fit my memory of the next day into Susan's, like two hands meeting, closing over each other, locking.

Wed., Mar. 7, 84: so upset today, like a damned baby. Ellen brought
me some groceries—

"And you owe me," I said, taking the receipt out of the bag and
handing it to her, $6.66."
Her hand drew back from the slip of paper. "What's wrong?" I
said.
"The amount. $6.66."
For a second I was puzzled, then began to laugh. "My God. I
didn't even realize." I looked at the receipt, the square purple
numbers. "Isn't that a laugh?"

—and I just started to cry, blubber, that's the word, and I don't even
understand why, and poor Ellen didn't know what to do with me—

"It's okay," I said, putting my arm around her shoulder, "Now,
now," such useless words; what comfort can anyone take from
such encouragements, *now, now; there, there; there now,* as
though it were some problem of time and space. "Tell me what's
wrong, Susan, what's wrong."
"I wish I knew," she said finally, turning her face away from me
and wiping at it with a paper towel. "Everything, everything."
"Are things okay with you and Whitman?"

—so I tell her the same old story about how W. has no patience with
me and how I just keep provoking him—

"And of all things we get into this argument about religion, and
all I want is for him to admit the possibilities, that maybe there's
something to be said for, well, sort of surrendering to spiritual
authority, that it really seems to work for some people, gives them
an answer." She stopped to blow her nose.
"It's really just another kind of determinism," I said, angry at
myself even as I said it, because it was a word that belonged with
Whitman, that had no right to interfere between Susan and me.
"Yeah? I suppose so. It's just a label. I guess all I want is for
Whitman to see that I have this *need* right now, for something to . . .
explain things, but he won't, he doesn't."
"What does he really want from you, do you think, want you to
be?"

—when she asked me what W. really wants for, from, me, I had to think about that, it's not as easy as that he wants me just to be a good wife, housekeeper, to be there for his needs, although I suppose that's all there, too, no, I suppose what he'd most like is just for me to be happy.

Happy. I do not remember her telling me that. I remember her saying Whitman wanted her not to make demands on him, not to bother him. But I do not remember her saying Whitman just wanted her to be happy. Of course, I think, re-reading the entry, she does not say she said this to me. Perhaps it is something she decided later.

Wednesday, March 7. Wednesday was the last night Whitman came over. When I think of it now it seems appalling, that in the afternoon I could have been at Susan's, the solicitous friend, and in the evening home to her husband, eager for whatever he would give me, telling myself all the time the two things could be separated, the way a good cook can separate an egg, careful not to get yolk into the white. But that is what I thought, that is what I thought.

He sat down at the kitchen table, agitated, rubbing his fingers as though they were cold.

"It's just crazy, Ellen," he said. "We can't go on like this."

My body went instantly still, like an animal in danger. *He is going to tell me it is over.* The kitchen pulled itself around me like camouflage.

"You know what I mean?" he prompted, when I didn't answer. "Crazy."

"I suppose so."

"So what should we do?"

"I don't know."

"You have to help me, Ellen," he said, angry, combing his fingers through his hair as I had never seen him do before.

"I . . . want you both, Whitman. I suppose I just want it to continue. I know that's not much help. It's you who has to decide."

He sat for a while with his fingers laced over his coffee cup, as though he were in prayer. He fixed his eyes on the corner of the table where I had left a small pile of supermarket coupons; I resisted the urge to get up and put them away, as though they were something personal and embarrassing.

Then Whitman reached over and slowly began to unbutton my blouse. I sat still, still, afraid to move. He slid his hands, damp from the steam from the coffee, to my waist. Then, clumsily, he knelt beside me and put his head in my lap.

"I can't decide, either," he said, his words snagging in his throat. My blouse drifted against his cheek. He closed his eyes. Looking down at him, I thought, *But he has decided.* He has decided to let it continue. I stroked his head, brushing his hair behind his ear. We must have stayed that way for five or ten minutes. What a strange picture we would have made, I think; and what title would the artist have given us—*Woman Comforting Man?* Or, depending on how far back he stood and on whose face he focussed, perhaps *Peace.* Perhaps *Despair.*

"The problem with Susan and me is," Whitman said finally, getting up and sitting down again at the table, "is that the things I still find interesting about her are also the things I hate."

I had no idea what he meant, but when I said, "For example?" he only shook his head a little, as though he were not sure either how to explain himself.

"Like Freddy, maybe?" I said, thinking, now is the time I could tell him, but I didn't; I didn't.

"Maybe," he said. "But our fights about him are . . . I don't know, almost like parts we have to keep playing."

I think now of the character Robert in Susan's play, and I wonder again if he was based on Whitman years ago and younger, and if later he hardly remembered when the arguments began or why, only that they were there, as he said, parts they had to play.

That was Wednesday, March 7. Wednesday was the last night Whitman came over.

Thurs., Mar. 8, 84: the way stars collapse, crumbling inward on themselves, trying to find the centre, become black holes. gravity. I think it pulls harder at me than at other people. heavy, heavy. W. in such a mean mood tonight, something about how the manager pulled him off loans to do tax returns for customers for the next month, and what did he know about other people's tax returns, he couldn't even do his own, and me saying, the understanding wife, as he slammed the dishes around, "don't take it out on me."

And here it is, the last entry. Friday, March 9, 1984. I put my hand over it, a gesture that protects, a gesture that hides. Friday was the last day I saw Susan. I remember it carefully, pausing on every detail. I had gone over in the morning, bringing her the asparagus fern I'd started for her because her old one had leaf mold ("got it from me, I bet," she'd said). She was just wearing her housecoat, but that wasn't unusual; lately she rarely bothered getting dressed until Whitman came home. And she had washed her hair—I remember noticing that because she'd been letting it go longer than she should. And what did we talk about? Plants. The movie on TV last night. RRSPs. Pencils without erasers. Nothing that was not ordinary, nothing that two ordinary women in Chilliwack would not talk about.

Then Susan said, "Hey, you've got company."

I looked out the window, and I saw two women turning up my walk. "They don't look familiar."

"J.W.s, probably," Susan said.

"I guess I should go see, anyway," I said.

"Okay. Thanks for the fern. See ya."

"See you," I said.

She was right; they were Jehovah's Witnesses, smiles embedded in their wholesome faces, their copies of *The Watchtower* held out to me for the price of my soul. "Not interested," I said tersely, going inside my house. What if I had gone back to Susan's? Would it have made any difference? No, of course not; how could it?

I lift my hand from the journal entry, slowly, as though something might scuttle out, escape. I read it over and over, looking for some last clue, not wanting to let her go.

> Fri., Mar. 9, 84: Ellen over and brought me a fern. W. still surly in the evening, got a little drunk, mad about work, at me, sympathy for each other, that's all we need, but where does it grow, where can we buy some.

That is all, all there is. *Sympathy for each other*, she says. The next page is blank, and so also all the others to the end of the scribbler, no final messages hidden in the margins.

I am filled with a sadness that has nothing to do with crying; it is the kind that makes me sit here for a long time, my eyes closed, listening to the soft breath kneading into, out of, me, over and over, making everything possible, pushing one moment into the next.

She did not know about Whitman and me. That is a mercy, at least. She didn't know. Of course it is for myself I feel relief too, because it will lessen my guilt, a little.

At last I get up, put the journal back in the box. My head feels thick, a fist of pressure between my eyes. I stand outside for a few moments; the sharp spring air feels as though it is scraping rust from my throat. The cat comes running up to me, and I see he has something in his mouth, a mole perhaps, or a mouse. He lays it at my feet, rubs proudly against my legs. A present, he is saying, I have brought you a present, a gift, a small death. I try not to be repulsed, to kick him away. He is doing what is instinctive. But why bring it to me first, as though I must approve? That is the corruption, not that he has killed it.

I go back inside, but the house feels close, stale, and, without thinking about where I want to go or why, I pick up my purse, go out the back door and get in the car. As I pull away, I can see the cat, eating. At least what he has killed will not be wasted.

Fifteen

I drive south down Yale road, past the restaurant with the thirty-five-cent coffee where Susan and I came so often, past Young Street where I can just glimpse the corner of the bank where Whitman works, over the freeway where I can see the big shopping centre, through Vedder Crossing, along Majuba Hill Road, and here suddenly is another piece of Old Yale Road, and Susan is saying to me again how one day we should drive into Vancouver on all the chunks of Yale Road there are left.

I am at the Sumas border crossing and in the customs line-up before I have time to think about it.

"Reason for your visit to the United States?" says the officer, her voice bored, without inflection, saying this hundreds of times every day.

"I don't know," I say.

"Pardon me?"

"Just a drive," I say then. It is the same answer, just in a formula she can recognize.

"Go ahead."

I drive on, but unfamiliar with the roads now, aware I am in another country, that Ronald Reagan is president here. I have heard that "Go home, cheesehead" has been spray-painted on windows of Canadian cars. Margaret tells me there are colonies of survivalists in Washington, to be careful not to stray from the main roads. Perhaps she is right, who knows? And what stories do they tell about us, I wonder. They do not spend all their time admiring Canadian medicare.

Perhaps this is how it all begins, a closing yourself off, withdrawing over borders, back to where it is safe, to your own country, your own town, your own neighbourhood, finally your own house, until you are Susan, a prisoner, and what difference does it make if the locks are on the inside or outside.

I try to reconstruct a conversation with Whitman, to explain why I may have come here. He was telling me about the Okanogan area in Washington, around Wenatchee, how pretty it is there in spring, the fruit trees in bloom. . . .

"We should go down there sometime," a voice said.

My voice? His voice? If I think about it I will know, but I stop myself, say out loud to the passenger seat, "What does it matter? What does it matter now?" This is my voice, but the words are Whitman's, angry in my kitchen, leaving me the box full of what he wants to forget.

The wind has blown the cloud and haze from Mount Baker, and it catches the sun magnificently. I drive toward it, stop at last at a town called Maple Falls, decide to have lunch. I have no American money, but they will have to take Canadian. I find a restaurant with a view of Baker leaning back from the windows, and I order something with french fries, and coffee.

A radio is playing loudly, Country and Western music ("the sound of a cow in heat," Gordon once called it), and the man in the next booth lights another cigarette with a kind of sexual aggressiveness because I have brushed away his smoke from my face. Still, it is not unpleasant to sit here now, so totally free of anything familiar, expecting nothing of myself. The waitress is friendly, brings me coffee refills every few minutes.

Outside the snow on Mt. Baker reflects the sun so purely it pulls wetness from my eyes. It is still an active volcano, I recall, in the same chain as Mt. St. Helen's, sisters under the soil, lava in their veins. It could blow up at any minute, bury us all. It is the way disasters happen, without warning. I remember the story of a distant cousin living in Oregon in the sixties, how they knew the tidal wave from the Alaska quake was on the way and they were warned to seek high ground, but she stayed on the beach, wanting to see it come, and was killed. It is the moment when she saw the change that I dreamed of for years, that moment of recognizing the difference between the beautiful and the deadly, the seeming and the being. But perhaps there is no difference. Nature is not like people.

I sip my coffee, stare with such bluntness at the man in the next booth that he shifts uncomfortably, but he does not put out his cigarette. I am not the volcano, the tidal wave, do not have that power.

When my lunch comes, I eat very slowly, and I think about Susan. I think about the day after her last diary entry. I had been getting ready to eat then too, when I found out. It was late in the evening, and I was leaning down to take the grilled sandwich from the oven. Out the kitchen window I saw the police car across the street. There should have been flashing red lights, a siren, I think now; the silence was like a trick. I set the sandwich on top of the stove, closed the oven door gently, thinking, it has nothing to do with me, with Susan, with Whitman; it is simply a police car, and it just happens now to be here.

I went outside. Whitman was standing by the car talking to the officer. I walked across the street. I must have been wearing only my robe. I may have been barefoot.

"What's wrong?" I said. *Everything, everything,* Susan's voice was crying.

Whitman turned away from me. He was leaning on the car, and he was taking deep gasping breaths, like an asthmatic.

"You live across the street?" the officer asked.

"Yes. What's wrong? What's happened?"

"You know the woman who lives here? Mrs. Jervis?"

"Yes. Yes. What's happened?"

"She, uh, she's been killed. It looks like she drove her van off Hope River Road, and, uh, well, the water's high this time of year. She's drowned."

I cannot remember my answer. I remember saying, "Whitman, Whitman," and how he did not seem to know I was there. I remember the policeman saying I should go home now, that someone would be over in the morning to take a statement, and I remember being back in my house, shivering and shivering and not being able to get warm.

And I remember, although I have tried so hard to forget, how finally a thin crust of sleep grew over my thoughts and turned them to nightmare, how a fever bloomed in me like a black flower in the middle of that night, dark throats of petals saying, *Susan is dead you can't bring her back think of the future Whitman is free now. Now Whitman is free.*

The next morning when the officer came to take my statement, I was quite under control, although my forehead still felt too warm. I had been dressed and sitting at the kitchen table waiting for over an hour, going over and over what I would say.

He was a short and stocky man, not the one I saw last night, with a flat childish face and a damp mouth, the close RCMP haircut that gay men have been wearing for the last few years. "She was a good friend," I said to him carefully. "I got to know her quite well since they moved in," and "Yes, she had been a bit depressed lately, not a lot, though; she was the kind of person who could laugh at herself, you know what I mean?" and "No, I can't believe it was, you know, that she'd do anything to herself. It must have been an accident, at night, the rain," and "No, I don't think she drank, not any more than most people, a glass of wine sometimes; why, do you think she had been drinking? Isn't there some test, you know, you can do to tell that?"

"Yes," he said. "There are tests. Now, let me see—" He peered into his little notebook as though the questions he had to ask were all written down. Perhaps they were. "How well do you know the husband?"

"Whitman? Oh, I don't know. Not as well as I know Susan. As I knew Susan."

"Did they get along okay? I mean, did she ever say anything to you about problems they might have had, any fights, if he ever hit her, that kind of thing?" He turned over a page in his notebook.

My hand, as I lifted my coffee cup, was quite steady. I could be excused the tremble in my voice, surely; a good friend had died, after all. "They seemed happy. He'd never hit her, oh, no. I'm sure I'd have known if there was anything like that."

"Well," he said, looking up, a dismissive smile on his young face. "I don't think there's anything else. Is there anything more you'd like to add?"

I thought for a moment, wanting to say something important and on the record, that would make things clear. "They loved each other," I said. "People don't stay together all that while if they don't love each other." It seems foolish now, to have said that, but then it seemed right, necessary.

"Yes. Well." He had closed his book, wasn't writing it down.

"And she was my friend," I continued urgently. "I can't believe she's dead. I can't even begin to think how much I'll miss her."

He stood up, uncomfortable. Probably he had never had to do this sort of interview before. I had the absurd feeling he was going to say, "Just the facts, ma'am," and I could feel hysteria gnawing at the edges of my control, mad laughter leaking out through the holes.

But he only murmured, "I know it's hard," moving toward the door.

"Yes, it's hard."

I could feel the tears bulging in my eyes, but I would not let them fall. I clenched my hand under the table, concentrating on the pain of my fingernails cutting into my palm. Somewhere I had read that this was a way of fooling a lie-detector. "Yes, it's pretty damned hard."

After he was gone I opened my hand, watched how long it took for the four red dents to rise out of the skin. And then at last I cried, because my friend Susan was dead.

Later, when I had finished, when I had drunk enough wine to make me numb, I would say to the chair the officer had been sitting in, "Wait. There's just one thing. She had agoraphobia, you know, wouldn't leave the house, so how did she get out on Hope River Road in the van in the middle of the night? It's something I don't really understand. Wait—"

"More coffee?"

I look up startled, at the black bulb of the coffee pot in front of me. "No, thank you. I should go soon."

"Okay." The waitress moves away, clumsy in her high heels. I cannot imagine working in them all day.

Two young women with a baby have come into the restaurant and sit at the booth across from me. The one who must be the mother lays the baby along the seat beside her, where it makes strange, strangled noises. The women take their coats off and look at the menu and order, and then they talk and laugh, the way Susan and I used to do, as they sip their coffee, looking down every few minutes at the fussing baby. The mother has on a thin silky blouse, and I notice suddenly that there is a wet patch on one of her breasts, and I realize that she must be lactating, that the baby's cries are pulling milk from her nipple. I cannot stop myself from staring. I think, for some reason, of Susan's hand, not Whitman's, on my breast, and something pulls at me too, something hopeless, like loss.

I make myself look away, and I finish my coffee quickly, close my eyes for a moment against the headache starting to butt against my forehead. I pay the cheque; the waitress does not hesitate over my Canadian bills, gives me back Canadian change. "No problem." She smiles with such an empty cheerfulness I almost feel like warning her, against her own life perhaps.

I drive back quickly, the car winding up the road I came on, Ariadne finding her way out of the labyrinth—no, that was Theseus; Ariadne only gave him the string, and he repaid her by abandoning her.

I am over the speed limit, I know, but I must get back. The sun is sliding westward; blades of light slash through the trees. Sun, shade, sun, shade: my headache drums to the beat. I put the visor down, but it doesn't help. Finally I am at Sumas again, tapping my fingers on the wheel as I wait at Customs.

"No, I didn't buy anything," I say.

She waves me on, as though I am not even worth words, and I head straight up to the freeway, and in less than an hour I am home, my key urgent in the door.

I tell myself I do not know why I am in such a rush, but that is not true. Somewhere, perhaps in the restaurant, I have decided that I must see Whitman, that I will not endure this silence. It has been over a week since Susan's death, and he has to tell me what happened. I have read what he gave me, have done what he asked. Now it is his turn.

I take the second folder of poems from the box, the short story "Choices," and the play about Freddy. I will ask Brenda to read them, I think, see if she thinks they might be publishable. I tuck the three photographs as well inside the folders I am keeping, and then I close up the box, fold the cardboard flaps into each other, but I have to do it several times before I get the sequence right, before they seal shut over the parts of Susan's life Whitman wanted me to see.

He does not answer the door. It makes me furious. I know he is home, can see his shadow like some huge moth through the lighted window. I am standing on his front steps, balancing the box against my chest with one arm, can feel curtains twitching back from all the windows on the block, the eager gossip of eyes on my back, and still he will not answer the door. I pound with my fist.

"Whitman," I shout, not caring. "Open the door. God damn you, open the door."

And finally he does. "I didn't know it was you," he says. I suppose it might be true. "Come in."

He is wearing a bathrobe, and although it is tied in front, the knot is so limp the robe hangs open all the way to the floor. Underneath, he has on terrycloth shorts and nothing else. There is

a smell about him of old alcohol, and he has not shaved for the last
day or so.

"Thank you," I say. I am still angry, but I can feel it leaving me,
though I would like to hold on to it, an amulet. "I brought this
back." I set the box on a chair by the door. "I kept some of the
poems and one of the short stories. And the play. I want to show
them to a friend of mine, and maybe she can say if they could be
published."

"Well," he says. "I really wanted you to keep everything."

We stand there awkwardly, the box between us. It is hard to
believe that only a little over a week ago our bodies moved together
in warm synchronicity. Now they stand like two chunks of
soldered sculpture, all angles and cold metal. I know he would like
me to go, but I will not.

At last he says, "Can I get you a drink?"

"All right," I say, quickly. "Whatever you have." I sit down on
the couch, force myself to lean back, cross my legs, look comfortable. He brings me a whiskey and soda, very strong, sits down
across from me and stares over my shoulder at the wall. Ropes of
smoke from his cigarette twist over his head.

"Did you read . . . everything?"

"More or less. There were a lot of rough drafts of things. I didn't
read those, but, yes, everything else. The two diaries." I stare and
stare at him, wanting to see what he is thinking, but he will reveal
himself to me as easily as a stone will give back light.

"You know, there were more diaries. I wonder if you found
them."

"I just gave you everything that was in the top drawer of her
filing cabinet." It is not, of course, really an answer, but it is all he
will offer.

"There was a play, too, with the things you gave me," I
continue, watching him. "About Freddy. Did you read it?"

He is startled. "About Freddy? No, no, I didn't." Surely, I think,
he cannot be acting; he is genuinely surprised. I wait for him to ask
me about it; he must be curious, but he does not, just sits there
staring past me with such concentration I have to force myself not
to turn around to see what is there. He stubs his cigarette out, hard,
crumpling it into a circle, and then immediately lights another,
from which he takes quick, nervous sips. I see with surprise that he
is using the ashtray Susan bought him, the one that says *Don't
Smoke* on the bottom.

"I have to know what happened, Whitman," I say finally. I am quite calm, as calm as when the officer came. I pause, waiting, but he says nothing, nothing. "You have to tell me. I didn't tell the police about the agoraphobia, I suppose you know that. I guess that could mean I'm withholding evidence. You've got to tell me."

Withholding evidence. The phrase sounds absurd, something that should be coming from the TV set.

"All right," he says quietly. He presses his hands together, pushes them between his knees, leans forward, looking at his lap as though there were a book there from which he is going to read. "It was all my fault. I guess you could say I killed her."

This is Whitman being dramatic, I tell myself; this is Whitman trying to shock me. I will not give in.

"I'm not about to believe you murdered Susan," I say firmly, the voice of a schoolteacher, the now-let's-have-no-more-of-this-nonsense voice.

"We had a fight," he says, his voice so low and thick I can hardly understand him.

"And?" I want to shake him, cannot stand the way he offers me a few words and then retreats.

"Okay," he says. And he looks up at me, his eyes brushing past mine. "We had a fight, earlier that evening. A really rotten one. I accused her of . . . all sorts of things, and she said I was treating her badly, ignoring her, and because I suppose it was true it just made me madder. I said she was using the agoraphobia as an excuse for not getting her life together, that she could leave the damned house if she just wanted to. And—she always does this when she feels in a corner in our arguments—"

I know what he will say, do not want to hear it, close my eyes against the name.

"—she started going on about Freddy, how things would have been different with him. She knows how I hate that. So I told her I could cure her once and for all of her goddamned agoraphobia."

He gets up, paces around the room. I am almost afraid of him, his hands that fling terse gestures into the air. His robe jerks around him, catching on the coffee table, the couch, like ragged parts of the story.

"So I grabbed her and, and, pulled her outside, into the van, and started it up and drove away. At first she was only mad, you know, but not wanting to make a scene because of the neighbours, and I was thinking, *there, damn it, it's working, she's outside,* like once my father when I was a little kid forcing my head into my plate of beans which I hated, saying, 'Some day you'll thank me for this,' and, Jesus, I can still remember swallowing them whole, the way they slid down my throat like worms. . . ."

He shakes his head a little, tight jerky movements, as though trying to chase away a buzzing insect. Then, confused, he looks back down at his lap, as if trying to find his place again in his book.

"Well, I drove out a ways on Hope River Road, her crying, begging me to take her back, and I said, really believing it, 'I'm doing this for your own good.' "

He begins to cry, horrible dry sounds. The tears run down his face, but he does not reach up to brush them away. I do not move, do not want to stop his telling.

Finally he continues, and his voice is slow, deliberate, a voice that has no tone, that is simply printing out words, the way a typewriter does. "No," he says. "That's not true." He hesitates. I hold my breath. I do not move. "I can't pretend I was trying to do her some goddamned favour, forcing her like that. God knows I'd like to believe it, but it's not true. I was . . . trying to hurt her, that's all, punish her for having that stupid sickness, for going on and on about Freddy. That's all. Just me getting mad, getting out of control."

He is silent again, picking at a thread that begins to unravel a seam in his robe. I want to lean over and pull his hand away from it. Then he tells me the rest.

"I park, two miles away, maybe, close to where . . . where she was found, and I hand her the keys, and I say to her, I can hear my voice, so gentle, 'You can drive back yourself, come on now,' and I walk back to the house. It was raining." He pauses, then adds, "Is that enough? Do you want to hear more?"

"No," I say. "That's enough."

He falls back, exhausted, onto the couch, wipes at his face with the sleeve of his robe, which he now pulls tightly around him. We are quiet for a long time. I am like a journalist, arranging the facts in my mind, getting the quotations right, not asking myself what I believe. I do not let myself think about Susan.

"And the police?" I ask. "What did you tell them?"

"I told them she just took the van and went out, for a drive. That was stupid; I could have told them the truth, but I just couldn't face what I'd done, I suppose. And once I'd said it I couldn't take it back, you know?"

I nod. It is somehow what I thought he would have told them, the assumption I made when I talked to the police, because it should, after all, have been the truth. "And did anyone ask about the agoraphobia? Did anyone besides us know?"

"Some of her friends in Vancouver, I guess. But they mustn't have known how bad it was. Nobody said anything about it at the funeral."

"So only you and I know about it. I suppose we're . . . safe, then."

"Safe." He turns the word down at the end, does not make it a question.

"It was an accident," I say. "That's all it was, an accident. An accident is nobody's fault."

To my surprise, he looks up at me and smiles, the kind of smile that pushes up his lower lip but that has nothing to do with the rest of his face.

We sit there for a moment longer, not looking at each other, and then I stand up to go; I have got, after all, what I came for.

"You don't have to leave," he says. He may even mean it.

"I should, really."

"You've no idea, Ellen, about the guilt, all that guilt."

"I have my share, too," I say.

"Not like me. Not like mine."

"I guess not." I go to the door, touch my hand on the box beside it. "Poor Susan." I will not think of her, her words dark in the box, under water.

"Just a minute," Whitman says. "There's something I want to give you." He goes into another room, and I prepare myself for some token he will bring me, something of Susan's that I will have to take.

There is a faintly sour smell here in the hallway, probably coming from the kitchen, the smell of garbage that has not been taken out. When he comes back, I think, I will offer to clean up his kitchen, but immediately I jerk back from the idea; he would think I was being pushy, was trying to replace Susan. The thought appalls me, too, and I feel a sudden panic about being here at all. I put my hand on the doorknob. Hurry *up*, I think. I notice a long and delicate silver thread lying along the carpet, and then I realize it is a slug trail. I track it with my eyes, and I see at its end the small dessicated body, not repulsive now that it is dead, lying like a single black parenthesis beside the closet.

When Whitman comes back at last, what he brings me, holds out to me, is a white undergarment. It looks like a brassiere. I do not take it, cannot believe he would want to offer me something like this.

"It's yours," he says.

And when I take my hand from the doorknob and reach for it, clumsily, I see that is *is* mine, remember how I left it here, such a long time ago. I am absurdly embarrassed.

"Where did you find this?" I ask. I can actually feel myself blushing, and Whitman's eyes watching me. Why is he giving this to me now?

"I can't remember, really. Somewhere in the house. I assumed it was yours."

"I'd forgotten about it," I say, pleating it in my fingers, gathering the silly straps into a lump. "I took it off once when I was here."

"Yeah. Well. I just thought you'd like it back," he says, shrugging, as though that is really all there is to it. Maybe it is.

He opens the door for me. "I wish you'd take this back with you too, you know." He gestures at the box but does not touch it.

"Is it that important to you?"

"Yes." And he picks up the box, quickly, and pushes it against my chest.

"Well, okay," I say, as though I had any choice.

Sixteen

"Well, how do *you* think she died?" Margaret is leaning intently across the table, her eyes like needles trying to thread themselves on my own gaze, which I have fixed in space just above her right ear.

"It was an accident, of course."

"Really, you think so? Well, I hope you're right."

Her voice is too loud, fills my pastel kitchen like a shrill colour, a shout of red or orange. Most of her friends are deaf, I tell myself; I must make allowances. On the phone this morning, waking me up, saying, *Can I come over*, it was so bad I had to hold the receiver away from my ear. My first thought had been that, my God, she has found out about Gerald—he has blubbered out some lie to Linda and she has sent Margaret over to confront me. Then I remembered what happened in the bookstore with Linda, and I decided, no, *that* must be it. Sitting at the kitchen table waiting for her I felt as I did waiting for the policeman: a calm that I painted carefully over myself, that would last as long as it needed to. When Margaret began asking me about Susan instead, I sighed with relief. But then I realized those questions could be even more dangerous.

"Why? Does it really matter now?" I ask, but I am stiff with caution. Susan could have told her about the agoraphobia.

"An accident is, you know, easier to accept than if it was . . . deliberate. And of course I'm thinking about her soul. You know people who kill themselves go to, well, the other place."

"Why do you think it could have been deliberate?"

"Oh, my *dear*," she says. "She was not happy. She told me herself she was feeling depressed. I'm surprised you didn't know that."

I sit back, exhale, try not to feel too relieved. It sounds as if this is all she knows. But Margaret is clever, good at making people confess.

"Yes, I guess she was. We didn't really talk about it a lot."

Margaret is pleased; now she can know more about Susan than I do. She takes another sandwich. Dong comes into the kitchen and rubs around her legs, grovelling for some of her sandwich which he wouldn't eat anyway. I notice he leaves a trail of hair on her slacks. Margaret lowers her voice so that it is only slightly above normal. "Well. She told me her life often seemed to have no meaning. She told me her poetry was important to her but nobody seemed to want to publish it. I said I would try to help. I know another lady, you see, Mrs. Berquist, you've met her, who's had her poems published, but when I read Susan's, well, it's all this modern stuff, and I don't know anything about that."

"Yes," I said. "It can be difficult." Susan never showed me her poetry, I think, but she showed it to Margaret.

"And she said sometimes she felt real closed-in, like, like she couldn't leave the house. Isn't that the strangest thing you've ever heard?"

She is watching, watching me. "Oh," I say, "I think most people feel a bit like that sometimes. More coffee?"

"Sure." She holds out her cup.

I pour the coffee into it with such precision I could be serving royalty.

"Well, I suppose so," she says.

She takes another bite from her sandwich, squirms back in her chair. I know it is finished, that I have won. Perhaps she was just playing a different game.

"You know," she continues, "I'm not one to force religion onto people, you know that, but Susan really was getting interested. Just a little longer—" She sighs. "Well, I think she might have been ready to find the Lord."

"Did she say so?"

"Well, she was coming to it. She had this deep *need*, you know—"

" 'For some imperishable bliss.' " It is a line from some poem, suddenly in my head.

Margaret thinks about it for a moment. "Well, yes, that's a way of seeing it. I don't really think it matters *why* people come to religion, their reasons, you know, just so long as they come. It's the end result that counts." Sometimes Margaret surprises me. I have always been more wary of her intelligence than of her ignorance.

"Mmmm," I say.

"What I found interesting about Susan," Margaret is still thoughtful, "was her feeling about Satan. She called it the force of negativity or something like that, but it was the Devil she was talking about, of course, evil, the anti-Christ."

"Really? Where did she think this . . . force was?"

"All around her, I suppose, but in herself, too. I wonder if she might have thought she might be, you know, possessed."

I cannot stand to go on. I do not believe any of this, but it may be circling truth, converging on it, like a predator.

For some reason I think of the story Claudia told me at Christmas, about the Baptist minister in the small Alberta town where her husband still has family. One Sunday the minister told his congregation that they would see a sign, very soon, of Satan's presence on earth, and that evening he shot his wife, his son, and himself. "Sick in the head, I guess," Claudia explained, but maybe he simply and logically decided a sacrifice like that was necessary to prove his point; the Bible is full of such expectations, after all. Believing in anything too much brings one closer to death.

"Well," I say brusquely, getting up and carrying our cups to the sink. "It doesn't matter now, in any case."

Margaret gets up too, knows she is expected to leave.

"I suppose so," she sighs. "Did you hear anything about how the funeral went?"

The funeral: Margaret had been furious at me for refusing to go with her. "You could go without me," I said, but she was too afraid of the drive into the city, of trying to find the Unitarian Church, which she was curious to see. I almost gave in, but then I saw how it would be, me sitting in the back row in my black suit, crying tears I had no right to. Besides, Esther Weissman would be there—I couldn't see her. No, I told Margaret, I'm not going to go. "So then I can't, either," Margaret said, sulking.

"No," I say now. "I suppose it went all right."

She nods. "It's the husband I feel sorry for," she says at the door. "They take it so hard."

She has said nothing about Linda or Gerald; it is something at least to be grateful for. Perhaps she is simply saving it for another time.

After Margaret has gone, I put on a sweater and go out for a walk. It is a beautiful day. It is spring. The sun is tugging blossoms out of the cherry trees the same way the robin just a few yards from my feet is pulling up an earthworm. It is a season of pulling things up, I think, no matter how much they would prefer to stay asleep. The daffodils are not quite open yet but are sticking out of their stems like thick yellow crayons; the crocuses like purple ones someone has stepped on are spattered all along the sidewalks.

The dandelions are starting to nudge up on the lawns, too, and soon Mrs. Schadel will be coming over with her blunt hints that I should "get after mine" because when they go to seed they will blow onto her perfect lawn, from which she will dig them and throw them over the fence into my back yard, where they will usually root again. It is an absurd little war we have each spring. We both feel we have won, but I win by doing nothing; it is the unfair victory of someone who does not care over someone who does.

I turn onto Menzies Street, walk north, cross the bridge at last to Hope River Road.

I feel like a student trying to solve a problem in Math, to balance both sides of the equation even though I have already handed in the test paper, know the exam is over. "This is Susan," I say out loud, tapping the forefinger of my left hand. "She is on one side. She is complicated. I have to add on the agoraphobia, and Freddy." I add two fingers. "On the other side," I say, jerking my right thumb into the air like a hitchhiker, "there is myself, and everything I knew and didn't tell." And Whitman, I think, where do I put him, subtract him from Susan's side, add him to mine?

Angrily, I collapse my hands into fists, shove them into the pockets of my coat. I cannot pretend we are a problem in arithmetic, with one right answer. And what good does it do to say *what if* (what if I had talked to Susan about seeing her mother; what if I had told Whitman about Freddy) and *then* (then they would not have had that last fight; then Susan would still be alive)? *If,* I think, the word that looks at us from the other side of the street, says, *I am a better history. Choose me.*

I look across the water knitting into itself the thick spring runoff. I cannot see our two houses from here, but I look at where they might be if there were no others blocking my view. I imagine Susan here, sitting in the van and looking across the dark at those two houses, so far away, and saying, "Ellen," saying "Whitman."

I look for the tire treads leading into the water. It was close to here, I know. The new grass is growing already on the banks, a clever rich green busy forgetting the white van that slid over it less than two weeks ago.

I sit down on the slope and close my eyes, try to be Susan as she sat here, crying in panic, try to prod loose the truth from this place. *I am in the van, thinking how I have to get home, have to get home, my hand shakes on the gearshift, it grinds and grinds, won't go into reverse, but now, at last, it slides into place, my foot jerks up from the clutch, and it is not reverse, the van lurches forward, goes down the bank, and I scream and scream—* Or the other way. *I cry and cry, cannot bear this pain, I shove the van into first gear, my foot lifts up from the clutch, releases, releases, and the van moves down the slope into the black water opening for me like sleep—*

I open my eyes. It is the green world spinning slowly around me again. A robin is singing for no reason at all.

I stare into the muddy water, but it gives me no answers. It does not owe me one. Susan does not owe me one.

I should go home, I think, but still I sit here.

Behind me I hear a car, and then I hear its tires grating on the gravel as it pulls to the side and stops. When I turn my head, I see it is a white van. Whitman gets out and walks over to where I am sitting. It is the first time I have seen him since I took the box over to his house and he told me what happened.

I look up at him, but I do not get up. I am not surprised to see him, for some reason, but I am surprised to see the van.

"When did you get it back?" I ask.

When he sees I am not going to stand up, he squats down awkwardly beside me. I notice how his pants pull tight across his groin, his buttocks, and I look quickly away, out at the water.

"Just this morning," he says. "The police were finished with it after about a week, but it was in the garage, getting cleaned up." When I don't answer, he adds, "The water and everything, you know."

"Why did you come down here?" I ask.

"Why did you?"

We are both silent for a moment, thinking, and then I say, "Maybe I needed to say goodbye." It seems close enough to truth.

He nods. Then he sits down beside me, although he is wearing a suit and must be aware he might get grass stains. I feel a surge of warmth toward him, but I stop myself from reaching out, touching his hand.

"That's what funerals are supposed to be for, to say goodbye."

"I'm sorry I didn't go. I thought about it, but I just, you know, felt I didn't have any right. Was it hard, making the arrangements?"

"The people in Vancouver did most of it."

"Was . . . Susan's mother there?"

"Yeah. And her brother. It was the first time I'd ever met them."

"Did you talk to them very much?"

"No. I mean, what was there to say?"

A lot, I think, but I only answer, "Yeah," and pick at the grass between my feet. "So why did *you* come down here today?"

"I don't know," he says. "I keep going over and over what it was like for her, right at the end, the last few seconds—" his voice splinters, "—the water closing in—"

"For me," I say, "it's just before that." I do not elaborate and he does not ask me to. We stare at the water.

"You know," he says, his voice deep but under control again, "on the police report they call this the Hope Slough. I thought it was called the Hope River. A slough, for Christ's sake."

"It seems like a river to me, too. It's part of the Fraser." We keep looking at the water, as though something might happen in it that we are afraid to miss.

"Ellen," he says, "about us. . . ."

I catch my breath. My fingers are squeezing a blade of grass so hard it snaps off.

"We can't, well, see each other. It's just that Susan is, you know, Susan is between us. We'd remind each other of her." He pauses, clearing his throat. "I didn't think I'd feel like this. I don't want to, but I do."

"I know," I say. But I don't, I don't, I don't.

"Do you understand? Do you see what I mean? That no matter how much I want to—" And he reaches out a hand for my knee, then pulls it back, turning it into a clumsy gesture that finally flutters to the grass, something too heavy for the air to hold.

"Sure," I say. My voice is raspy, a voice that is struggling with tears. I cannot trust it to go on. I swallow and swallow again, determined I will not let Whitman see me cry. I pick up a stone and throw it feebly. It curves into a listless parabola and lands in the water.

"Please don't hate me," he says quietly.

"I wish I could," I say. And we are quiet again for a moment. Whitmas shifts a little, pulling his leg up, and perhaps it is because I think he is going to leave, but I can hear myself saying suddenly, "One of Gordon's sons, he's older than I am, came over to see me a few nights ago. He wanted me to sleep with him."

It is such a pitiful plea, I want to cover my head with my hands and say, *I take it back; forget I said that,* but I will not humiliate myself further. I say, trying to make my voice light, "It was rather funny."

"Did you want to? Sleep with him?" Whitman's voice is carefully unemotional. He will not give me even a trace of jealousy, of possessiveness.

"No," I say. "No, of course not." *Of course not.* I am pleading again, obsequious. *Of course not* means how could I want anyone else when I want you?

I look at his hand lying limp and neutral in the grass beside me, the hand he is telling me he will never put on me again. And for a moment Gerald's hand is on my shoulder, and I feel a tremble of desire, and I can see, with a tense horror, the Geralds with their simple needs stumbling into my future, and my taking whatever they offer because Whitman is gone.

"Look," I say, taking a deep breath, desperation making me calm. "I guess all I want you to know is that I don't want things between us to end. For a while, maybe, that's all. Susan didn't know about us. We had nothing to do with . . . what happened."

"That's the problem, you see. She did know."

"What?"

"She did know. About us."

"But the journals. . . . There was nothing. . . ." I will not believe him. It cannot be true. He is lying, lying.

He stares across the water, and I stare at him. In profile his lips twist a little, and then he continues. His words head forward, and the wind from the water blows them back into my face. "Susan had a way, a way of not admitting things to herself if she didn't want to face them."

I think of Freddy. Oh, God. It is possible. Yes, it is possible.

"That last night, when I left her out there in the van, she shouted after me as I started to walk away, 'Go back to Ellen, then.' And I just walked on and pretended I hadn't heard. But the important thing is, don't you see, that she had admitted it to herself. She couldn't pretend any more. That's what I have to live with, my walking away and her last words to me, as I left her in the van knowing the truth about us, her last words were, 'Go back to Ellen, then'."

"My God," I say, my voice barely a whisper. My fingers dig into the soft earth as though it were liquid. Dirt squeezes up under my nails. My eyes are thick with images of Susan, us laughing and being friends together over our endless cups of coffee, and for how long was the truth waiting, ready to jump across the synapse, trip her suddenly into awareness? I see her in the van, shouting, "Go back to Ellen, then," her hands clenched on the steering wheel and holding that horrible knowledge.

"So can you understand now? I see you, and I see Susan in the van, watching me walk away, to you. And how I left her there alone, to deal with that . . . admission."

"Yes," I say numbly. "I understand."

"I didn't want to tell you," he says. "There didn't seem to be any point, both of us . . . suffering with that."

"Yes," I say.

"Of course," he says, hesitating, "there's a possibility that she didn't really know for *sure*, that she meant it only as, kind of, go back to Ellen because that's where you borrow your books and talk about Skinner. . . ."

I realize he is trying to make it easier for me, to give me a way out if I want it. But ever since meeting her mother I should have understood that Susan might have known about us, that if she could change the truth about Freddy, she could do the same with Whitman and me. Perhaps I have been like Susan, pushing away knowledge too shameful to face.

"No," I say. "You don't have to try to give me other explanations."

"Maybe I need them, too," he says. "Gentler explanations."

We are quiet then. The air around us is rich with the green smells of spring. It kneads into our lungs without asking if we want it, as though it knows our answers cannot be trusted. A swallow hops to the grass only a few feet in front of us; we are sitting so still he must think we are something that grows here. Somewhere down in the water a frog blurts out a throaty message; I suppose it has something to do with mating. Nothing answers.

And then I think, I might as well tell Whitman about Freddy; it does not matter now. The story is eager in my mouth, but as the first syllables form around my tongue, I hear Whitman's words again: *I need them, too. Gentler explanations.* I cannot tell him. It is not becaue I want to protect myself from his anger, his saying, "Why didn't you *tell* me?" and turning away from me, which in any case he has already done, but because I need to give him, too, those gentler explanations. He has enough guilt without having to replay all the quarrels, especially the last one, about Freddy, and realize that they were arguing about a fantasy. Freddy is Susan's secret I will have to carry away with me, out of Whitman's life. Perhaps it is as unselfish an act as I am capable of.

Suddenly Whitman says, "There's something—" But then he stops.

"What?"

"No, it's nothing. Nothing important."

I want to insist, *What? What?* but I know he has decided not to tell me. He stares resolutely away from me. It makes me angry, that he would hold out what he is thinking and then snatch it back.

I do not know how long we sit here, saying nothing, pulling around ourselves our separate blankets of grief and guilt. *I want you both,* I said to Whitman once, it seems like years ago, and now I have lost them both. I give a little shudder, and Whitman looks at me, as though he had forgotten he was not alone.

"It's getting cold," he says. "I should get back." But he does not get up. "Can I give you a ride?"

I start to say yes, thinking of the long walk, but then, perhaps to show us both that I will be strong, I say, "No, I'd rather walk."

He stands up, brushing his clothes. A shrivelled leaf falls from his jacket into my hair. He picks it off, holds it out to me foolishly, like a gift.

"Sorry," he says.

I pretend I think he is talking about the leaf. "That's okay. The trees are making new ones."

"April is the cruellest month," he says, and I can tell from the lighter sound of his voice that he is smiling. I look up and smile back.

"It's still March," I say. I take the leaf from him, careful that our fingers do not touch.

"Yeah. Well." He looks toward the van, pushing one foot a little in that direction. "I'm off then. I'll see you."

"Sure," I say.

He gets into the van, slams closed the door. I do not turn around. Then I hear the door opening again, can hear the soft sound of Whitman walking up behind me. I close my eyes. *Let him tell me he can't let me go.*

But of course that is not what he says. "Ellen. About the cat. It just occurs to me that his trial week is over. You know."

For a moment I have no idea what he is talking about, and then I remember. Dong. I swivel around and squint up at him. The sun is behind his back, and he appears to me like a black featureless tree.

"Oh, yes," I say. "Well, what do you think? Do you want him back?"

"No," he says.

"Okay," I say, relieved. I would miss the cat now. He is something alive around the house, something that gives me affection if I give him food, a simple agreement but satisfying. "If you're sure."

"I'm sure," Whitman says. "He's just something else to, you know, remind me."

"You can't give away everything that was Susan's," I say. I am trespassing, and I know it is none of my business, but I stumble on. "There are things you should hold on to—"

"Like yourself?" The words are like two small stones thrown into my ears, but thrown without feeling, as though they were simply there in his hands and he had to make them go away. His face is a black blister in the sky as I stare up at him, trying to see.

"I didn't mean that," I say calmly, although I suppose he may be partly right. I remember how when I heard his footsteps behind me I closed my eyes and thought, *please, please, please.*

"I know you didn't," he says softly. "I'm sorry." He shifts his weight, awkwardly, and the sun lurches out from behind him. I put my hand up to shade my eyes, but I can see him no better. He is still only something large and black and faceless, his words floating down now like ashes, conclusively.

"It's just that . . . you can't help me, Ellen. I have fifteen years to deal with. I won't run out of memories. I wish I could. Don't make it harder on us. Just . . . we have to let it go, be over. Don't you see?"

There is such desperation in his *Don't you see?* that I can no longer not understand. *Don't you see?* It is a teacher giving up on the child who seems too dull or obstinate to comprehend something so obvious to the teacher that he cannot simplify the explanation any further, so obvious that he tosses the pencil down and can only insist, *Don't you see?* His voice is a wall leaving no ambiguities, no spaces into which I can dig my fingers and hold on. *Leave me alone,* he is saying. *Go away.*

"I do see, Whitman, I do, really."

"I'll never forget you," he says, his voice so stiff and formal and the words so corny that laughter rolls up from my throat and rattles onto the spring air.

I take a deep breath and struggle with what I know is the fringe of hysteria ready to drop its red cloth over me. "I didn't mean to laugh," I say. "It's not funny. God knows, it's not funny." I look away from him then, turn my body back a little to face the water, giving him permission to leave.

"Well," he says. "I should let you go."

The laughter almost runs from my mouth again. *I should let you go,* I think; how appropriate. It is one of those phrases of dismissal that is always said by the person who most wants the visit to end, but it gives an illusion of courtesy.

"Yes," I say. I do not look up.

I can hear the gravel grate under his shoes and then the door of the van opening, closing.

The van starts quickly, on the first touch of the ignition, as though it had not sat submerged in these waters for hours such a short time ago. If metal had memory, I think, what would it tell us? Perhaps it would forget too, out of carelessness, out of need, out of tiredness. Metal fatigue: I have heard the phrase, metal that is old and tired and stressed.

Whitman pulls the van back onto the road. I do not look around. He drives away, slowly. I hear the little hiatus as he shifts into second gear, and I listen for the drop into third, but he is too far away; the acoustics of the city have already absorbed the sound.

I breathe in, very deeply, then out, emptying myself fully of air before I inhale again.

"Well," I say out loud, "that's that." Whitman is gone. I am the movie camera drawing back, back, until the lonely figure sitting by the side of the road is only a speck, its emotions now so small they cannot possibly matter. The music swells up and lingers and then the lights go on and people sigh and brush at their eyes and go home.

The sun leans into the west. *Go back to Ellen, then.* Susan sat here in the van and said that, then sank back in the seat with the horror of what she knew flooding over her. I go over and over it, waiting for the hurt to lessen, but it does not happen.

I think again of Freddy. At least I did not tell Whitman about him, and it gives me a small lurch of warmth, that I have kept Susan's secret, that I have for once done the right thing and for the right reasons.

The cold and damp from the ground have been climbing up into me as though I were a piece of blotting paper. When at last I stand up I am stiff and wet, and my knees crack like ice when you pour water on it. I look for a moment more into the water. I am still holding the leaf Whitman has given me and, aware that I am being theatrical, I throw it toward the water. A breeze catches it and whirls it away, and I cannot see where finally it lands. For some reason this makes the tears burn at my eyes. I turn and start walking home.

I have not gone far when suddenly a large, black dog comes out from one of the yards and stands on the street in front of me, growling, baring his teeth. It is that part of town where the lots have begun to thicken into acreages, where urban becomes suburban, where the ordinary rules of proximity to neighbours are no longer obeyed, and the dogs run loose. I have, in fact, been bitten by one on this same street several years ago. I am rigid with fear.

The dog has yellow eyes, and they look at me with what I imagine must be pure hatred. They remind me of the look Gerald gave me, standing at the door, calling me a C.T.

The dog moves slightly towards me, stiff-legged. I can see how full his mouth is with teeth. And suddenly I am no longer frightened. I am furious.

"Damn you," I yell. "Damn you."

I can feel the adrenalin leap in me, making me dizzy for a second. I pick up a rock from the side of the road and throw it. It lands short but makes him stop, take a step back. I bend down and fill my left hand with rocks, drop some in my pockets. My second rock hits him on the shoulder, and I shout with joy, something primal and powerful, not my own voice.

I throw rock after rock, and most of them hit their target now. I advance on the dog, and I know I have won, can tell from his posture, the way his tail and ears are lower, the way his feet move unsteadily back, back. And suddenly he turns and gallops away, down his driveway, back to the big house for which someone has created dogs like this.

Even after he is beyond my range, I heave more stones at him, do not want to let go of my power, my exhilaration. I have won, and I whisper, "Damn you, damn you, damn you" like a celebration. Perhaps I am out of control again, I think, like in the bookstore, some madness leaping out of me. But no, this time I am *taking* control; it feels quite different.

Finally I walk on, a bit reluctantly because I have fought for the right to be here and do not want to relinquish it. I am at the bridge before my heartbeat returns to normal.

By the time I get home I am shivering, my small triumph over the dog almost forgotten, and I open my door eagerly, unbuttoning my coat to the warm air. I walk through the kitchen, touch things, as though I have been gone a long time. When I am warmer, I make myself a hot rum. The cat rubs himself against my leg, making the half-purring, half-meowing noises that mean he is hungry. I spoon out a lump of fishy cat food, saying the silly things he seems to like to hear, "Oh, good kitty, are you hungry, what a pretty kitty you are." He waits in the patient way Susan taught him until I am finished, and then he begins to eat, noisily.

I wander into the living room, sit down in the chair facing the TV set, but I do not turn it on, only sit there staring at its blank grey face. I become Susan in front of her TV, watching fantasies, while across the street Whitman is making love to me, and the part of her that knows this squashes the knowledge flat, a balloon that panic can inflate. *Go back to Ellen, then.* My God. I close my eyes, and for a while the tears leak out from under my lids, until I tell them to stop because they can do no good for any of us now.

I sip my rum, and when the cat is finished eating he comes over and cleans himself a little and then leaps up into my lap. I stroke and stroke him. It is supposed to lower one's blood pressure, petting a cat. I pay no attention to the hair that floats up into the air, clings to my sweater. I stroke and stroke, feel under my hand the vibration of that small, determined motor. His paw twitches in sleep, a dream of running.

For a long time I sit here, a middle-aged woman with a cat on her lap. The light thins, is slowly being pulled from the corners of the room, is being wound up somewhere like yarn into a big sunny ball for another part of the world. Twilight, this is called. "Twilight sleep," the nurse said to my mother, as she injected the morphine. My mother, who used to say, when she was frustrated or joking with us, "Well, I give up."

Seventeen

It is the next day, and I am mowing my lawn, or trying to. This is not fun. The lawnmower keeps choking on the thick grass, and I hate the feel of sweat as it gathers on my shoulders, my stomach, between my breasts. Mrs. Schadel gives herself an excuse to take something out to her garbage can so that she can walk past me and give me a smug smile, as though I am doing this because of her, but I smile back pleasantly, telling myself there is no reason to feel annoyed.

The mower sputters off again as it gags on a heavy clump of grass, and I leave it off and lean for a few minutes on the handle, wiping at my forehead. One of civilization's jokes, I remember Susan saying of lawns. I look across the street at her house, at where she used to live, and wonder what she would say if she could see me now, being a proper neighbour at last. I notice an old blue truck, the air above it crinkling with heat waves, is parked across Whitman's driveway, blocking his van, and I think that if he comes out now and wants to go somewhere he will be angry. Who would park that way, when the whole street is practically empty? Then my hands clench on the mower handle and I catch my breath, because I see the Alberta license plates on the truck and I recognize it instantly as the one that belongs to Esther Weissman, the one in which she took me to see Freddy.

I stand there numbly for several moments, not knowing what I should do. When at last I decide that I should simply go inside and wait until she leaves, it is already too late. Esther Weissman is coming out the door carrying what looks like a cardboard box full of clothes. Behind her is a young man, probably her son, although he looks nothing like Susan or his mother. He is dark, although he may just be sunburned, and he is wearing a cap with "Pool" stitched onto the front; his hair stands out from under it like a frill. He is carrying another box, and I can see sticking out from it the ribs of a lampshade half-covered with macrame. It is something

Susan started once and never finished, "during my Macramé Period," she said. "I made half a dozen plant hangers, but the plants in them always died, so they just hung around empty until Whitman said I had to take them down, they reminded him of nooses." They are probably in the box too, I think.

I simply clutch my lawnmower handle and stare at Esther Weissman and her son, in that odd animal way that thinks immobility is a better defense than movement, and I watch them walk to the truck and put the boxes in the back. Whitman, I can see now, is at his door, and he is looking at me, wondering, I suppose, why I am standing here staring so rudely, as though this were any of my business.

Esther Weissman straightens up, and then she looks directly at me. I can see the way she pauses, the fumbling in her mind for why I look familiar, who I am. Then she remembers, and she smiles widely at me, and so of course there is nothing I can do except curl my lips into a smile and walk the few steps across the street to where she is.

"Well, hello," she says.

"Hello," I say. "It's good to see you again."

"Yeah," she says. "Ellen, isn't it? Ellen . . . Grey."

"Yes," I say. From the corner of my eye I can see Whitman watching us. He starts to move slowly and reluctantly down his walk toward us. Of course he does not understand why I should be here, interfering. Now he will have to find out that we have met before.

"This is my son, Howard," Esther Weissman nods toward him, and we give each other awkward smiles and say hello.

"I'm so sorry about Susan," I say.

"Yeah." She shrugs, looks away from me. There is a moment of silence, both of us expecting the other to say something more. "Howard and me, we stayed in the city a bit longer after the funeral, I got a sister there. There was no reason to rush back, Howard got the crops all in early this year."

Howard smiles at us modestly. "Not much run-off this spring," he says.

"And now you're on your way home?" I say.

"Yeah," Esther Weissman says. "Whitman said we should stop by on the way back, pick up some things of hers."

Whitman is standing beside us now, listening to what we are saying. I hate how my body responds to his being here, how I am beginning to perspire in that strange way that is no longer the simple sweat of exertion.

"Have you two met before?" he asks. Perhaps it is only because I expect it that his voice sounds cold and accusatory.

"Oh, yeah," Esther Weissman says. "Ellen came up north to see me once, not all that long ago, I guess, a couple weeks is all."

"I went up to Dawson Creek," I say, as though he would not remember. Perhaps he doesn't. I am something he is trying to forget, something he would like to have put in a box too, and given away. "Their farm isn't far from there."

"I see." A chilly wind whips around us, making us all shiver.

"Well," says Howard, slapping the side of the truck lightly. "I should get that tire fixed. Where was that garage, did you say?"

"Just a few blocks up on Yale Road," Whitman says, pointing.

"Where on Yale Road?" Howard asks.

"I can come with you," Whitman says. "It won't take long."

"Well, I can wait here for you then," Esther Weissman says. "Visit with Ellen, maybe."

"Sure," I say. "I can make some coffee." Whitman looks at us both uneasily. I can tell he does not want to leave us here together, but now he does not really have any choice. "Don't worry," I say. "We'll be okay. Go ahead."

"We won't be long," he says again. And then Howard opens the passenger door and waits for him to get in, so he has to go. Howard trots around to the driver's side and jumps in, and then he drives quickly away. I can see the two boxes they have put in the back bounce around, and I start to say they should pack them more carefully for the ride home, but I stop myself in time; I have no right to say anything.

"Howard's in a hurry to get back," Esther Weissman says. "We wanted to get to Prince George by tonight, but I think maybe that's too far for one day."

"Yes," I say. "It probably is. Well, come inside."

I lead her to my house, and she says something about how big it is, although compared to the other houses on the street it really is rather small. I apologize for my messy front yard, and she laughs and says she could never understand city people and their lawns. Inside, while I make the coffee, Esther Weissman looks around my kitchen, at the pale walls with only one picture on them, and she nods, not knowing, I suppose, what to say about all that wasted space. We sit listening to the growing rumble of the kettle, watching the steam begin to thicken the air above the spout.

"It must have been such a dreadful shock for you, hearing about the accident." I emphasize the word *accident* slightly, to see if she might question it, to see what she has been told.

But she only sighs and says, "Yeah. I still don't believe it, really. When your kids die before you do, well, that's supposed to be one of the hardest things."

"I'm sorry I didn't go to the funeral," I say. I fumble in my mind for excuses, and what I finally say surprises me because it is, at least, part of the truth. "I think I was afraid of seeing you there and of just not knowing what to say."

She nods, as though that is a perfectly acceptable reason. I go over to the stove and unplug the kettle and make us our coffee. When I come back to the table with the cups Esther Weissman says, looking at me in her intent way that is really a stare, "You didn't tell Susan you'd been to see me, did you?"

"No," I say. "I tried to bring it up, but she just didn't seem, well, ready, so I decided maybe it was best not to."

"That's good, I suppose. Although we'll never really know."

She sighs and looks down at her large fingers that she wraps tightly around the coffee cup, as though they were cold. She lifts the cup to her mouth in both hands, and then she sets it down again without drinking from it and says something that astonishes me.

"You know, about Freddy. Well, I didn't tell you all of it. He raped her."

I simply stare at her. "Raped her?" I say at last.

"I didn't tell you that part of it before."

"Raped," I say again, as though it were a word in another language, one I have heard before but do not understand. Esther Weissman only nods, so I say, "My God. What happened?"

"It was at their place. We're neighbours, you know, we had to be friends and help each other out, so when both their cows dried up at the same time I sent Susan over once or twice a week with some milk. We had a lot, the separator milk especially, just would've given it to the pigs. She liked to go, it gave her a chance to drive, she just got her license. Well, this one time she came back from there her clothes all dirty and her shoes lost somewhere, and she's just hysteric, crying and crying and not wanting to tell me what happened. I finally phone Clara, and she tells me. They had some other people over there and they saw it too, she couldn't deny it.

Maybe she wouldn't have anyway, I don't know. They heard Susan screaming and when they finally found her she's way back in one of the cow stalls in the barn, and he's on top of her, his pants down around his feet—you know, and it takes all three of them to pull him off. Susan she gets up and pulls her clothes together and runs and runs, they said."

We say nothing for a long time. The fridge clicks off and the silence is like something thrown on the table in front of us. *Runs and runs.* I cannot bear the image; I turn my head to the side, wincing, as though someone is about to strike me. I suppose I thought there might be more to the story about Freddy, but not this, not this.

"I guess it helps to explain things," I say at last. "Why she needed to make up that other story about him."

"Do you think she really believed it herself?"

"I suppose so. When something is too hard to face, you can make up a more . . . tolerable story."

"It was *Henry*, you know," Esther Weissman says, her voice suddenly angry, saying *Henry* faster and louder than her other words. "He made it so much worse for her. But what did anyone know of rape in them days, anyways? If you were a good girl nothing like that could happen to you. And Susan, she was a bit wild, kind of sassy to the teachers and to her dad, no worse than most her age, I suppose, and Freddy was a good-looking boy even though he had no brains. So Henry, he blames Susan, he says she deserved it for being friendly to him, flirting with him, he called it, he says she led him on, and everybody else, well, they like that story, too, although there was talk of putting Freddy away somewhere, an institution.

"Well, Henry, he doesn't hit her, I give him credit for that, there's some that would have, but maybe there's worse things. He locks her in her room for a week and says he can't stand to look at her, and that she better pray and pray because the Devil is inside her. He won't let me go in to her, and I guess she never believed I wanted to. By the end of the week she was, I don't know. She did her chores and she finished her school and got good grades, but she was a different girl, just, well, really keeping to herself, quiet. Now there's people you can get to help you, social workers, but then there was nobody. She just had to get better by herself. And so she went off to university, I told you that part, and Henry, he was glad to get rid of her, said no man around here would want her, anyway."

"I suppose," I say lamely, just to fill the sudden silence, "it's a good things at least she didn't get pregnant."

Esther Weissman taps her coffee cup for a moment with her fingertips. Her nails are cut so short that no white at all shows. Then, as if she has suddenly decided, she says, "Well, to tell the truth, maybe she did. I was never really sure. She missed her period for two months, and it might not have been anything, but I don't think so. I didn't want to take her to the doctor to find out—if he said yes then she'd be, you know, trapped. So I took her to old Mrs. Bergman, we called her the *Kraut-Frau,* it means like Herb-Lady. Women would go to her as much as to the real doctor, especially for any kind of, you know, female troubles." She pauses, waiting to see if I understand.

"And she gave Susan something to make her period start again," I say.

"Yeah," she says, pleased at the way I had put it, "to make her period start again. And it did. So, you see, I was never really sure."

"It's lucky there was someone like the Herb-Lady around," I say, wanting to reassure her. They used to call women like that witches, and kill them, I remembered someone telling me. Susan.

"Yeah," she sighs. "She was a good woman. Now nobody knows all that stuff any more. Everything comes in pills and bottles and makes you sicker."

"Poor Susan," I say. "What a horrible thing to carry around with her all these years."

"Yeah. Isn't it." She does not make it a question.

"Why did you decide to tell me about it now?"

She thinks about it for a moment. "Well, before, I guess I thought I should still, well, protect her, maybe. Even showing you Freddy was retarded was kind of dumb, I guess. Afterwards I wished I hadn't. Maybe I wanted you to understand, but not understand everything. Anyway, now I figure it's best just to have it all out in the open. Maybe now people *should* know. I started to tell Whitman about it, too, in the house just now, but he already knew."

"What?" I must have misunderstood her. Of course he knew about Freddy, but only the Freddy Susan invented for him.

"He already knew. About the rape and everything."

I am stunned. It simply makes no sense. "But . . . how? Did Susan tell him?"

"No, no. He said there was some friend of Susan's from high school at university with her—that must of been Janie Klemchuck, she was the only other girl who went to university that year—well, anyway, Whitman knew her, I guess, and she told him. Anyway, it makes me feel a bit better, that he knew, because then he would've, you know, understood. He seems like a nice enough fellow."

"He would've understood," I echo dully.

"Why? You don't think so?" Esther Weissman asks, alert to the strangeness of my voice.

"Oh, no," I say. "Of course it would have been better. If he'd understood."

"Yeah, I think so," she says, relieved. "I mean, then he would've had some, well, sympathy for what she went through."

"Yes," I say, taking a sip from my coffee. Nothing makes any sense. How could Whitman have *known*, and pretended to her all those years that he didn't?

"Well, anyway," Esther Weissman sighs, "she's at peace now, I guess."

"Yes," I say. "That's true."

We sit there quietly for several moments, sipping our coffees. I listen for the sound of the truck coming back. After a while, I pour us another coffee, and we talk about what the winters are like in Chilliwack and about how the Pope will be visiting B.C. and how neither of us care a lot but it will be nice for the Catholics. I listen for the sound of the truck coming back.

Finally I hear it. Esther Weissman does, too, and she picks up her purse and says, "So, I guess we'd better get going. Howard won't want to wait. He wants to get to Prince George tonight."

"Yes," I say. "Well, have a good trip." I stand at the door, do not walk out with her, cannot imagine how I would face Whitman, who is getting out of the truck and saying goodbye to Howard.

"Okay. And come up to see me again sometime," Esther Weissman ways. "You know where I live." She smiles and waves and then goes over and shakes hands with Whitman, and then she gets in the truck and they drive away. I do not see the boxes bouncing in the back, so perhaps when Howard and Whitman were at the service station they rearranged them.

After a moment I hear the sound of Whitman's door closing, and I know he has gone inside. I stand in my doorway a little longer, someone who cannot decide on something as simple as whether to go in or out. Dong comes up to me and sniffs at my shoes, and I look down at him with such desperate affection I feel tears nudging at my eyes. I pick him up and take him inside, where he twists to get down, but I do not let him go; I take him to my chair where I stroke and stroke him, murmuring foolish things, until at last he gives in and sinks down on my lap and begins to purr. I am absurdly grateful, as though I have been given something I don't deserve.

"He raped her," I say. I close my eyes and let my head sink back, but Esther Weissman's voice pushes at my ears, twists into horrible images in my head. I get up, quickly, setting the cat on the floor, and get myself a glass of milk. Milk is supposed to calm one. I drink it all without taking a breath, although the cold grates at my throat. I set the glass down on the counter, then turn back and rinse it out in the sink. I barely know what I am doing.

Finally I go back to my front yard and start up my lawnmower again. I do not feel like mowing the grass, but I do not know what else to do. My mind is so full of confusion that even pushing a lawnmower back and forth will be difficult for it to understand. The mower stalls again and again as I shove it over the tall grass, and again and again I start it up, will not allow either of us to give in. I am afraid to stop because then I will have to do something else, think about something else. Sweat runs into my eyes, down my legs. She was raped. And Whitman knew.

I have almost finished, have only about two more rounds to make, when Whitman comes out of his house and walks across to the white van. He fumbles for a moment with his keys, and, without thinking at all of what I am doing, as though this is what I come back outside for, I walk briskly across the street to him. As he opens the van door he sees me coming toward him, and I can tell by the way his eyes quickly shift to the van again that he is considering the possibility of leaping inside and driving away before I reach him, in a desperate pretense of not having seen me. But it is too late. I am standing in front of him, flushed and panting, my hair in wet strands across my face and neck.

"You knew the truth about Freddy," I say.

"What?"

"You knew that he raped Susan, that the story she told you about him was just all made up."

Whitman looks down at his keys, flips them with his thumb around the ring, one by one. At last he says, "What did Mrs. Weissman tell you?"

"Well—" I decide that I will have to be fair, will have to tell him that I knew part of it, too. Perhaps he has already realized that.

"When I saw her on my trip north she only told me that he was retarded, but I didn't know about the rape, my God—she just told me that now. And that you'd found out about it years ago, right when you first met Susan, I guess."

He kicks lightly at the tires of the van. "I started to tell you about it, you know, on the riverbank that day. But then I thought, what's the point?"

Yes, I remember. I remember, too, how I had decided that what I knew about Freddy was a secret I would keep, would protect Whitman from. And all along he knew, knew so much more than I did. I feel betrayed, I suppose, and foolish—selfish emotions, but there is also anger, anger most of all, because I think of Susan and all her shame about provoking Whitman and how for him their arguments were not about the same thing at all, how he must have felt not jealousy, but something deliberate, something chosen.

"Why didn't you tell *Susan* what you knew?" I demand.

"Why didn't you?"

And of course he has the right to ask me that. But I will not let myself be intimidated into letting my own guilt exonerate him. "I tried to," I said. "I just . . . she didn't want to discuss it, and it really was none of my business. But if I'd known about the rape, well— that makes it so much more serious, don't you see, not just some little lie she made up. Anyway, I only knew about it for a week," I persist. "You knew for fifteen *years*. Why did you go on playing this game, this cruel game, with her? Why didn't you get her some counselling, some help?"

"That's the question, isn't it?" he says, reaching over and rubbing at a smudge on the van door. "Don't you think I've had to ask myself that, too?"

"And what do you answer yourself?" I say, surprised at how cold and unsympathetic I sound, at how his answer has not disarmed me.

Whitman finds another smudge and prods at it, dirtying his fingers which he then rubs together until the dirt turns to dust and drifts down toward the driveway, disappearing in the air before it reaches the ground.

"I guess," he says, "it was just something I started doing, the pretending. Maybe sometimes I even forgot that's what it was, it became such a habit, just the easiest thing, you know, to go along with Susan's version of things. It was what she expected."

"Yes," I say, "I can understand that." And I do understand, how easy it is to get trapped into things, a small wrong choice becoming irreversible. And haven't I, and Esther Weissman, only done the same thing, telling ourselves it was what Susan wanted, needed? My anger against Whitman begins to seep away. Perhaps we were all only participants in each other's failures.

But then he goes on. "And," he hesitates, squinting up at the sky, the sun heavy on his face, "maybe . . . maybe I didn't believe it really was rape. I mean, the way Susan told it—"

"But you must have known she made that story up, to protect herself, because the truth was too horrible to face." I cannot believe he doesn't see that.

"Well, yeah, maybe." Whitman shrugs, looking intently over my shoulder down the street, as though he were expecting someone. "But, oh, I don't know. Freddy was retarded, okay, but Susan was friendly to him. Maybe she led him on."

I am suddenly so furious again that I want to kick at him. Does he think it was Susan's fault?

"Don't be so fucking stupid," I say.

Whitman's mouth actually drops open a little as he stares at me. It must seem to him as though it is Susan standing here, not Ellen, Ellen who is polite and deferential and has always let him make the rules. I feel instantly embarrassed, but I do not apologize. It seems like the right thing to have said, although perhaps not by me.

"I'm not stupid," he says, a child's denial. His face is shut like a clamp.

"Over this you were," I say.

"What do *you* know about it?" he says, angry now, too.

"I know what *rape* means," I say.

"For God's sake, Ellen," he says, jerking his hands from his sides as though he wants to use them for something more than a gesture, then letting them drop stiffly back down. "Maybe I just began to believe what Susan wanted me to believe. Is that so wrong? Why do you want to blame me? What good does it do now?"

And he is right, I suppose. It does no good, whether it is myself I am blaming or him.

"I guess so," I say, quietly. "Well." I make some futile little movement with my hand. "I guess that's it, then." I have delivered my anger like a piece of mail, and now it is time to leave. I turn to go.

"Ellen," he says. I stop, but I do not turn around. I remember how we sat on Hope River Road, and how much I wanted him not to end it between us, how my heart lurched when I heard him come back and say "Ellen," just as he has now, and all he asked, of course, was if I wanted to keep the cat. I struggle with myself not to feel that again, that shiver of hope, and I almost succeed; this time I can almost walk away.

"Yes?" I say.

"If I had thought it would help Susan for us to talk about it, I would have told her I knew about Freddy," Whitman says. I turn to face him. "Do you believe that? It's important to me, that you believe it."

"I think so," I say. It is the best I can offer. *I think so* withholds something, but, still, it means, *probably, yes.* It is all he can expect.

"It's the truth," he says. He looks down at his hands, which are playing nervously with the keys to the van, and then he looks up at me and says again, "It's important to me, that you believe me."

I nod, although I am not sure what I am agreeing to. He smiles at me a little and I smile back at him, the same kind of smile, sad and ironic.

"I guess," I say, "I just don't understand you. Susan and you both."

He looks at me then with an expression that is so open and eager that I know I have said the thing he most wants to hear from me. Of course. Why should it surprise me?

"Yeah," he says.

"Well," I say. "I better get back to my grass." And I turn and walk back across the street.

Behind me I hear Whitman start up the van, back it out of his driveway. I hear the clash of gears as he tries too quickly to take it out of reverse and put it into first. When he gets it at last into gear, he accelerates rapidly, not risking even the small loss of speed it would take for him to shift into second before he gets to the stop sign at the end of Macken.

I do not feel like finishing the lawn, so I drag the lawnmower behind me like some resisting child to the house, and I leave it by the door and go inside. Esther Weissman's coffee cup is still on the table, and I take it quickly to the sink and wash it and put it back in the cupboard, as though that could make me forget that she has been here, forget what she has told me. I have tried so hard for the last weeks to smooth down in my mind all that has happened, to put everything in its place, make everything coherent, and now Esther Weissman scatters it all again. I remember when I first saw Susan and Whitman moving in across the street, how I thought they were just ordinary people.

I get out the coffee again, and while I stand waiting for the water to boil, I think about Susan, about all those years of building around herself another story, like a room to keep herself safe. Were there times when the truth began to seep in, the way it had about me? And Whitman *knew*. All those years, and he said nothing. Even if the reasons he has given me are true, still it seems to me like such a bizarre way to live. I remember the character Robert in Susan's play, and I wonder again if that is how it might all have started, if for Whitman/Robert jealousy was something feigned because it was a way of excusing anger, telling himself that was only what was expected. I wonder if Whitman has ever had to shout something incomprehensible at someone in a bookstore because all the secrets he was guarding wanted to be free.

Then I think of what he said about the rape, that it might have been Susan's fault, that she might have led Freddy on. *Led him on.* They were her father's words, too. Perhaps she was afraid that would be how Whitman would feel, the way her father felt, so she never dared to tell him, constructed instead the more acceptable story, for all of them. "Men," I remember her saying, "I'm so sick of being a victim of goddamned *men*," and the way she slapped the steering wheel with the palm of her hand. I hear myself saying to Whitman, *Don't be so fucking stupid.* It makes me smile a little, thinking of the look on his face, and probably on mine. But he *was* being stupid, saying rape is some form of seduction. I begin to get angry again, but then I take a deep breath and tell myself it is not up to me to judge him; he has given himself the explanations he thinks are necessary. It is not as though I think he does not have to suffer enough. I still care about him. It is not easy to make that stop.

My head begins to throb a little, as though all the pieces of knowledge I have about Susan and Whitman are drifting loose in my head, electrons in a tired atom, full of soft and pointless collisions.

The water is boiling, and I make myself the coffee and take it into the living room. As I walk past the telephone it starts to ring, startling me so that I spill a little of my coffee on my slacks. But I decide not to answer, and there is silence after the fifth ring. Of course I immediately begin to wonder who it was. It might have been (I cannot stop his name) Whitman, or Brenda (but I know I am only adding her name to try to fool myself). Why would Whitman be phoning? I must stop being absurd. He has nothing more to tell me that I want to hear.

But perhaps to prove to myself that it could have been Brenda after all, I sit down on the chair beside the phone and dial her number.

When she answers she sounds tired, as though she might have been sleeping, but I do not apologize. "I want to come up this weekend," I say. "Are you free?"

"It's not a good time for me, really," she says. "I've got report cards to do, and I'll be out most of Saturday."

"Sure," I say. "The next weekend, maybe." I am disappointed, even a little hurt, but I do not let her hear it; I cannot expect Brenda to be available to me whenever I want her. Brenda is not Susan. I will have to get used to that.

As I go into the living room and sit down on the chesterfield beside a book on reincarnation I began to read last night, I wipe a little at the dark wet blot on my pants where the coffee spilled. It is not a serious stain, not something permanent. But as I brush at it, there is a word in my mind, *scissors.* Where does it come from? I try to track it back, make the associative connections between *stain* and *scissors.* And then I remember.

Before Christmas, it must have been, early December. Was it something I skimmed over in Susan's journal, or was that a day she did not record? I almost get up and bring the journals out of the study to check, but then I decide, no, it is time to leave them, time to see things my way alone.

I am at Susan's and we are playing *Trivial Pursuit.* I am better at it than Susan ("I've just lived longer," I say), but not much, and we are enjoying the game. The worst category for both of us is "Sports."

"What's the only NFL team without decorations on the sides of its helmets?" I ask.

"Oh, come *on*," Susan wails. "Who the fuck cares?"

"The Cleveland Browns. Everybody knows that."

And then it is I who land on orange, and Susan asks, "How many yards from goal line to goal line in Canadian football?"

"Good grief. Forget it."

"But that's Canadian content. You should know."

"Do *you?*"

"Oh, of *course* not!" Susan shouts. "Why don't they have categories that would give women a chance? Things like 'Cooking' or 'Child Care' or—"

"You'd do well on those."

"Don't be rude. I mean typical women. Or 'Household Hints.' "

"Household Hints?"

"Sure. There could be questions like, 'How do you get garlic smells off your hands?' "

"*I* know that. With lemon or vinegar."

"You see? We may be onto something here. We could patent a whole new game, call it 'Hausfrau Pursuit.' "

"How about, 'How do you get grease stains out of clothes?' "

"With a scissors," Susan says.

" 'Give three uses for styrofoam egg cartons.' "

"Uhh, something to put styrofoam eggs in, and, uh, let's see, a sexual aid, and a bra for a pig. We should be writing these down, you know. How's this one: 'How do you train a dog not to shit on the carpet?' "

"With a gun." I am surprised to find such silliness in myself. I can feel for a moment what it must be like to be Susan, to look for a new answer simply because the old one has been used before. Imagination: that is all it is. I have always been afraid of imagination, I think, of what it could make me see, make me want. Now it seems as silly as being afraid of laughter.

And suddenly Whitman is home. I usually leave before he gets back from work, but the time has passed too quickly today, and here he is, staring at us as we sit at the table, giggling guiltily.

"*Trivial Pursuit,* I see," he says, gesturing at the game spread out on the table. And to my amazement he comes over and sits down with us. "Can I play?"

Susan and I look at each other in surprise. "Sure," Susan says. "Let's start a new game."

"I don't want to interrupt," he says, polite.

"No, no," we reassure him, our voices tumbling together, "we were finished."

"We were inventing different categories," I add.

"Sports," Susan says, drawing out the 'o' lugubriously. "We were doing too awful on it. 'What NFL team has no decorations on its helmets?' that kind of things."

"Oh, everybody knows that," Whitman says.

"*You* know?" Susan and I say together.

"Lord no," Whitman says, embarrassed because we did not understand he had been joking. "Who would know something like that?" So we all laugh in relief, and Susan sets up the board for a new game.

And like three children we sit and play. The game goes for over an hour, but none of us wants to quit. The dice rattle over the board, and we shout or groan over what they tell us; we surrender to chance, happy atheists. Sometimes Susan or I look shyly up at Whitman, who gives comic answers to questions he doesn't know, and then we look at each other, our eyes saying, *Well, who would have thought he could be such fun?* and then one of us rolls again and gets an easy question and the other two shout, "Not fair!"

I cannot remember who won. I remember it was a day I loved them both, and in the same way.

I feel a kind of excitement now, as though I have just understood something important, but I am not sure what. It is a memory where there is no pain, perhaps that is it.

For these last weeks I have been like a child outside a house trying to look through a window that is too high for her; she jumps up and down, seeing things in quick glimpses, pieces she has to put together later to make a whole reality, but she is always an outsider, and there are things she can never really understand, that belong to the people who live in the house. I have been rummaging through Susan's life, trying to fit everyone into it as though it had to be done, but maybe all I need to take with me is one good memory, uncluttered with history or motive, one good memory, where we are all simply the people we are pretending to be.

I pace around the house, can feel my lips moving as though they must articulate this. Finally I sit down on the chair by the phone, although there is really no one I want to call. The cat jumps up into my lap, and I stroke him absently. One good memory. To take with me. Yes.

My hand falls to the phone book, rests there a moment, and then I pick it up, begin flipping through it. No reason, I tell myself, but I know I am looking for something, something I am not yet ready to use but might be soon, and then I can tell myself it's not as if I hadn't been considering it before. Here. Pages and pages to choose from. Real Estate Agents.

I stand up, dump the cat from my lap. He wakes up only enough to land on his feet, a survival reflex.

Across the street, Whitman turns on his light. Like this, I whisper, pushing my thumb slowly on my own kitchen switch, and the light leaps into the room. Then I go around to all the windows, pull closed the curtains. They are eyelids, I think, not stopping others from looking in, but stopping me from looking out. For a while that will be necessary.

Leona Gom

Leona Gom was born in 1946 on an isolated farm near Hines Creek in northern Alberta, where her parents were homesteaders. She received a B.Ed. and M.A. from the University of Alberta in Edmonton, where she taught in the Department of English for two years. She is now teaching English and Creative Writing at Kwantlen College in Surrey, B.C., where she has been editor and poetry editor for the past ten years of the literary magazine *event*.

She has been published in dozens of literary journals and anthologies in Canada, the U.S., and Australia, and in 1980 her book *Land of the Peace* won the Canadian Authors' Association Award of $5,000 for best book of poetry of the year.

Her poetry books include:

Kindling, Fiddlehead Press, 1972
The Singletree, Sono Nis Press, 1975
Land of the Peace, Thistledown Press, 1980
NorthBound, Thistledown Press, 1984
Appropriate Behavior, forthcoming.

Housebroken is her first novel.